# SUBMITTING TO TWO DOMS

Cowboy Doms Book Five

BJ WANE

Published by Blushing Books
An Imprint of
ABCD Graphics and Design, Inc.
A Virginia Corporation
977 Seminole Trail #233
Charlottesville, VA 22901

©2019
All rights reserved.

No part of the book may be reproduced or transmitted in any form or by any means, electronic or mechanical, including photocopying, recording, or by any information storage and retrieval system, without permission in writing from the publisher. The trademark Blushing Books is pending in the US Patent and Trademark Office.

BJ Wane
Submitting to Two Doms

EBook ISBN: 978-1-64563-103-3
Print ISBN: 978-1-64563-111-8
v1

Cover Art by ABCD Graphics & Design
This book contains fantasy themes appropriate for mature readers only. Nothing in this book should be interpreted as Blushing Books' or the author's advocating any non-consensual sexual activity.

## Chapter 1

*Curiosity killed the cat.* That could also be said for her concentration, Kelsey mused as yet another soft cry echoed up from the lower floor and distracted her from the numbers on the computer screen before her. *Do not leave the office tonight, no matter what.* Due to the secluded location of this private establishment, her foster father had insisted on driving her tonight and dropping her off with that dictate, one Jared Markham, the owner, had reiterated before leaving her alone in his office to audit the club's books. *Twenty-nine years old and Jordan still keeps an overprotective eye on me.* She shook her head ruefully. It was hard to get upset with either Jordan or his wife, Theresa since they were the closest thing to family she'd ever known.

A shiver racked Kelsey's body as the suspicious sound of leather snapping against bare skin reached her ears, the high-pitched shriek that followed making her jump. She didn't know much about her accounting firm's new client except that Dominion was a private club and the only time she could audit their books was in the evening as there was no one around during the day. But putting two and two together was easy and she knew, just knew she was inside a kink club for the first time. Growing up in Philadelphia, she'd heard all about the decadent social pleasures Pennsylvania's largest city boasted.

"It's none of my business. Focus, girl," Kelsey lectured herself as she calculated the debit column for the third time. Odds were, the long dry spell since her last relationship ended contributed to her mind insisting on straying toward those foreign sounds. *I mean, really, who shrieks like that during sex?* Not her, that was for sure. As much as she loved doing the horizontal nasty and missed getting naked and sweaty with a hard male body, her orgasms had never rendered her a mindless ninny nor were powerful enough to draw a cry out of her.

She made it through the debit column before a low moan resonated upstairs, sounding as if it had been wrenched from a tortured woman's throat just outside the open door. Kelsey glanced out into the hall and at the rail along the catwalk circling the lower floor. *What could one peek hurt? Just enough to satisfy my curiosity so I can concentrate on work.*

"Oh, hell, why not?" she muttered, pushing back from the desk. She wouldn't get any work done at this rate. Her sneakered feet were quiet on the carpet as she stepped into the hall and sidled over to the far corner where she could stay partially hidden. She knew she shouldn't be risking this. If caught going against a client's instructions, she could lose her job, and the last thing she ever wanted to do was disappoint the McAllisters who had taken her in and kept her after the second foster family in five years turned her back over to the state.

Kelsey's life before the age of five was as murky as the Hudson River, her only memory that of holding a small black puppy while angry male voices followed by a series of loud, unexplainable noises filtered through a closed door. She remembered nothing else, not even how she ended up a ward of the state. No one had claimed her then and no one had stuck with her in the twenty-four years since, not those foster parents or counselors poking at her memory between the ages of five and ten, and not one of the four men she'd enjoyed a relationship with in the last ten years. Only Jordan and Theresa, who never let the fact she wasn't biologically theirs matter. She would do anything for them, including putting up with their ever watchful, overprotective concern that could, at times, stifle and irritate the hell out of her.

*I'll make it fast*, she promised herself. Just a quick look, enough to answer the plaguing questions each of those sounds kept popping up. Leaning sideways, she peered down, her knees almost buckling at what she saw. The dimmer lighting didn't hide the odd contraptions both men and women were bound to or the apparent pleasure they reaped from their partner's attention and the public exhibitionism. Weren't they embarrassed? she wondered, gazing down upon the pale, stripped bodies on display.

Kelsey shifted her eyes around the room and zeroed in on a tall man standing right below her, his face revealing displeasure as he appeared to rebuke the blonde who trembled before him wearing nothing but a sheer, thigh-length slip. She could only catch snippets of the man's deep voiced lecture. "…attitude… not acceptable… know better… I'm disappointed.…" The young girl paled at that last utterance and tears pooled in her eyes as she lowered her head.

Slapping a hand over her mouth, Kelsey watched wide-eyed as the girl slid her hands under her slip and lowered her panties to mid-thigh. With a barked order, the man snapped his fingers and pointed to the arm of the sofa next to them. Other people milled about, some pausing to watch as the subdued girl turned and positioned her hips on top of the arm, the slip inching up, baring her butt as she braced on her elbows and lowered her head to the sofa seat. Kelsey's legs gave out and she squatted down, which wasn't far considering at five-foot-two she was already halfway there.

She wasn't surprised when the man pulled his arm back and

swatted the blonde's butt, but the ripple of shocked awareness warming her body with as much heat as she imagined those fleshy cheeks were feeling did. *Oh, that's just wrong.* Kelsey groaned as the girl lifted her butt and pushed back, as if begging for more, which he delivered with enough force to jiggle the rounded globes. "Knock it off you two," she hissed under her breath when her nipples puckered in response to the scene. "This *is not* our thing, so don't get any ideas." But when the next spank reddened the under curve of the girl's right buttock and her stomped bare foot in reaction earned her a sharp-voiced reprimand and a smack that pushed her forward on the seat, Kelsey's long neglected pussy spasmed and went damp. Fisting her hands, she rolled her eyes and cast a quick look down between her bent legs. "You too, you slutty bitch. Behave!"

If she didn't get back to work soon, her own butt might be in trouble, but she couldn't seem to pull herself away from that one scene. Not understanding why those two enthralled her, she forced herself to scope out some of the other activities. The two women kneeling at a man's feet with their heads bent over his straining cock was certainly eye-catching and worth ogling for a few moments, as was the woman writhing under her raised, chained arms as two men dropped melted wax onto her nipples. Kelsey's nubs heated and pulsed even though she couldn't imagine ever agreeing to try such a painful thing, her body's continued betrayal giving her something to think about. But two men? Well, what red-blooded woman didn't fantasize about that ultimate pleasure? She wondered if she would shy away from such an offer if she were ever lucky enough to get one.

Her gaze followed one man's hands as they stroked down the young woman's waist and thighs before trailing up the insides of her spread legs. A shudder ran through Kelsey as he cupped the woman's bare labia, her head dropping back as her hips thrust forward into the cupped palm. She had never considered going further than keeping her pubic hair neatly trimmed but witnessing the woman's reaction to such a light touch on that sensitive skin gave her one more thing to think about.

Unable to resist another look before getting back to work, she gazed back at the spanking scene and flinched every time the man bounced his hand off the poor girl's bright red butt again. *Oh, that's wrong too*, she thought again, this time with a gasp before biting her lip. It wasn't the tormented young woman's eager acceptance of the hard spanking Kelsey criticized – to each his own, whatever floats your boat and all that – but the tingles racing across her own cheeks, raising goosebumps in their wake from witnessing those punishing blows.

With a well-aimed swat right between her legs, the man brought the girl to her toes with a startled cry just as Kelsey heard a soft footfall behind her. Before she could come to her feet with a plausible excuse, a hard hand cut off her surprised gasp, the tight pressure sending a wave of cold terror through her. *Why do these things always happen to me?* was her first thought.

Whimpering in fear as he drew her up and tried to walk backwards with her back held tight against his front, she forced herself to recall the self-defense moves her foster parents had drilled into her over and over starting the first week she'd come to live with them. Digging her nails into his bare arm, she drew blood as she thrust her right foot behind his right ankle and yanked forward with as much strength as she had in her leg. Caught off guard, her assailant stumbled, loosening his hold enough for her to wrench free and let out an ear-piercing scream.

"Fucking bitch," he swore, making a grab for her arm.

Panting, Kelsey put all her fright-induced adrenaline and momentum into swinging her body around, intending to deliver a back kick to his kneecap. Her aim was off due to his towering height and her foot snapped against his upper thigh hard enough to knock him back a step. In horrified disbelief, she watched him flail his arms out as he hit the rail, his overcompensated efforts to regain his balance forcing him backwards. Kelsey rushed forward and made a grab for his arm as footsteps pounded up the stairs. But neither her nor the people rushing to her aid were fast enough and he landed on the floor below with a sickening thud.

Shaken to the core, Kelsey inched forward and peeked over the rail, the sight of his awkwardly sprawled body threatening to bring up the nausea roiling in her stomach. *Oh, shit.*

---

KELSEY STRAINED to hear what was going on outside the office where 'Master' Jared had ensconced her over an hour ago after rushing to her side at the rail. She twiddled her thumbs around and around, a nervous habit she had no desire to break. No one should have as much bad luck as her, either in being in the wrong place at the wrong time or as the target of some creep's malicious designs, it was never clear which. Wasn't an attempted kidnapping during her second-grade field trip enough? Or the late-night break-in through her bedroom window in her second foster home three years later that ended with that perp getting hit by a car when the alarms scared him off? Her life since the McAllisters had taken her in had been incident-free, thank God. And now, this. She supposed she should feel some relief in having two FBI employees on her side but fretted over causing trouble for either Jordan or Theresa.

Sirens had heralded the approach of law enforcement and, she assumed, an ambulance, well over an hour ago now. Since she hadn't heard those blaring alarms signaling a fast return to a hospital, she knew her would-be attacker was dead. She shuddered, guilt and sadness overriding relief. To be responsible for another person's death, regardless of the circumstances, was a burden she wouldn't wish on anyone.

Louder voices neared the door and Kelsey recognized Jordan's. She hoped Theresa was with him. Her foster mother often took her side as a teenager. Of course, eleven years had passed since she'd needed a buffer against getting into trouble with her foster father. The door swung open and, regardless of worrying over disappointing or angering either McAllister, she jumped to her feet and flung herself into Jordan's outstretched arms the moment he entered. When he hugged her in return, whispering, "Thank God you're safe," and then transferred her to Theresa's warm embrace, she broke down into sobs.

"I'm so proud of you, Kel," Theresa crooned, smoothing back her blonde hair. "If you hadn't kept your head and remembered everything we taught you…" Her voice caught and she tightened her arms before releasing her. "But you did, and that's what counts, right?"

Kelsey sucked in a deep breath and brushed the tears aside with the backs of her hands. "If you say so. Do you know what he wanted? Was he looking for money or…" She paused, unsure if she should reveal she knew what sort of establishment this was.

Jared walked in just then and lifted one dark brow at her dangling question. "Maybe you think he broke in here wanting a sneak peek and you were in his way."

She flushed and looked away from the censure in all three of their gazes, but caught the quick, unnerving glance between Jordan and Theresa, one she'd witnessed off and on over the years and didn't understand. Irritation crept in and she resorted to sarcasm. Fisting her hands on her hips, she squared her shoulders and looked back at them, drawling, "Well, what do you expect? You people aren't exactly quiet down there."

Jordan rolled his eyes, a gesture she had picked up, much to his amusement. "You're coming home with us until we know more about this guy and can figure out what he wanted."

Kelsey shrugged, more relieved by his order than annoyed. "Fine by me. I don't relish spending the night alone." She still quaked inside and prayed she could sleep without nightmares haunting her.

"*MONTANA?*" No way. Enough was enough. Kelsey jumped to her feet and started pacing in front of Jordan and Theresa who were seated on the sofa in their den while trying to ignore the sensitive tingling erupting over her labia with each shift of her silky panties against the newly bared skin. She'd finally given in to that plaguing curiosity yesterday and had been enjoying the tantalizing sensations having a denuded crotch evoked until just now when the couple dropped that bombshell on her. She had agreed to stay with them and work out of the house this past week in deference to their concern for her, but this was carrying their over-protectiveness way too far. Not since she'd first come to live with them had they gone to such extremes in keeping close tabs on her.

"No. There is no reason to send me away just because you don't know what, or even who that guy was after." They had identified the man who broke into the club last week and unearthed his reputation as a thug for hire. The problem was, since he was dead, there was no way to know who hired him or for what purpose. Was someone targeting the club, or one of its members and she happened to be in the wrong place at the wrong time, like when she was a kid? Or had he been after her specifically, and if so, why?

Throwing up her arms in frustration when they remained quiet, she snapped, "There is no reason for anyone to come after me. I'm a nobody, and no one knows that better than you. I love you, you know I do, but this is asking too much. *Montana*? Who the heck goes to Montana? There's nothing there but cows."

Theresa stood and padded across the plush carpet to grip her upper arms and halt Kelsey's movements. "Thousands of people visit Yellowstone each year, but regardless, sweetheart, we know how upsetting this has been for you. You're not sleeping, and the stress of not knowing is making you irritable. We get it, we really do. But, Kelsey, I couldn't bear it if anything happened to you." Her voice wobbled and Kelsey panicked seeing the tears swimming in Theresa's green eyes. "It would tear me apart. We love you too, and you know that."

*Crap.* The woman knew just what trump card to play, and when. Kelsey believed her foster mother. Theresa couldn't feign the naked emotion written on her face, and both she and Jordan had demonstrated how much they cared for her in numerous ways over the years. Would it be too difficult for her to repay their kindness and love by giving in to this demand meant to ensure her safety? Maybe, when she thought of leaving her beloved city with all the noise, pollution, rude people and the best food and entertainment anyone could ever want for the boring, unpopulated, backwoods west.

She glanced at Jordan and saw the same love and determination to protect her at all costs reflected on his face. "You do know the odds of that guy being after me are next to none, right?"

Theresa stiffened, and Kelsey noticed she didn't turn around and look at her husband. These two had always harbored secrets, but given their professions as FBI agents, she understood and never questioned them. If she felt excluded at times over the years and hurt from their obvious attempts to keep things from her, she sucked it up as a small price to pay to stay a part of their lives.

"We know, Kels." Jordan sighed and stood. "But in our line of work, we've learned not to take unnecessary risks, and where you're concerned, we've always drawn a hard line we know you don't understand. I'd say I'm sorry, but I'm not. You have come to mean too much to us to ever be sorry for putting your safety first."

Have they always played so dirty, or was this a new tactic now that she was older and more independent? Either way, it didn't matter. She would cave, she always did. But, God, she didn't want to go to Montana.

"Fine. I'll go since you took it upon yourselves to clear it with my boss for me to work remotely." That also rankled. "But give me a time limit. I refuse to leave my home for an indefinite period." There, exerting an ounce of independence made her feel much better.

Theresa squeezed her, her smile coming through her voice as she replied, "Thank you. It won't be bad, I promise. We have some friends who run a small dude ranch. You'll have fun."

*A dude ranch?* Could this exile get any worse? "How long, Theresa?" she reiterated, pulling out of her arms.

"Give us a month. Will you do that?" Jordan asked.

"A *whole* month? What am I supposed to do in my spare time? Muck out smelly stables?" A shudder of revulsion rippled down her spine. *Eew!*

Theresa laughed, wrapped an arm around her shoulders and steered her toward the kitchen. "It won't hurt you to repay their hospitality by pitching in to help, but I'm sure they won't ask you to. Greg and Devin are former agents and have experience with keeping an eye on people in trouble. I'm sure we can convince them to welcome you as a guest for a few weeks."

Kelsey narrowed her eyes as a small thread of hope blossomed inside her. "You haven't asked them yet, have you? A possible reprieve." She threw her fisted hand up in the air with a wide grin. "*Woo hoo!*" The unsure look Jordan and Theresa exchanged offered her an even bigger boon. Neither of them was as sure of her welcome on this dude ranch as they let on.

---

GREG YOUNG EYED HIS FRIEND, Dan Shylock from across the table. The Barn, their private club, was still quiet with him, his partner, Devin, Dan, the Dunbars and the sheriff the only ones here at the moment. They'd just finished a short meeting regarding the club's newest members, Kurt Wilcox and Mitchell

Hoffstetter, and were enjoying a drink before opening the doors. He didn't know much about either man other than Kurt and Caden were old high school friends and Kurt had recently returned to the area after a twelve-year absence. Mitchell was the new, much-needed doctor in Willow Springs and both were experienced Doms.

He relished the few hours he and Devin spent here every Saturday night, socializing with friends and indulging their ménage kinks with willing submissives. But now, Dan just informed them he and Nan were going to tie the knot, following in the footsteps of first Caden then Grayson and shortly after him, Connor.

"We were hoping you would hold out longer. Soon there won't be anyone left to play with if this keeps up." Shaking his head, Greg sighed as if disappointed, but in truth, was happy for the lawyer. He and Devin had enjoyed the pleasure of Nan's submission before her recent commitment and knew what a lucky man Dan was.

"Doubtful," Dan returned. "Besides, after five years, we decided we knew each other better than most couples when they marry."

"When it's right, it's right. I took way too long learning that the hard way," Connor put in. Kicking his long legs out, he leaned back in his chair, eying Greg and Devin from under the lowered brim of his Stetson. "You two have never lacked for female attention."

Devin lifted one dark eyebrow and nodded at Connor's left hand. "Neither did you, but there you are."

"Jealous?" the younger Dunbar taunted.

The men all laughed at that, but only Greg knew just how low the odds of his best friend and business partner settling down with one woman were. He had rebounded faster than Devin after the fuck-up that prompted them to leave the Bureau five years shy of full retirement. Taking a smaller pension had been a small price to pay for losing a protected witness but, unlike Devin, Greg refused to let one failure keep him from having an open mind about the future.

"As delightful as we find your wife, there hasn't been a relationship either of us has envied," he answered for both himself and Devin. "Who would indulge the girls' fantasies of submitting to two men if we split off and restricted ourselves to one woman?"

A wry grin twisted Caden's lips as he pushed his chair back and stood. "I can't wait to see which one of you caves first." Looking toward the front doors as they opened, a smile stretched his leathered face, softening his gaze. "And there is my lovely, pain in the butt wife now."

Grayson shifted the toothpick he was chewing on to the corner of his mouth as his lips curled. "What has Sydney done this time?" he asked, keeping his gray/green gaze on his wife as she and her friends headed toward their table.

Caden fisted his hands on his hips and shook his head in mock disgust. "I should know better than to ask her to do anything except cook, but we brought in a newborn who lost its mama overnight and needed hand feeding."

Greg and Devin might still be new Masters in the club, but in the eighteen months they'd been members, they'd heard enough rumored stories about Sydney's penchant for spoiling animals to know she'd taken her husband's instructions a step further than he wanted.

"And?" Dan prompted as Nan settled on his lap wearing an eye-catching tight, leather dress with crisscross straps down the sides. All the Doms enjoyed the slender brunette's taste in fetish clothing.

"And I returned at lunch to check on the calf and was he in his stall in the new calving barn? No." He shook his head. "How the hell she managed to get him into the mess hall is beyond me, but there he was, lying on a pile of blankets in front of the fireplace, all snug and content, with the dogs guarding him."

"I couldn't leave him alone out there," Sydney said, padding up to her annoyed husband with Tamara and Avery joining Connor and Grayson. "There are no other calves in there right now, and he was missing his mom. Really, Caden, have you no heart? At least there he could see me in the kitchen and know he wasn't alone."

Caden blew out a breath, as if giving up trying to reason with her. "That's okay, darlin'. I felt better after you spent ten minutes over my lap. Come on. You can help me behind the bar."

Maybe Greg hadn't been totally honest a few minutes ago, he pondered, watching the couple walk hand-in-hand across the hardwood floor to the circular bar in the center of the converted barn. Surely that wasn't a pang of envy tightening his abdomen. Like Devin, bachelorhood suited him just fine, or, it had until they'd joined this club and witnessed the downfall of each of their friends in the last year and a half. But ever since he and Devin helped Dan coax Nan back into the lifestyle she loved after a traumatic experience rendered her incapable of embracing the erotic pain she got off on, he'd been as discontented flitting from submissive to submissive as Dan was during Nan's long, unexplained absence. Watching how the lawyer had taken advantage of his and Nan's close relationship, both here at the club and outside this sex-charged atmosphere, to aid her in healing before resulting in their now fully committed relationship had started him on contemplating the merits of such a bond.

"You look good, Nan," he said now, pleased to see the shadows haunting her gold eyes were fading more and more with each day that had passed since she'd returned from testifying against the bastard who had abused her. That sexy dress conjured up the feel and taste of her soft skin as she had writhed in bondage.

"Thank you, Sir." She leaned against Dan, her face flushing

with arousal as her fiancé slid his hand up the inside of her bare leg, her thighs falling open to give him unfettered, unabashed access to wherever he wanted to go.

"Putting that asshole away for twenty years agrees with you," Devin remarked as he pushed his chair back and stood. "But since your Master has gone all possessive of you lately, I'll excuse myself." He looked toward Greg. "Coming?"

Nodding, he rose as Connor nudged Tamara up, saying, "I'll take the first shift monitoring upstairs. You're with me, sweetie."

Greg smiled as Tamara narrowed her eyes at Connor's back as he tugged her toward the stairs leading up to the loft. Everyone knew how it irked her when he called her sweetie, which, of course, was why he did it. "One of these days, his teasing will land him in more trouble than he's aiming for."

"Can't tell him that." Grayson hefted Avery over his shoulder and smacked her upturned butt then lifted a hand to them as he strolled toward the spanking benches near the back.

"We'll catch you two later." Greg turned to ask Devin what, or who he had in mind for tonight when his phone buzzed from his back pocket with an incoming call. Pulling it out, he checked the caller I.D. and glanced at Devin with a cautious expression. "It's McAllister."

"No."

Devin's quick, unequivocal reply didn't surprise Greg. "You don't know what he wants. Maybe he's just checking in." Even Greg didn't believe their ex-boss at the Bureau would call just to chat, but he wasn't as opposed to talking with Jordan as much as Devin.

"He's not. The answer's no," he bit out, tightening his jaw.

The phone buzzed again. Ignoring his friend's glower, he brought it to his ear as he strode toward the back doors for a quieter place to talk. "Hello, Jordan," he answered as he opened the glass slider and stepped out into the cool, September evening air. "To what do I owe the pleasure of hearing from you again?"

## Chapter 2

If possible, Devin would slam the sliding back door shut as he followed his soon-to-be ex-friend and partner outside. He was so annoyed with Greg for answering Jordan McAllister's call he didn't even spare an appreciative glance toward the two young women enjoying the bubbling hot tub. The nip in the air, a hint fall was sneaking up on them fast, did nothing to cool down his hot temper.

"I'll have to discuss it with…"

"No," he interrupted Greg, refusing to hear what favor their ex-government boss wanted from them.

Greg glared at him but his annoyance didn't come through his smooth reply. "Yeah, you heard right, but if I agree, he can just ignore her. I need to think about it. I'll call you back in the morning." He ended the call, leaned against the rail and crossed his arms. Looking toward the hot tub, he stated with polite firmness, "Give us a few minutes, please."

"Sure, Master Greg." Mindy, a regular at the club, and her friend, an attractive redhead Devin didn't know, both stood and stepped out of the heated water.

Devin snatched two towels off the bench and tossed them

over to them, the water sluicing down their naked bodies distracting him for a moment. He might be pissed, but he wasn't brain dead. He waited until the door closed behind their towel-wrapped forms before rounding on Greg again, who still lounged against the rail, giving him *that* look, the calm under the surface but annoyed mien Devin knew only too well.

"We retired early for a reason," he reminded Greg, moving to stand next to him, facing the night-shrouded trees several feet from the deck as he leaned his forearms on the post. "We swore we were done, and agreed to start over without looking back, without regrets."

"And yet the regrets are still there." Greg sighed and ran one hand through his wavy reddish/brown hair. "You recall the foster kid Jordan and Theresa took in, the young girl they talked about?"

"No." But of course, he did. He remembered way too much of his years as an agent. Jordan once showed him a school picture of the cute blonde whose large blue eyes dominated a small face.

"Stubborn ass. Anyway, she's in need of a safe place to hang for a while after an attack at a job site. They're asking us to take her in until they know what's going on, if she was the target or just in the wrong place at the wrong time."

Devin shook his head. "No. They can find someone else."

"It'll only be for a few weeks," Greg persisted. "And we're about as far off the grid from Philadelphia as you can get."

Pushing off the rail, he leveled an angry glare toward his best friend. "No, and God damn it, you know why." He turned and took two steps toward the doors, intending that to be the end of it since he refused to go down that road again.

Greg's next words halted him with his hand on the knob. "I'm thinking of saying yes."

Devin looked back and replied coolly, "You do that, but leave me out of it." Storming back inside, he went straight to the bar and ordered a beer from Caden.

Handing him the cold bottle, Caden's shrewd eyes took in his disgruntled face. "Having a bad evening?"

He took a long pull on the cold brew before answering, "Not until just now. If you want, I can spell you early." It had pleased him and Greg when the owners of the club invited them to act as monitors, which included keeping an eye on the lighter scenes that took place on the lower level while tending bar. The offer signaled their trust in Devin and Greg. None of them knew about the tragedy that ended their FBI careers on a sour note.

"I've only put in twenty minutes but if you're willing to step in, go for it."

"That works for me, too, Master Devin," Sydney called out from the other side, her green eyes sparkling with excitement.

An amused grin tugged at his lips. Caden's girl possessed a knack for getting herself into trouble and a straightforward, irrepressible charm that was hard not to like. "Looks like my timing is good." Striding toward the end of the circular bar, he lifted the hinged end of the top and beckoned Caden forward. "Go, take care of your wife. I've got this."

"Okay, if you're sure." Caden paused as he went to move past Devin. "Let me know if you need anything."

He nodded, reading between the lines. "Thanks."

Taking a position behind the bar, Devin spotted Greg coming back inside. The tenseness in his shoulders eased as Greg headed toward him without hesitation. Their friendship dated back twenty-five years and in all that time, neither of them had allowed their differences to put a dent in their close bond.

"I thought you wanted to scene together tonight," Greg said, bracing his hands against the bar.

"And I thought you had more sense than to consider taking another protective duty job." Just the thought of being responsible for keeping someone safe from an unknown threat again produced a ball of nausea in his gut. One failure along those lines was enough.

"They don't even know if she's a target. Hell, Devin, we didn't need to meet her or see the McAllisters with her to know how overprotective they were and apparently still are." Devin folded his arms in what Greg dubbed his brick wall stance, refusing to listen. Throwing up his hands, Greg snapped, "Fine. I'll change the subject. Do you want me to wait for you?"

"No, go ahead. I'm not in the mood tonight."

Shaking his head, Greg muttered, "Stubborn ass," and shifted his green eyes to scan the room for a needy sub.

"We've already established that." Brett and Sue Ellen strolled up to the bar and Devin turned his attention to the couple that still appeared happy with wedded bliss after almost two decades. "Master Brett, what can I get you two?" The twenty-four-seven Dom/sub lifestyle the two were committed to kept him from asking Sue Ellen directly. It wouldn't be an easy relationship to maintain for that long, and was one Devin himself wouldn't care for, but who wouldn't envy their obvious devotion and the contentment always reflected on their faces?

Brett smiled and flicked one of his wife's pierced nipples left bare by the leather chest harness that crisscrossed around her breasts with two short straps hooked to the attached collar. "Sue Ellen has grown fond of screwdrivers, and I'll take a beer. How's it going tonight, Dev?" He cast a questioning look toward Greg who walked past them leading Mindy toward the stairs.

"We're big boys," Devin drawled with a crooked smile as he poured orange juice in a tall glass before adding a shot of vodka. "We can, and often do hook up separately." He and Greg had favored ménages ever since a horny college girl invited them both up to her room one night following a frat party. Being the equally horny, red-blooded young guys they were, they never thought to turn her down. Thanks to Becky Dalton, they had discovered the thrill of teaming up together and were still indulging their penchant for threesomes fifteen years later.

"I know. I was referring to the disgruntled look Greg just aimed your way." Brett took the beer Devin handed over and sipped before saying, "It's not often he looks put out."

No, between the two of them, Greg was easier going, slower to rile than Devin. But push him too far and his anger wasn't a quiet rumble like his but a loud explosion that would send a smart person stumbling back until he cooled off. "He and I are disagreeing on something." He shrugged. "We'll work it out."

"Oh my God, Master Brett, you *have* to tell me where you bought Sue Ellen's harness," Nan exclaimed as she and Dan joined them. "Does it have hooks in the back too?"

Sue Ellen giggled at her enthusiasm for the fetish attire and looked up at her husband, seeking silent permission to speak. Brett nodded with an indulgent smile, twirling his finger for her to turn and show the other couple the different possibilities of her new gift. Talking to Dan, he fingered the metal ring behind the neck and then the one in the center of the back strap. "Two different loops to hook cuffed hands to in back as well as the center D ring in front of the collar."

Dan yanked Nan in front of him and reached around to cup her bare breasts and tug on her clamped nipples. Somewhere along the way, he had divested her of the PVC dress, leaving her wearing only a black, leather thong. Devin leaned against the backside of the bar and watched the two couples converse, admitting to the benefits of two people knowing each other well. Even though he and Greg were strictly heterosexual, their long-lasting friendship held some of the same benefits as a committed couple, such as having someone who knew when to push, and when to back off.

Sighing, he glanced up at the loft and, even in the dim lighting, caught a glimpse of Greg binding Mindy on the St. Andrew Cross. The two of them met in middle school in Bozeman after

Devin's father died and his mother moved them to Montana to live with her parents on the family ranch. Greg had helped him acclimate to being the new kid, taught him to ride, herd cattle and skip stones over water when they discovered they were neighbors. Growing up in Phoenix, those activities were as foreign to a city boy as the French language he had struggled to learn.

They remained glued at the hip all through school, attending the same college, fielding the constant inquiries about their sexual orientation, sometimes with humor, other times with thinly veiled angry sarcasm. After joining the FBI, they were assigned to different field offices and worked different cases, getting together back here in their home state several times a year while continuing to apply for an assignment together. When they finally got it, it had ended so badly, they'd walked away from their careers to start over with a small dude ranch, as far away from corruption as they could get.

Devin huffed an exasperated sigh. So much for escaping the long arm of the law they'd sworn to protect and uphold all those years ago. Always willing to champion the underdog or come to the defense or protection of someone in need, Greg wouldn't change, and Devin didn't want him to. He knew deep in his gut Greg would agree to Jordan's request, and wouldn't fault him for wanting to help. Just as he knew he wouldn't cave and offer to assist him. If that made Greg the better man, then he had no problem with that. He hadn't earned his friend's nickname of stubborn ass for nothing. Greg could take full responsibility for the McAllisters' foster daughter, but no way would he risk that heartache again.

---

"WITH THIS BEING the end of the season, the timing is good." Greg held the phone in one hand and a steaming cup of coffee in the other as he leaned against the kitchen counter. Devin sat at a stool at the island, his glower unchanged from last night when they had returned home and parted for their separate suites.

"The cabins are full and booked for the next two weeks," Devin argued.

Waving his arm toward the spacious great room behind Devin, Greg reminded him, "We have more than enough room here. She can stay in one of the spare bedrooms and she'll be working, so she won't be underfoot. What can it hurt?" He didn't know why he continued to try and change Devin's mind; he wasn't going to budge. Still, he preferred not agreeing to Jordan's request without some concession from his partner. In his current mood, he would have the girl shaking in her shoes the minute she arrived and it sounded as if she had enough to fret over.

Downing the last of his coffee, Devin carried his cup over to the sink and rinsed it out. "It can't hurt me because I'll have nothing to do with it, or her. I should be back by mid-afternoon."

Frustrated, Greg watched him walk out without saying anything else. Maybe the trail ride today would cool him down. They led guests on guided trail rides through the woods, winding their way up to the flat tops of the rolling hills surrounding their five thousand acres. From there, outdoor and wildlife enthusiasts could enjoy a view of Montana's wide-open prairie grasslands spanning hundreds of miles and the picturesque mountains along the skyline. Through binoculars and telescopes, they scouted for a glimpse of bison or elk grazing on the range or tried to capture a sighting of black bear or bighorn sheep along the mountain edges.

Pulling up Jordan's number, Greg strolled toward the floor-to-ceiling bank of windows in the great room and leaned his shoulder against the corner to gaze out at the incredible view he never tired of seeing. The wide-open meadows, still lush and green with a spattering of wildflowers, were backed by the rolling hills Devin would be riding through today. The jagged peaks of the Crazy Mountains rose above the shorter hills in the distance, the endless blue sky blanketing the entire, breath-catching vista. His ex-boss picked up, his relieved voice pulling Greg's mind off the stunning panorama.

"I was hoping to hear back from you this soon," Jordan said.

"After how our last assignment ended, I'm wondering why you would trust us." It would likely surprise Devin if his partner knew about Greg's misgivings in accepting responsibility for the McAllister's ward, one of his doubts centered around why Jordan would come to them with his favor.

"Do you forget how many times we told you that wasn't your fault? Hell, Young, both you and Fisher were wounded protecting that witness. Considering you were outnumbered two to one, it's a damn miracle all three of you didn't die."

"That doesn't negate the fact she died on our watch."

"No, and I can only imagine how difficult that must be to live with, but there's still no one I would trust Kelsey with more than you two. Not only do Theresa and I have every confidence in your abilities, your place in Montana is perfect. *If* she's a target, there's no trail that can lead anyone to her there."

Greg ran a hand through his hair, watching Devin mount up and lead six of their eighteen guests toward the hills. "Just because she was assaulted doesn't mean someone's after her. Couldn't it have been random?"

"Not with the dead perp's rap sheet. He was either after her or someone at that establishment and she was in the way. Theresa and I can concentrate on investigating all possibilities if we know Kelsey is tucked away someplace safe." Jordan paused and then whispered with a catch in his voice, "Please."

"Yeah, okay, bring her on out. Like you said, we have the room." Greg gave him the information on the small private airport where he would meet them in a few days, as soon as they could arrange a private flight. He didn't relish dealing with Devin's sour attitude and hoped the girl would stay to herself as much as possible.

KELSEY TRIED hard to keep from letting her disgruntlement show as the small government jet touched down and the view out her window was nothing but a wide expanse of barren land. Okay, the tall grasses were kind of pretty the way they swayed in the breeze with the bright sun highlighting the colorful scattering of wildflowers. The mountains looming in the background looked closer than she imagined they were and reminded her of the trips to the Cascade Mountains the McAllisters had taken her on during her teens. As much as she'd enjoyed those summer vacations, she never could imagine living in such a rural environment. She shuddered thinking the next four weeks were going to drag by.

"I hope you're not sorry you didn't pack more," Theresa commented as they stood on the tarmac waiting for the eager young man to unload her suitcase. Tall and lanky, Kelsey guessed him to be in his late teens, probably working at the private airport while attending college. Although, where he would go to university around here was beyond her. This area gave the term 'a whole lot of nothingness' new meaning.

"I'll be fine. It's not like there will be anything to do or anywhere to go that would require more than my jeans, right?" She pulled her sunglasses out of her purse and put them on, as much to shield her eyes from the sun as to hide her discontentment with a situation she could blame on no one but herself. If she hadn't let curiosity get the better of her, that man would have continued on with whatever nefarious deed he'd planned and she would still be home, going through her days without guilt eating at her from causing his death.

As if being in the wrong place at the wrong time wasn't bad enough, she'd spent the last ten days plagued by hot, sweaty dreams of being bound and tormented into a sexual need she didn't understand, dreams where she'd been the one on the receiving end of some man's dominant control. Once her exile was over, the first thing she intended to do upon returning home was look up an old boyfriend who would be willing to give her a booty call. She just hoped she lasted that long.

The only thing she knew about her hosts was they were retired agents. *Just what I need, two more father figures looking over my shoulder all day for the next month.* She wished she didn't care about the McAllisters so much, otherwise she could ignore their fretting and unsubstantiated worries. There were worse things than having people love you, like being abandoned at the age of five.

The largest truck Kelsey had ever seen pulled into the parking lot and from the name Wild Horse Dude Ranch stenciled in black against the maroon side, she assumed her ride to her temporary home had arrived. *Oh, wow.* She paused in reaching for her suitcase to ogle the tall, lean cowboy sliding out from behind the wheel. If he's an example of the employees working on the ranch, her stay was looking up, way up. Her mouth watered as she eyed long legs incased in tight denim and the ripple of muscled forearms and bulging biceps below a short-sleeved, tautly stretched forest green T-shirt. Much of his tanned face was shadowed by the lowered Stetson, but she could still make out a rugged jawline, sculpted lips and the curl of thick brown hair clinging to his corded neck.

"Maybe this won't be so bad after all," she whispered to Theresa as she drank in the man's long-legged sexy stride.

A smile of relief touched Theresa's mouth. "He is eye-catching, isn't he? And Devin is just as easy on the eyes."

Kelsey whipped her gaze toward Theresa in surprise. "Huh? You mean *he's* one of the retired agents you asked to put me up?"

"Yes, dear. Who did you think would pick you up today?"

Certainly not anyone who looked like the man walking across the tarmac toward them. "I don't know. Maybe one of their employees."

"No way." Jordan grabbed her bag and looked down at her

with a frown. "We wouldn't turn you over to just anyone, not even an employee of someone we trusted. Besides, their ranch is small compared to most resorts. There's only an older couple that takes care of the cooking and reservations and the stable manager who live on site. A few cowhands are there throughout the day. Greg," he held out his hand to Kelsey's host as he approached, "I can't thank you enough for doing us this favor. This is Kelsey. Kels, Greg Young."

"Welcome to Wild Horse, Kelsey." Greg tipped his hat and Kelsey's pulse spiked at the shrewd look in his moss green eyes. *Oh, dear.* This was not a man who missed much. It was a good thing he couldn't see her toes curling inside her sneakers.

Smiling, she hoped he wouldn't notice her sudden nervousness as she shook his hand. "I would repeat Jordan's thanks for having me, but since I don't see the need for this trip away from home, I won't bother lying."

Jordan rolled his eyes. "She's not happy with us, but I promise she'll be no trouble. Isn't that right, Kelsey?"

Jordan only used her full name when he wanted to make a point. Feeling like a chastised teen again, she shuffled her feet and twirled her thumbs, wishing she didn't always feel so guilty when either McAllister showed even a hint of displeasure with her. "Of course not. You won't even know I'm around, Mr. Young."

Cocking his head, Greg thumbed his hat back, giving her a crooked smile that brought about a quick spasm between her legs. *Crap.* Her instant attraction meant it would either be a very long, frustrating few weeks or a very enjoyable short vacation. His response tipped the scales toward the latter.

"Call me Greg and let's hope that's the case, Kelsey. I had enough trouble getting my partner to sign off on this favor." He switched his gaze to Jordan. "Inside is a pretty decent snack bar. Why don't we wait with you while your plane is refueling?"

Kelsey breathed a sigh of relief she wouldn't have to be alone with this man just yet. Every time those piercing eyes swept her way, the warm rush spreading through her body grew hotter and she didn't know which urge tempted her the most – to sidle closer or inch further away. When he turned his full attention to Jordan and Theresa as they sat down to eat hamburgers inside the terminal, she found herself growing irritated because he *wasn't* paying attention to her. Yep, it was going to be a long few weeks.

Less than fifteen minutes later the ground crew signaled they were done refueling the jet. "It looks like our plane is ready and I imagine you need to get back, Greg." Jordan rose and held his hand out to Theresa. "Ready?"

A wave of uncertainty assailed Kelsey, a sense of abandonment she knew was ridiculous. She wasn't a scared five-year-old found walking alone in a strange neighborhood again. The landscape now surrounding her might look foreign, but the McAllisters would never leave her someplace unsafe or with someone they didn't trust. But it wasn't home and she wanted to be here no more than this man's partner wanted her to be.

Theresa stood with Kelsey and wrapped her in a tight embrace. "Try to have some fun, okay? Look at this as a vacation and we'll have you back in no time."

She sighed. How could she let them leave thinking she was unhappy after all they'd done for her? "I'm sure it'll be quite the experience."

"A good one." Jordan hugged her and then turned back toward the plane with a hand on his wife's lower back.

Greg reached to clasp Kelsey's elbow while taking her suitcase from Jordan with his other hand. "Relax, little bit. I don't bite and I won't let Devin try. She'll be in touch." He nodded to the couple and waited with her while they re-boarded the plane. Puzzling as it was, she found comfort in the nearness of his big body and the snug grip of his calloused palm against hers as he slid down her arm to grip her hand. He might be a stranger, and she might be feeling an irrational qualm of abandonment, but she couldn't deny the escalating urge to press against that ripped body and lose herself in mindless, sweaty sex.

A shiver racked her body as he turned and tugged her toward the truck. "Why Wild Horses?" she asked as he opened the passenger door, tossed her bag in the back and hoisted her up onto the seat as if she weighed nothing.

"We named our place after the Pryor Mountains Wild Horse Range, which lies south of us about sixty miles." Kelsey held her breath as Greg reached in front of her and drew the seatbelt across her lap and chest, his rugged face close to hers, his arm pressing against her abdomen. "They're a sight to see, if we get the chance to take you down there. Sit tight."

He slammed the door and she exhaled on a *whoosh* and a delicate shiver. They just didn't make them like him in the northeast, at least none she'd ever met. She shifted on the seat, the glide of her silk panties over her bare flesh causing those distracting, warm tingles again. If her wayward thoughts and heated reaction to Greg's nearness, slight touch and/or look continued, she might fare better letting her pubic hair grow back to help lessen the effects of her stirred-up libido.

"Do you ride?" Greg asked, sliding behind the wheel and starting the massive truck.

A rueful smile curled her mouth. "I ride the subway, does that count?"

He chuckled, the amused, deep rumble curling her toes again. If this kept up, she would need to see a podiatrist when she returned home. "No, that doesn't count. We have a horse clinic next week and if I have time, I'll take you up. You can learn a lot in those few days." Changing gears, he turned onto a long, barren stretch of highway and veered from the subject as easily as he shifted the truck's gears. "Tell me about the attack on you. Are you sure he didn't say anything that would give you a clue to what he wanted? Where were you at?"

Surprised Jordan didn't tell him, Kelsey slid her gaze out the window to hide her expression. "Other than calling me a name, he didn't say anything. I was at a client's office, working on the books," was all she said about that.

"That's what Jordan said, but sometimes, after the adrenaline has settled, small things pop up in your recollection. If you think of anything else, let me or Devin know right away."

"I thought your friend didn't want me here." She didn't know why that bothered her; she didn't even know the man.

Greg shrugged, the move drawing her eyes to his broad shoulders. "Doesn't mean he won't keep you safe, if need be."

Kelsey shook her head, returning her gaze out the window and on the blur of wide-open prairie whizzing by. "There won't be a need. I'm no one of importance, just someone who seems to draw the crazies." She didn't see his sharp look, or the frown tightening his eyes.

## Chapter 3

Greg couldn't wait to see Devin's face when he got his first look at Kelsey Hammond. While he was a connoisseur of all body types, his partner possessed a special fondness for the petite ones, and Kelsey was about as small as they came. Her head barely reached his chest as they were walking to the truck, putting her around five foot two, and if she weighed a hundred pounds soaking wet he would eat his hat.

Out of the corner of his eye, he watched her changing expressions as they neared the ranch, those he could see with her face pressed to the window. She appeared even unhappier about being here than Devin was, but after catching the look in her face-dominating blue eyes as the McAllisters hugged her goodbye, Greg felt a tug of sympathy for the girl. There were issues there, maybe more than just getting over an assault and dealing with a possible threat against her. Devin might be a sucker for the long blonde, almost white hair and diminutive body type, and Greg already felt compelled to help her cope with her current circumstances, but that would be as far as their association with their temporary houseguest would go. They'd made the mistake of getting physically involved with a woman they were assigned to protect once, and her death still haunted them.

Kelsey sat up straight with a gasp, pointing out the window. "Those aren't cows."

Greg smiled at the surprised accusation in her voice. "No, that's a herd of bison. Never seen buffalo before?"

She turned and looked at him with wide eyes that could deliver a sucker punch if he let his guard down. "Not out my window. Shouldn't they be… contained or something?"

"There's plenty of land for them to roam free, at least around here. You can join one of our trail rides while you're here and get a closer look. Here we are." He pulled through the wooden arched entrance, never tiring of seeing the low-lying acres, rolling, tree-lined hills and rough-hewn buildings he and Devin had put so much effort into. Nodding to the left, he said, "That's the social hall. Mary and Les Ingram do all the cooking for the daily buffets and tend the reservations desk. Feel free to walk over this evening and introduce yourself. They know you're coming. There's a pool table and game table, if you play."

"I do, but it's been a while." She blew out a breath, the heavy sigh a sign those entertainments weren't enough to appease her. As he continued driving down the unpaved road, he saw her frown at the three stables off to the right.

"What?" he asked, pulling to a stop in front of their two-story, log cabin home.

"Is this it?" Kelsey waved a hand toward the window with a shake of her head. "I didn't see a nearby town between here and the airport."

"Because there isn't one. We lie north between Willow Springs and Billings, both about a forty-minute drive from here. People come to the ranch to get away from everyday life, which is why the McAllisters think it's a good place for you to stay until they can learn more about who your assailant was after. No one knows you're here or that we've stayed in touch with our former boss."

Shaking her head, her tone laced with disbelief, she asked, "What the heck do you *do* all day and night?"

His mouth curled in amusement. She was such a city girl. "This time of year, we work twelve to fourteen hours a day except Sunday. Camping season lasts from May through mid-September and once we close the ranch activities for the winter, we still rent out the cabins for those who want more privacy and a rustic retreat while here to ski, or just a quiet winter getaway. Devin and I also spend a few months visiting our families during the worst of winter. From the look on your face, you're not an outdoors person."

She lifted one slim brow. "Only to walk from store to store when I'm shopping."

He shrugged, unconcerned with the stark differences in their daily lives. She would have to make the best of what they offered for the time being. "Sorry, no shopping around here. We can take you into Billings one day, if we can spare the time." He slid out of the truck, not surprised Devin wasn't around to greet them. Grabbing her suitcase from the back, he jerked his head toward the front door. "Come on in. I'll show you your room and you can get settled while I check in with Devin."

---

KELSEY'S JAW almost dropped as she entered Greg's home. The tiled entry gave way to the largest, two-story room she'd ever seen in a house. A place like this would cost in the millions in Philly and there was something appealing about the wooden beams above and the floor to ceiling rugged stone fireplace in front of them. She tried to keep up with his long-legged stride as he led the way past the open kitchen sporting a hanging rack of copper pots and pans dangling over a gray concrete counter-topped island but didn't mind the view of him from behind. The man looked as good going as he did coming, making her warped mind wonder what he looked like when coming in an altogether different way.

*Pull your head out of the gutter, girl.* Even though Greg had shown her every courtesy on the long drive out here, he hadn't expressed a hint of interest in her other than as a temporary guest. Since she was currently dealing with worse things, that didn't bother her.

"My rooms are on the opposite side of the house and Devin's quarters are upstairs," Greg said as he veered down a long hallway. "There are two guest rooms separated by a bath at this end. You can pick either one." He set her bag down in the hall and lifted his hat to run his fingers through his hair before settling it on his head again. The girls and slutty bitch tingled with warmth and Kelsey decided she must be in desperate straits over being stuck here if she found even that simple gesture sexy. *Settle down!* she scolded her happy places as her body seemed to dance a jig at the thought of spending time in the wilds with nothing to do but ogle the man doing a favor for her foster parents. Cocking his head, those moss green eyes turned sharp and assessing without warning. "What's wrong?"

She wasn't dumb enough to ask him what he meant. "Nothing, just jet lagged." She waved a hand toward the first room. "This will be fine. Go on back to work. I take it I'm not a prisoner and can walk around and acclimate myself."

"So long as you stay within close proximity to the house where one of the hands can see you from the pastures or the barns you can go where you please. Let someone know if you want to hike through the woods, then stay on the paths and don't venture far enough you can't see any of our buildings. Don't bother the guests and don't enter any of the enclosed pastures or corrals. We have livestock that aren't broke in yet."

"Gee, I'm glad I'm free to roam around," she drawled with as much sarcasm as she could muster up. "Do you honestly think there are worse hazards and risks out here than in Philly? I thought you lived there when you were working for Jordan."

"Devin did. I was in Albany until we were paired up on a case, and yes, there are wilderness hazards a city girl like you could fall prey to. Here." He pulled a pre-paid cell phone from his back pocket and handed it to her. "Stick close and you'll be fine, but if you need help, I've programmed my, Devin and our stable manager, Tom Weston's phone numbers in there. Tom lives in the apartment above the largest barn and is always around when Dev and I are either out for the day with guests or away from the ranch."

Something akin to panic dug its claws into Kelsey's abdomen at imagining him leaving her alone here for so long. It was a struggle, but she managed to fight off the need to beg him not to take off anywhere without her. That alone was a testament to how much out of her depth, alone and abandoned she felt in this place. At home, she was comfortable spending time alone, even going to movies or somewhere to eat by herself when she wasn't with friends, coworkers or the McAllisters.

"Hey." Greg reached for her and wrapped a thick, muscled arm around her shoulders. Naturally, the girls and the slutty bitch took the friendly hug to heart and reacted to the press of that large body and the steady thud of his heart beneath her ear by going all warm and tingly. "Relax and let yourself enjoy this time. Who knows, you may end up liking it here enough to book a vacation next year."

Kelsey huffed a laugh and stepped back, both surprised and a touch piqued when he released her immediately. "Let's not get ridiculous. Go away. I need to get settled and send a note to my boss. You *do* have internet out here, don't you?"

He tipped his hat down and started back up the hall, tossing over his shoulder, "Why, no ma'am, we still use smoke signals to communicate. Didn't Jordan tell you that?"

"Moron," Kelsey muttered, her lips twitching as she heard the front door close. She wondered if Devin Fisher was as sexy and easy to be around as Greg.

An hour later, she discovered Devin was nothing like his friend and business partner. Her bedroom window offered a stunning view of the mountains and tall pines as well as the barn closest to the house. Putting away her clothes in the small dresser next to the four-poster bed, she caught a glimpse of another tall, broad-shouldered man leading the biggest horse Kelsey had ever seen into the stables. Ink black hair brushed the back of his neck below an equally dark Stetson.

"Oh my," she breathed as her traitorous body sat up and took notice when he turned around and her eyes were automatically drawn to the way leather chaps framed his pelvis. If all the men around here were that panty-melting, she wouldn't get bored, just needy for a diversion from all this space and quiet. "Behave, damn it," she scolded herself out loud. "I'm not some horny hussy lusting after every man I see." But if she became desperate, she suspected she could easily become one.

Turning from the window, Kelsey set up her laptop on the desk and sent her boss a quick e-mail stating she would get back to her accounts tomorrow, once she acclimated to the time change, and all the other differences from Philly she was stuck enduring for the next month. The good news was she wouldn't have to give up her daily walking regimen. Instead, she would have to adjust to stumbling her way over forested terrain instead of strolling city blocks window-shopping fun stores calling her name. If the jerk that accosted her weren't already dead, she would be tempted to go back and kill him for that alone.

The mid-afternoon sun shone high in a cloudless blue sky by the time she left the house to stretch her legs. Curiosity pulled her toward the barn, and the man she'd spotted entering a short time ago. She'd seen a few other cowhands milling about, two riding out in a field where a small herd of black cattle grazed. Two horses, both sporting coats in varying shades of reddish brown that reminded her of Greg's hair, were busy chowing down on a bale of hay in the corral next to the largest barn. Even from several feet away they appeared huge, with rippling muscles every time they shifted their long legs. She had to admit they were beautiful creatures as she entered the stable and took in the tall, regal equine heads hanging out the long row of half doors to their stalls.

The murmurings of a soft, deep voice resonated down the aisle as Kelsey strolled across the wide, neatly swept concrete floor, keeping her distance from the horses sticking their noses out toward her. She passed ten stalls lining each side by the time she rounded the corner at the end of the row and spotted the dark-haired man who caught her eye from the house running a brush along the side of the black beast he'd led inside.

"Feels good, doesn't it, boy? Mind your manners and I might have a carrot or two for you."

Some impish part of her prompted Kelsey to ask, "What happens if he doesn't behave?"

The man turned slowly, as if her sudden presence didn't surprise him. Nudging his hat back, she got a look at his midnight blue eyes, a shiver skating under her skin at the cool assessment he subjected her to before answering.

"A firm hand is needed when dealing with bad behavior, especially if it's destructive. You must be Greg's temporary guest."

The emphasis he put on Greg's name didn't bode well for this man welcoming her on the ranch. She tried not to take it personally but couldn't help the tight clutch in her chest that reminded her of other people who hadn't wanted her around for long. "Kelsey Hammond, and you won't even know I'm here," she tried assuring him.

"Since you'll be residing in my house, that's doubtful, but

mind the rules and we'll get along fine. I'm Devin Fisher, Greg's partner."

*Oh, dear.* Considering the low hum of awareness spreading through her, the same response she got around Greg, the odds of the two of them getting along fine weren't in her favor. What was it about this man that stirred her even though he made it clear he was none too happy about having her around? Whatever it was, it pushed her into goading a response from him other than that frown between his eyes. "Your partner? Greg didn't mention you two were a couple."

Devin blew out a disgusted breath, as if he'd dealt with that misconception once too often. "We're not. We're friends and business partners. Now, go away. I need to finish brushing Thor. But stay close. I'm not in the mood to come searching for you."

Kelsey halted in mid turn to say, "Which is it, go away or stay close? I can't do both."

Her buttocks clenched as he narrowed those dark eyes. *Whoa, where did that come from?* she asked herself as the image of the man she'd watched delivering a spanking to that young woman a few weeks ago popped into her head, that stranger wearing the same expression as Devin's face now conveyed. It was way too easy to imagine Devin treating her to the same punishment if she pushed him too far. Instead of that thought acting as a deterrent, her body tingled in reaction and with as much enthusiasm as she had to Greg's nearness. *Crap, it really is going to be a long few weeks.*

"Ms. Hammond, do us both a favor by turning around and trotting out of here. Now."

"Fine. I'm going for a walk." She grumbled but let a small smile curl her lips. "But I'm telling Greg you were mean to me."

---

DEVIN REFUSED to smile as he watched Kelsey twitch her cute ass and skip down the aisle and out the stable door. She put on a good front, but there had been no mistaking the insecurity lurking in her bright blue eyes. He doubted his curt words were the cause, so why the sliver of guilt tightening his muscles? Greg had a lot to answer for and the number one infraction was not telling him their temporary houseguest was the exact body type he favored. He'd been drawn to the petite ones since puberty. There was something about their small, dainty stature that tugged at the macho, overbearing side of him. Add in Kelsey's feisty nature that was at odds with the lost, uncertain expression in her eyes and he knew keeping his distance from Ms. Hammond would be a battle. Good thing he was adept at winning, even if he found her pixie, fey appearance and striking white/blonde hair tempting. Not to mention that look in her eyes that conveyed she wasn't as sure of her cocky acceptance of her circumstances as she let on.

He had only to remember another pair of blue eyes, those staring lifelessly up at him as he and Greg refused to give up on trying to stop the flow of blood pumping from a nicked artery they'd failed to prevent. Even after they'd thrown their bodies over Catherine Valdez to shield her from the spray of bullets two masked gunmen aimed their way as they broke into the safe house, one bullet had managed to hit her. And one was all it took. He and Greg had each suffered three hits before taking the assailants out, and they'd learned how much more painful the guilt of losing a witness was compared to the physical agony of getting shot. The fact they'd given in to Catherine's pleas and joined her in her bed that night hadn't helped to ease their conscience.

Thor shoved his head against Devin's shoulder, demanding his treat. "Yeah, yeah, I've got it right here." He held the carrot out to the stallion, stroking his hand down Thor's sleek neck. The three-year-old black had been his first livestock purchase two years ago when he and Greg settled here in Montana and had begun plans for the ranch. That last case had taken an emotional and physical toll on both of them, and they'd decided to retire and return home to lick their wounds and start over with a new career. The two of them had hit it off ever since middle school, grown as close as brothers and stayed that way despite living most of their FBI years in separate cities. They rarely fought or disagreed, but that might change over the next few weeks if Greg's insistence on having Kelsey here interrupted the peaceful existence Devin had found on their ranch.

"Do you have a new guest?"

Devin turned at his barn manager's question, waiting until Tom reached him before answering. "That was Kelsey Hammond, the girl Greg mentioned would be coming to stay for a few weeks. She's a city girl, so if you can keep an eye on her when she's wandering around, I'm sure he would appreciate it."

Tom rested a hand on Thor's flank, cocking his head with a small grin and shrewd glint in his brown eyes. "Greg's got himself involved with a city girl?"

With a derisive snort, he replied, "Not involved other than as a friend doing a favor for a friend and she's about as green as you can get." And he sure as hell hoped it stayed that way. "She has instructions to stick close and since she didn't seem overly thrilled with being near horses, I doubt she'll venture out of the house much, except maybe to wander over to the clubhouse."

"I'll be sure to pass it on. I'm heading out to bring in the mounts for the fishing excursion tomorrow so I can get them saddled and ready first thing in the morning. Anything else you need before I call it a day?"

Devin opened the stall gate and slapped the black's rump to prod him in. "No, thanks. How about a game this evening?" He and Greg often sat down to a game of poker in the evenings if they weren't on an excursion. Sometimes a guest or two would join them, but most often it was just them, Tom and maybe a few of the cowhands.

"Sounds good. I'll meet you at the social hall later. Be sure to introduce me to your houseguest."

"Greg's houseguest."

Tom gave him a two-fingered salute off the brim of his hat and smirked as if he didn't believe that reiterated statement. Devin scowled, watching the older man stroll back out and grab the tethered reins of his horse. For a sixty-something-year-old man, he swung up into the saddle with the ease and agility of a much younger cowpoke. The part-time manager's job that included the upper level apartment in the barn fit into Tom's semi-retired schedule and offered him the flexibility to help out his older, disabled brother. Devin could trust him to watch out for Kelsey if Tom was nearby when she was walking around. As long as she didn't get in his way or cause trouble, they would get on fine the next few weeks.

---

KELSEY DELIVERED a kick to a large stone as she came out of the stable, trying hard not to get upset over Devin's lack of enthusiasm toward having her at the ranch. After being abandoned at the age of five and shuffled through the foster care system for the next five years, she thought she had developed a thick skin against personal affronts. God knows she'd gotten enough practice shrugging off hurtful disappointments as an adult every time a relationship had ended without a commitment. The only people who had entered her life and stuck by her for the long haul because they wanted to were the McAllisters. Strolling past a row of small, neat cabins, she headed toward a path in the woods, admitting she wouldn't trade Jordan and Theresa for the world, even though they pawned her off on two hunky strangers, one of whom wished she were far away from here. At least Greg seemed okay with having her around for a short time.

The late afternoon temperature had already dropped to a pleasant seventy-four degrees, but as she entered the dense, tree-shaded forest, the much cooler air drew a shiver. Making sure to glance behind her every few yards to ensure at least one of the buildings remained in sight, she followed the well-worn trail up a steep slope. The hike reminded her of the two mountain trips she'd taken with Jordan and Theresa over ten years ago. Damn, time flew by once a person reached adulthood. Where had her twenties gone? Here she was turning thirty in a month, and had nothing to show for the past decade other than earning a degree in accounting. *Whoopee!* Could she get any more boring or have less to show for all those years? Where was the excitement, the sense of adventure or accomplishment?

The closest she'd come to an exciting, memoir-worthy experience was that fifteen-minute, voyeuristic, eye-opening ogling episode that had landed her in trouble and then out here in the wild west. Coming upon a gurgling mountain stream, she sat on a fallen log, waved to the two men sitting on the opposite bank with fishing poles in one hand and a beer in the other, a secret grin curling her lips. Her life up to that point two weeks ago might have been dull, but she would swear those few minutes were worth the hassle of being exiled out here in the middle of nowhere. Her dreams since that night were more electrically charged and lust inducing than any of her four affairs. *Sorry guys.* She figured it served them right for not sticking around.

Kelsey took a few minutes to wonder what there was about fishing that some people found enjoyable. She wrinkled her nose as one man reeled in a writhing, silver fish, wrestled the hook out of its throat and then tossed the slimy critter back into its watery home. *What was the point?* Finding no answer to that riddle, she stood, brushed off her seat and turned back to the path that had led her to the oddly soothing spot.

As she started back toward the buildings still within her sight, her thoughts returned to those erotic scenes she'd spied on two weeks ago, and from there to her two hosts. She had no trouble picturing Greg or Devin in the roles of those dominant men, or herself as either man's plaything. A ripple of taboo lust coursed through her at the images popping up in her head. *Yeah, I wouldn't mind being labeled a plaything for the right man, for a short time.* For someone who valued her independence, that was a startling admission, but one she refused to shy away from. After all, what else did she have to look forward to for the next month other than her fantasies?

Kelsey was so immersed in her thoughts, she didn't see the tree stump until she went sprawling over it. A quick twist of her right ankle sent a shaft of pain up her leg and brought tears to her eyes. *Shit, shit, shit!* Struggling upright on her left leg, she took a moment to lean against a tree, catch her breath and adjust to the ache throbbing in her lower joint. *Just what I need to endear myself to the two men who don't want me here.* Shaking off her frustration, she hobbled along the path, putting as little weight on her right leg as possible.

By the time she emerged from the woods, the sun had lowered to a narrow, burnt-orange sliver on the horizon, sweat rolled down her spine and her jaw ached from keeping it tightly clenched against the discomfort. A quick scan of the surroundings showed no one was around to witness her humiliating hobble across the wide, green lawn between the cabins, barns and the guy's cabin home. Just as she reached the steps leading to the porch, the front door swung open and Greg's frown turned to a look of concern as he took in her awkward stance and pain-filled face.

"What the hell have you done?" He trotted down the steps and stopped to gingerly examine her swollen ankle.

"Ow," she drawled with sarcasm, refusing to screech or whimper like a damsel in distress. "It's fine. I just need an icepack and to elevate it tonight."

Shaking his head, Greg rose and pinned her with a narrow-eyed glare. "You need something all right. Come on." Before she could grasp his intention, he swooped her up in his arms, cradling her against that wide, muscled chest.

Pressed against his hard frame with the strength in his arms bunched under her legs and behind her back, those pesky, panty-melting fantasies returned in Techni-color. Too bad they were obliterated as soon as they entered the great room and she encountered Devin's derisive look of censure.

He took one swift glance at her ankle as he moved by them, tossing out, "That needs to be wrapped," without pausing on his way to the hall stairs.

Kelsey couldn't help it. She was hurting, in more ways than one, and he was being a prick. Without thinking, she stuck her tongue out at his back, not taking notice of the mirror until Devin turned slowly and regarded her with a cool gaze and one raised brow. "Careful, baby. My bark is just as bad as my bite."

Greg sighed and lowered her onto the sofa, his green eyes full of reproof. "Little bit, you need to tread more carefully through the woods and around here."

"Or what? Will you send me home?" she asked with a hopeful look and tight twist of her heart.

Running one broad palm down her hair, Greg's face softened as he stepped back. "The McAllisters are worried about you. It's not right to challenge their motives for sending you away when you know it's for your safety."

Guilt trickled through her and she leaned back with a nod. "You're right, but Devin doesn't want me here."

"No, he doesn't, so don't push him. Stay put while I get a wrap and ice pack." Pulling over a stool, he lifted her leg onto an ottoman and pushed up the bottom of her jeans with a low whistle. "Let's hope you didn't do more damage by walking on it instead of calling me to come get you." He pivoted and left the room before she could form any kind of reply to that rebuke.

Greg returned carrying his supplies, a frown creasing his forehead as he looked down at her propped-up foot. "What?" Kelsey asked, her eyes going to his hands. A shiver danced down her spine as she imagined those long fingers touching her again. Coupled with that potent green gaze, she prayed she could keep her thoughts from veering into those lustful fantasies that now included his and Devin's faces.

He nodded toward her ankle. "If that swells any more, you won't be able to get your jeans off." His look turned sardonic as he stated, "You can either let me cut the leg up the middle, thus ruining them, or take them off now. Your choice."

*A chance to get his attention on her semi-clad body? Why not?* Kelsey grew warm at the thought, the girls and slutty bitch saying *yes, please!* Cocking her head, she gave him a small smile as her hands went to her waist. "We're both adults with a modicum of restraint, right?"

His lips twitched as he looked her over from his towering height. "I am, but I'm not so sure about you. You look like you're about twelve."

Kelsey lifted her hips and shoved the jeans down as she wrinkled her nose. "If you knew how tired I am of hearing stuff like that, you wouldn't tempt my annoyance by repeating it. I'll have you know I turn thirty in a few weeks, on October second."

His shoulders stiffened and then a wry grin lit up his eyes. "I turn thirty-eight on the first and Devin on the third. That puts you in between us." *And won't Devin just love that coincidence?* Greg shoved aside thoughts he had no business thinking about Kelsey and stooped before the stool.

Being as gentle as possible, he worked her jeans off and set them aside to wrap her ankle. Even swollen, she had dainty joints and feet. But, damn, the girl sported a pair of killer legs. It took every ounce of his considerable control to keep his eyes on his task and to stifle the urge to glance up those smooth legs to peek under the hem of her blue blouse. *Panties or thong?* That was a question best left unanswered if he intended to keep her out of his bed, which he did. He couldn't help but be amused by the taunting curl to her soft lips as she had shimmied the jeans down her legs, or note her lack of embarrassment, proving she wouldn't let her unhappiness about her circumstances keep her down.

"You okay?" he asked gruffly, noting her wince and twirling thumbs as he pinned the end of the wrap.

"Yeah, thanks. It's sore, but I'll manage."

Laying the icepack on her ankle, he pushed to his feet, wishing there was more he could do. "It'll be fine in a day or two if you baby it. Devin and I will be gone most of the day tomorrow, starting early, so you'll have the place to yourself and can get plenty of rest." Greg tried not to let the flash of hurt on her face get to him. For all her outward bravado, she still possessed a thread of insecurity that tugged at his dominant urges, and that was something he refused to give in to. "I'll get you a plate at the buffet. Anything you don't like?"

Kelsey glared at her propped-up foot, as if it was her appendage's fault she couldn't join everyone at the social hall. "No, I eat everything. And thanks, again."

"I don't know where you put it, but I'll load you up." When she narrowed her eyes, he pivoted and left the house thinking he might have bitten off more than he'd been willing to take on when he agreed to Jordan's request for help.

## Chapter 4

"The girl is trouble already." Devin glared at Greg as he entered the social hall and the two of them headed to the buffet. He tried keeping his annoyance from showing since their guests were scattered around the tables and in front of the fireplace enjoying the evening meal, but damn, it was difficult. Not here a full day and Kelsey was already proving to be a nuisance. It sure as hell didn't help she wasn't shy about revealing her disgruntlement with his attitude, or that his hand and cock both itched to connect with her soft flesh.

"Cut her some slack," Greg replied, grabbing a plate at the front of the food line. "She just twisted it. By morning, I suspect the swelling will be almost gone and she'll only have to baby it for a day."

"We've got the all-day excursion tomorrow, so you better hope she sticks close and keeps off her feet since you won't be around to watch her." Devin scooped a large serving of pulled pork onto his plate, smiling at Mary as she came out of the back kitchen carrying a tray of pies. "For me? Mary, you shouldn't have," he teased.

"And I didn't, so don't get any ideas. One piece until

everyone has a chance to get theirs." Setting the tray at the end of the row of dishes, she shook her salt and pepper, curly-haired head and her finger at him. "I mean it, both of you. The guests come first."

Greg added a spoonful of mashed potatoes to his plate, winking at their motherly employee. "Of course, Mary. We always put our paying customers first. This plate is for Kelsey though, so I get dibs on getting a second piece for me when I return from delivering her dinner. She hurt her ankle earlier and is sitting up at the house with it propped up."

"Oh, the poor dear, what a way to start her vacation. Here, I'll take it and introduce myself. You sit down and eat with Dev."

Devin shrugged at Greg as Mary plucked the plate from his friend's hands. "You know it's easier to let her have her way." Short and round, they both watched her waddle across the room to the doors, noticing she added the largest cut of cherry pie to the food Greg had piled on her plate. "I doubt that girl can get through half of that, and then Mary will be upset over the waste."

Greg picked up another plate and started filling it as he replied, "I wouldn't bet on it since she told me she eats everything." He nodded toward a table that still had two empty chairs. "Let's join the Colters."

Devin followed Greg to the table, hoping acting the dutiful host would help keep his mind from shifting to the petite blonde with the wide blue eyes who was sprawled on his sofa. Since he didn't plan on getting friendly with Greg's guest, he sure as hell had no business picturing her in his bed or tied down over a spanking bench at The Barn.

Three hours later, Devin straightened from sinking the eight ball in the corner pocket and winning a game of pool against the Colter brothers who were new to their ranch this summer. The retired professors enjoyed fishing, hiking and shooting pool with him, swearing one of these evenings they would beat him.

Returning his cue stick to its slot on the rack, he said, "Sorry, fellas. I'm calling it a night. You're signed up for the trail ride in the morning, aren't you?"

Jed, the oldest by a year, smirked. "Yes, but we don't need as much beauty rest as you."

Devin returned his grin without touching that remark. "Good night." Lifting his hand as he pivoted to leave, he noticed the room had cleared out and the buffet was cleaned up. Stepping out into the star-studded night, he spotted Greg by the firepit, along with a few guests and Mary's husband, Les strumming his guitar along with Tom. Their poker game would have to wait until another night; entertaining the guests always took precedence. Greg nodded as Devin jerked his thumb toward the house, indicating he was turning in. The longer trail rides left at the crack of dawn.

The faint strains of guitar picking tunes followed him along the path, but his mellow mood evaporated as soon as he noticed Kelsey sitting on the front porch, her foot propped on the rail. Seeing her looking so alone as she gazed toward the small group around the fire tugged at something inside him he had no intentions of acknowledging, let alone delving into.

His displeasure at finding her still up came through in his tone as he climbed the steps to the porch. "What are you doing up? Considering the long day you've had, you should have been in bed two hours ago."

Tilting her head back as he stood over her chair, her sarcastic drawl slithered under his skin. "Gee, Dad, I'm sorry. I didn't know I had a curfew."

Devin wasn't into age-play, but damned if her words didn't conjure up a scenario that had no business popping into his head. Narrowing his eyes, he growled, "Be careful, little girl, or you just might find yourself on the receiving end of 'Daddy's' ire, and it won't be your ankle left aching." Spinning on his heel, he stormed inside before she could taunt him into another unacceptable response.

Kelsey's pulse jumped and tingles raced across her buttocks as she watched Devin enter the house. She didn't know what came over her every time he revealed how undesirable he found her presence at his ranch. Maybe she goaded him to hide the hurt his cool indifference evoked, or maybe he just got to her on the same sexually aware level as his friend and partner. Whatever the reason, she'd better get a handle on it before he made good on that threat. Then again, considering the tight pucker of her nipples and the quick spasm between her legs his irritated line produced, there could be worse ways to pass the time here than provoking the one who didn't like her while cozying up to the one who did.

She'd enjoyed meeting Mary earlier as much as she had the older woman's cooking. Without a doubt, the pulled pork, smoked turkey, coleslaw, corn and pie were the best she'd ever eaten. Either that or her trek into the woods along with the continuous fantasies weaving through her head all day conspired to build up her appetite to the point anything would taste like the best she'd ever eaten. Mary told Kelsey about her husband, Les and their jobs that included cooking the food for a morning and evening buffet for a maximum of twenty guests and taking reservations. In the fifteen minutes she spent with her, Kelsey learned the cabins were booked solid during the summer months and that the 'boys' were the best employers anyone could work for.

The surprisingly soothing guitar music ceased and she glanced toward the glow of the firepit to see the small group dispersing. Lowering her foot, she stood and hobbled inside, making her way to her room and her lonely bed.

Kelsey awoke with the remnants of another bad dream about a man falling to his death before her eyes still troubling her, dashing her hopes the change of scenery might set her mind at ease from feeling responsible for her assailant's demise.

The quiet house and still throbbing ankle didn't improve her mood. Less swelling apparently emphasized the discomfort but she managed to work her jeans back on with little effort, her thoughts straying to the way Greg had taken great pains to avoid looking at her bare legs as she'd sat in front of him in her panties and top. She didn't know whether to take that resistance as a compliment or an insult. Thank goodness she'd had enough wherewithal to resist the urge to taunt him by spreading her legs. But, damn, the temptation to do so had been there in spades.

Shaking her head at the sorry state of her wayward thoughts and needy body, she glanced out the window, hoping the sun provided as much warmth as it appeared to by early afternoon because she had no intentions of staying holed up inside, alone all day. But first, coffee and work. Limping into the kitchen, she was wondering how many cupboards she would have to snoop through to find a cup when she smelled the rich aroma of a freshly brewed pot. A warm fuzzy spread around her chest as she hobbled up to the counter and saw the note propped against a coffee mug next to the full carafe.

*A serving of this morning's breakfast casserole is in the oven and Mary will bring you lunch around noon. Stay off your foot. G*

The warm fuzzy disappeared as she read that last line. She was a grown woman, damn it, perfectly capable of knowing if her ankle required continued babying by this afternoon. If it did, she would keep it up and risk going stir crazy. Greg telling her that rubbed her the wrong way and it took reminding herself they were doing a huge favor for her foster parents and she needed to respect their turf. If she didn't care so much for Jordan and Theresa and weren't so grateful for the way they'd taken her in and continued to be there for her after she had aged out of the foster care system, she wouldn't have agreed to come here in the first place. *I mean really. I'm a nobody, always have been. Why they would think that man was after me specifically is beyond me.* But they had insisted and she was stuck here for the time being. She may as well make the best of it.

Now, why did her head dive into the gutter at that last thought, as if making the best of this situation meant trying to lure one of her hosts into her bed a few times?

With effort, Kelsey switched gears and focused on work as she downed breakfast and carried a refilled cup of coffee to the desk in her bedroom. Arranging the chair in front of the computer so she could prop her foot on a small stool, she settled down to concentrate on numbers and get her mind off her hormone-driven lust.

By mid-afternoon, Kelsey's work was done for the day and, other than a dull ache and a little puffiness, her ankle was much improved, and so was her mood. Shutting down the computer, she slipped her feet into her sneakers and bent to lace up just the left one, leaving the right loose to accommodate the leftover swelling. Picking up the plate Mary left with her, now empty of the thick ham and cheese sandwich, she made her way slowly over to the social hall. She glimpsed several hands through the big barn's open doors, their laughter echoing in and out of the cavernous building. Shielding her eyes, it was easy to pick Greg out of the small group of riders winding their way through the herd of lowing cattle out in the pasture. He sat a head taller than anyone else on a horse that appeared large enough to carry a man of his size with ease. Even with the ranch activity taking place, she found the area quiet compared to early afternoon in downtown Philly.

A tall, lanky man with thinning gray hair and a welcoming smile greeted her from across the room of tables and chairs as she entered the hall. "Hi there. You must be Kelsey."

"I must be. And I bet you're Mary's Les." Their voices resonated in the large space devoid of anyone else except them. The buffet table sat empty, the fireplace unlit and the dead animal heads adorning the walls looked sad.

"Have been for forty-five years," he boasted without pausing in running a dust cloth down one wooden leg of the pool table. "You're as pretty, and as little as she said."

Suppressing a sigh, Kelsey returned his smile and held up the empty plate. "Thank you. I'm returning this."

"Just set it up on the buffet. Mary went to Billings for supplies and lunch with our daughter. You need anything else?"

Envying the other woman's excursion away from this wilderness exile, she shook her head. "No, thank you. I'm just going to walk around a bit. I'm stiff from sitting all morning."

She shuffled over to the buffet and Les frowned with a look aimed toward her ankle. "Don't overdo. The boys would take any more harm coming to you personally."

*The boys can kiss my ass.* Kelsey stifled the spurt of irritation that produced that thought as well as the lust the image produced. Pulling open the door, she said, "I won't. It's almost healed. See you tonight." She stepped back outside, the faint whinnying from the horses out in the fields along with high-pitched tweets coming from birds flitting about in the trees greeting her. A slight breeze ruffled her hair and loose tee shirt as she strolled toward a corral holding three horses. The fresh, open air and lack of industrial noise was a vast cry from the crowded city where she worked and lived, and was almost creepy. She'd take the hustle and bustle of people jostling along the sidewalks and the clamor of bumper to bumper, impatient traffic any day. At least among the masses, she knew what to expect.

Leaning her arms on the fence rail, she eyed the horses, taking note of how large they were when this close to them, and wondered what the people who came here found so appealing about the animals. Curious, she held out her hand only to have it yanked back by a calloused grip before the biggest horse reached her.

"Sorry, ma'am," the man said, dropping her wrist. "But you don't want to get the attention of these three. They haven't been broke yet, and Red there would take it out on your hand once he discovered you weren't offering a treat. I'm Tom, the manager. Greg mentioned you might get antsy today, Ms. Hammond, and the boys don't want you getting hurt again."

Kelsey's annoyance with 'the boys' was growing by leaps and bounds as she realized Greg must have told his employees to keep an eye on her. "I appreciate their concern," she drawled. "Thank you for your timely intervention." She cast a wary look at the horses that appeared so docile. "Do you have any I can get to know? I need something to do in the afternoons, and I figure learning to ride might be fun." *Not.* Even though she doubted she would find much enjoyment in that activity, it was better than sitting on the porch twiddling her thumbs every afternoon while everyone else was out doing their thing.

A smile creased Tom's leathered, lined cheeks, crinkling his brown eyes shaded by his hat. "Come with me. Cleo is a small mare, a pretty bay roan with a sweet disposition. She would be perfect for you."

"What's a bay roan?" she asked, following him to the next barn and the attached corral around back.

"That's a horse whose coloring is a mixture of red and white hair all over." Pointing to a petite mare with large doe eyes and a grayish coat with hints of red, Tom whistled then said, "This is Cleo," as the little horse trotted over with a toss of her head. "Here." Pulling a sugar cube out of his pocket, he handed it to Kelsey. "Hold it out to her with your hand flat so you don't get nipped."

Cleo's velvet soft mouth tickled Kelsey's palm as she took the sweet treat and she felt her attitude toward the equine species shift into the positive column. After getting Tom's nod, she reached out a tentative hand and stroked her nose and then down her soft, corded neck.

"If you want, I can saddle her and walk you around a little."

Tom looked down at her feet and bit his lip. "How's the ankle today?"

She'd never earned such fretting attention from so many people before and it left her unsettled. "It's much better, just a little lingering soreness. I'm game to try, if you don't mind."

"Nope. Give me a minute to get a saddle."

Kelsey found riding more entertaining than she'd imagined. Seated atop the dainty mare, she enjoyed the view spread out for miles as Tom walked them around the corral. Once she settled into the rhythm of Cleo's slow, smooth gait, it was easy to relax. She could feel the shift of Cleo's muscles against her legs with each step and realized how powerful even a smaller horse could be. As long as she didn't look down and see how far away the ground was as it moved beneath her, she got a kick out of this new experience.

"You're a natural, Kelsey." Tom smiled up at her as he brought them to a halt. "Want to take her out to the field? I'll be right by your side."

"As long as you don't move away from me too far." She reached out and stroked Cleo's silky neck. "She's a sweetie but I still don't trust anything that's this much bigger than me."

Tom snorted and shoved his hat back. "I hope you're just referring to animals since most of the human population over the age of ten is bigger than you."

She gave him a mock scowl. "Ha, ha. Good things come in small packages, or haven't you heard that before?"

He chuckled and tugged Cleo toward the rail where he tethered the reins, saying, "I think it'll be good for the boys having you here. Sit tight and I'll go get my horse."

Over the next thirty minutes, Tom gave Kelsey riding instructions in a field away from all other activity, teaching her how to steer her horse and control how fast she wanted to go. She kept Cleo to a steady, slow pace, not ready to try anything faster. They spotted a small group of white-tailed deer and took a moment to watch their graceful run across the prairie as the sun's brightness dulled to an amber orange with the start of its descent. Squinting her eyes, Kelsey saw Devin's group of riders merging with Greg's and then head their way, her pulse jumping as they neared and Devin and Greg's piercing eyes settled on her.

"Is that the group Devin took out trail riding all day?" she asked Tom.

"That's them." Tom flipped her a proud grin. "In two weeks, reservations drop in half and you'll be able to accompany an excursion by then. Maybe not such a long one though. Do you want to wait up for them?"

Kelsey's heart thudded with anticipation as she nodded. She didn't know which man fired her up more or what accounted for her interest and sudden obsession with sexual fantasies. It could stem from the stress of being accosted and then responsible for a man's death, or escorted out here to Timbuktu, away from everything and everyone she knew. But as the group neared and she damn near drooled watching Greg and Devin handle their huge mounts with a combination of strong control and coaxing, soothing strokes, she pinned all of her wayward thoughts on lust-driven hormones. *I can live with that*, she mused with a sigh as they approached and the ripped, corded muscles of both men's forearms rippled as they pulled back on their reins. Her face heated as she wondered if those lean muscles would bunch if either man swung his arm and cracked his palm against her butt.

*Crap, pull your mind out of the gutter. There are people around.*

The first words out of Devin's mouth cooled the rush of heat their nearness evoked, his sharp tone once again laced with censure.

"You were supposed to stay off your ankle today."

A deeper blush stole over her face as the eyes of strangers shifted her way, his cool reprimand rubbing her the wrong way. Tightening her hands on the reins, she replied evenly, "I am off it. Can't you see I'm sitting down?"

"Devin." Greg nudged his horse between Devin and Kelsey. "Go on in. I'll follow with Kelsey." He waited until the group was out of earshot before turning to Tom. "How far did you get with lessons?"

Tom reached over and patted her arm. "She's got a good seat and has steering down perfect. Just needs practice before she can take Cleo any faster than a walk."

Kelsey nodded. "There. Tell that to Mr. Grumpy. And, my ankle is fine."

"Good to hear." Before she realized his intent, Greg moved alongside her and plucked her from the saddle, settling her in front of him on his massive beast of a ride without breaking a breath. "If you'll take Cleo back, I'll give Kelsey a faster ride on in."

Saluting his boss, Tom grabbed Cleo's reins and waved as he trotted behind the other riders. The dizzying effect of being transferred from one horse to another with such ease and speed cleared Kelsey's head as Greg wrapped one thick arm around her waist and pressed her back against his wide chest. With her butt nestled against his groin, another sensation took hold, this one more to her liking. Wiggling her hips, she turned her head enough to grin up at him, catching his frown from under the rim of his hat.

"I like this seat much better." She meant the flippant remark as a tease, but when the hard, thickness of his cock jerked against her butt, a slew of other possibilities ran through her head.

"Sit still and hold on to the pommel." His guttural growl sent a frisson of excitement running down her body and her grin widened.

"Why? You've got a good hold of me." Kelsey didn't know if it was the pleasure of being this close to such a freaking sexy male body or the desire to see Greg smile at her that prodded her into pushing his buttons. Whatever it was, she was enjoying this turn of events in her afternoon.

"Because I said, and I'm the boss as long as you're here." He placed her hand on the pommel and nudged the horse into a walk. "Did you like riding Cleo?"

She nodded, her head rapping his chin. "Sorry, and yes, more than I thought. Probably because I didn't have as far to fall off." She cast a quick look down and shuddered.

His deep chuckle went through her, clear to her toes. "Cherokee is big but well-behaved. You won't fall."

Unable to help herself, she rubbed her butt against his crotch again. "You sure?"

Greg brought the hand holding the reins up and gripped her chin, turning her to face his disapproval, which only made her smile wider "Stop that," he scolded. "You'll distract me and that's not wise, in more ways than one."

"You're taking the fun out of my first ride." Kelsey feigned a pout.

Releasing her chin, the arm around her waist turned into a steel band. "Behave and I'll take you for a real ride."

"*Ooh*, promise?" Whether it was the accumulation of stress, unhappiness and lust that prompted her to keep pushing him or just plain orneriness, Kelsey didn't care as a sudden thought struck her. What better way to pass the time here than with a hot and heavy affair? It would be the first time she entered into such a relationship knowing there would be an end date and the two of them would go their separate ways. How much more freeing, and enjoyable could such a liaison be when the risk of getting hurt is taken out of the equation? The more she pondered the idea, the more she liked it.

"Be careful, little bit, or you might incur consequences you aren't prepared for." With that warning, Greg kicked his booted heels against the horse's sides, sending the steed into a trot that jarred her as much as his words.

Kelsey exhilarated in the faster clip that blew her hair into her eyes and bounced her against Greg, wondering if it was just coincidence both men had now hinted at spanking as a way to stop her from goading them. Were they idle threats, or were they serious? God help her, she was tempted to find out. If she could entice one of them – Greg being her best shot – into an affair, that penchant would fit right in with her vivid imagination and fantasies of the past two weeks.

Squeezing her side, Greg stated above her head, "Ready? Here we go." Another nudge to Cherokee's heavily muscled flanks and the stallion took off in an all-out run.

With her hair whipping around her face, the evening air cooling her heated flush and the ground below them whizzing by, her exultant laugh rang loud and clear. Who would have ever thought this could be so much fun? Maybe it was the tight hold of a sexy cowboy that was responsible for sending her senses soaring. Either way, by the time they galloped up to the barn, she could feel the strain in her legs from gripping the sides and the rapid beat of her heart pounding against her chest. Greg pulled on the reins, controlling and slowing the huge animal with admirable ease, his equally large body swaying in tune with hers as Cherokee tossed his head in a vigorous shake, his long, shade lighter mane brushing against her arm.

"He seems awfully winded," she commented on a deep breath, noticing the horse's labored breathing and heaving sides as Greg brought him to a halt at the corral rail by the stable.

"He's fine." He dropped his arm and patted Cherokee's long neck. "We spent most of the day at a sedate pace, so he's glad for that short run. Don't let go until I have hold of you," he warned as he dismounted.

Kelsey missed the comfort of his embrace and strength as soon as he slid off, but then those large, calloused hands reached up, clasped her waist and lifted her down with as little effort as he'd exhibited when hauling her off Cleo onto Cherokee. Accidentally on purpose, she fell against him as soon as her feet touched the ground, loving the hard contact of all those chest muscles against her front as much as she had pressing against her back a few minutes ago. As soon as her nipples flattened against his taut pectorals, the girls puckered into turgid tips and the slutty bitch showed her glee with a surge of damp heat. Who was she to continue telling her body no?

A quick glance proved they were the only ones around. With a coy smile and blatant batting of her eyes, Kelsey brushed her chest against his, shivering as he narrowed those heart-melting green eyes and sucked in a deep breath that shifted his tense muscles over her nipples.

"I don't know what you're playing at, Kelsey, but knock it off," he warned. "It's not happening."

Cocking her head, she trailed her fingers down his corded, tanned neck. "What's not happening?"

"Anything between us while you're here. We're responsible for you, and we take our responsibilities seriously." Greg reached up and pulled her hand down. "Now, be a good girl and return to the house. I'll escort you to dinner after I see to Cherokee and get washed up."

Grabbing the reins, he pivoted and led the horse into the stable, Kelsey following on his heels with another taunt. "Fine, but Devin made it clear he wasn't responsible for me, so I'll just see if he's interested in helping me pass the time in this boring place so I don't go stir crazy."

A laugh burst from Greg as he pulled the saddle off and opened a stall gate. He didn't want to see her hurt by what would be Devin's much harsher rebuttal to her wiles, so he sought to caution her. "If you think you'll get anywhere with him, you're sadly mistaken."

Flipping that long, blonde hair, she glared at him with sparks in her bright eyes. "It's my mistake to make, isn't it?"

He swore as she spun around and took two steps toward the open door, twitching that cute ass he was sure, on purpose. He understood she was put out by her circumstances and that the ranch offered little in the way of pastimes she was used to. But that was no reason to break his vow not to involve himself on a sexual or personal level. She tempted him, he wouldn't lie, but not enough to go down that slippery road again with a woman he'd sworn to protect.

After ensuring they were alone in the stable, Greg decided an example of those consequences he mentioned wouldn't threaten his resolve if he delivered just enough to deter Kelsey from her set course and spare her the embarrassment of Devin's reaction. Reaching her in two, long-legged strides, he grasped her hand and tugged her back into the stable.

"You need to heed my warnings better, and remember, I don't bluff." Ignoring her startled gasp, he yanked her into the crook of his arm, pinned her against his side and delivered five rapid swats on her upturned, jean-clad butt, putting just enough force behind them she would experience a twinge of discomfort and nothing more.

"Hey! What? *Holy shit!*" Kelsey's strident cry ended on a gasp, and much to Greg's surprised annoyance, she lifted her ass for the last slap, as if embracing the humiliating experience instead of balking at it.

Helping her upright, he kept hold of her upper arms as he gauged her reaction. Fuck if the rose hue blooming on her face and dilation of those large eyes didn't hold a hint of excitement. Not only he, but Devin would be hard pressed keeping their hands off her if they learned she possessed a submissive streak and she kept up with her cock-teasing innuendos.

"You need to get any thoughts of pushing one of us into entertaining you with sex out of your head, little bit. It's not going to happen. Now, run along and let me finish seeing to my horse."

## Chapter 5

Whoever said *fantasies were best left unexplored didn't know what they were talking about.* Every step Kelsey took toward the house stirred the warm tingles still racing across her butt with one word resounding in her head. *More.* All that from a few light swats, just enough to make her wonder what her response would be to harder spanks, to the crack of Greg's large, calloused hand on her bare flesh. A shiver trickled down her spine as she entered the house with the image of her lying across his hard thighs with her pants pulled down running through her mind.

"Oh, for crying out loud," she muttered as the girls and slutty bitch let her know with soft pulses how much they liked that idea. Leaning against the door, she closed her eyes, wondering how far she was willing to go with pushing either Greg or Devin into sex. The fact she couldn't decide which man she was drawn to and itching to get down and dirty with most should give her pause. But it didn't, just the opposite kept happening. She liked both men and was in enough of a needy turmoil due to the upheaval in her life that had landed her here that she would settle for the diversion of either man's attention.

"What's wrong? Did Greg reprimand you for not staying off your ankle today?"

Kelsey opened her eyes and glared up the stairs at Devin who stood in the shadows at the top. His cool, taunting tone hurt, prompting her to disguise that undesirable emotion any way she could.

"No, in fact, he rewarded me for knowing when I was healed enough to walk on it. I do believe I could get into this spanking proclivity you two seem to enjoy." Shoving away from the door, she strode toward her room, smiling when his low curse reached her ears.

Devin was nowhere around thirty minutes later when Greg stood ready to escort Kelsey to the social hall, and as happy as she was for the warmth of his hand resting on her lower back as he held open the door, another part of her wished they were both willing to spend time with her.

A sigh escaped her as they stepped out into the evening air, the sound catching Greg's attention. "Are you okay?" he asked, casting her a probing look from under the brim of his hat while slowing his stride to match her shorter steps.

"If you're referring to that 'reprimand'," she finger quoted the last word, "then yes, I'm fine. It's not as if you hurt me." Nope, just gave her enough to leave her aching for another lesson, one harder and longer enough to satisfy her curiosity instead of adding to it.

"If you refuse to heed that warning, you won't get off so lucky the next time. I made sure you were settled afterward before letting you go, so why the sigh?"

"Why does Devin dislike me so much? He doesn't even know me." Kelsey's stomach rumbled as she caught a whiff of tantalizing aromas emanating from the open doors to the dining hall, but as they entered the crowded, noisy building, she preferred an answer before food. Pausing, she looked up at Greg, waiting for a reply.

Removing his hat, he tossed it on a hook next to several others and raked his fingers through his thick, wavy hair. "He doesn't dislike you, he just doesn't want the responsibility for your safety. And, before you ask, his reasons are his own and for him to tell."

"Aren't you both responsible for the safety of all your guests?" she returned, smiling when he frowned and tried to work through the logic of her question. "See, you don't have an answer, do you?"

"You make a good point, little bit, except our other guests aren't hiding out from a possible assailant."

She shrugged, pivoting toward the buffet across the room. "There's no proof I need to be either. Thanks for walking me over." Flipping him a cheeky grin and finger wave, she left him standing there with a rueful twist of his lips.

---

DEVIN FINISHED HIS MEAL, struggling to keep his mind on the guests at the table and their conversation instead of straying toward the sound of tinkling laughter coming from the table next to them. Not even two days, he thought in disgust as he eyed Kelsey's animated face and sparkling eyes, and she was wreaking havoc on his intentions to remain immune to her presence. Greg's knowing smirk from another table didn't improve his mood. He knew his friend didn't want to take the same risk they'd both taken the last time they were in charge of a woman's safety any more than he did, but he also knew Greg didn't blame himself for their charge's death as much as Devin did. Deep down, he knew they'd done everything humanly possible to protect Catherine Valdez when the surprise attack had occurred, but a part of him would always question whether they were distracted that morning following the first and only time they'd spent the night in her bed. After being brave enough to agree to testify against her corrupt boss, she hadn't deserved to go out that way.

Kelsey tossed her head and laughed at something one of the men sitting next to her said, all four people at her table appearing captivated by the girl. There was no denying she had a way about her that, when coupled with the fey appearance of her petite features, drew people in. And then she bit into her thick burger, closed her eyes as she chewed then slowly opened them with a sigh as she swallowed. *Jesus*. As if the look of bliss on her face wasn't enough to stir his cock, she had to raise a fry to her mouth, dart her tongue out to savor a lick of salt and then nibble on the slim potato with small white teeth. When she shifted those wide, guileless blue eyes his way he swore under his breath, damned sure her antics were for his benefit. Pushing back his chair, he hardened his determination to stay clear of the girl and let her remain Greg's problem.

"Anyone for a friendly pool wager?" Devin asked the young couple who would be checking out the next day and Otis and Silas, two of their long-term renters. It didn't surprise him Silas was the only one eager to join him at the billiards table.

"I'm in. I owe you a rematch, boy."

Devin grinned, replying in kind. "Come on then, you can give it your best shot, old man."

An hour later, he and Silas were finishing up their game with each readying to make the winning shot when Kelsey strolled up with a Cheshire cat grin Devin didn't trust. Leaning a hip against the pool table, she cocked her head as she took in the placement of the last three balls, her pose distracting him as he bent at the waist and lined up his shot.

"You won't make it at that angle," she said, her tone laced with amusement.

"Hey, don't give him any pointers. Save them for me. I'm old and need all the help I can get against these young sharks." Silas winked at her from the other side of the pool table and

Devin shook his head at both of them from his position at the end.

"Nice try, but I've been watching your moves. You're good enough on your own," Kelsey retorted with an engaging smile.

It surprised Devin she caught on to Silas' bullshit so fast and he couldn't help but be amused by the older man's disgruntled expression and grumbling reply. "I used to have a way with the ladies. Sucks to get old."

Devin flicked a look toward Kelsey and told her the truth. "He says that a lot. Shouldn't you be getting back to the house and putting your foot up?"

"Shouldn't you give me a little credit for knowing when I need to turn in and put my foot up?" she shot back.

Silas threw his head back and guffawed, setting his cue stick on the table. "Good for you, girl. This one's yours, Devin. *I* am ready to turn in. Otto and I plan to be at the creek with poles in hand by sunup." The two best friends had booked the entire month of September for the last three years, spending most of their time fishing all day and shooting the breeze with other guests in the evenings.

"It's a draw. We'll settle the matter next time. Goodnight, Silas." Devin frowned as Kelsey reached for the rack, placed it on the felt tabletop and started grabbing balls to put inside the triangle. "What are you doing?"

Leaning across the table, she plucked up Silas's cue stick and straightened with a wicked grin. "One game, you and me. We each name our own prize if we win. I want you to give me my next riding lesson if I beat you."

*She was challenging him?* Devin never could resist a dare and maybe it was time he demonstrated who held the upper hand between the two of them. "You're on, and if I win, you ignore me, stay clear of me, don't talk to me for the next few weeks." He regretted his words the instant they came out of his mouth, the flash of pain in her eyes cutting him to the quick. Sliding his gaze away from her expressive face, his eyes connected with Greg's stormy green glare. The social hall had cleared out except for a few people playing cards in front of the fireplace, so at least he had spared her the humiliation of anyone else overhearing his callous wager. "Look, Kelsey…"

She lifted a hand and shook her head. "Fine, you're on. I'll even let you go first."

"Good enough." Maybe this was for the best, Devin thought as he bent and took aim to break. He needed to hold on to his resolve not to have anything to do with her, and it would be much easier to accomplish that if he won and she abided by their wager. His gut clutched at that but he refused to acknowledge the odd feeling of dissatisfaction it conjured up as he pulled back and started the game with a clatter of balls spreading out across the table.

Fifteen minutes later, he blew out a frustrated breath as Kelsey sunk yet another ball, increasing her lead by two. There were only four balls remaining and the eight. Unfortunately, she was the high ball after he choked on the eight. She was good, he'd give her that, but he wasn't above playing dirty to get out of the bind she wrangled him into. There was no way he wanted that small body pressed against him as they rode Thor, or even the responsibility of sticking close to her as she rode Cleo. Cursing Greg, who stood leaning against the wall with a glower on his face this whole time, he strolled behind her as she lined up to sink the ten. Thinking just to distract her enough to screw up her shot, he slipped in a tight squeeze of one buttock without slowing, surprised at the malleable fullness of her cheek. She jumped and missed, but that didn't seem to bother her since she flipped him a cheeky grin, swaying her hips.

"Feel free to do that again."

A laugh burst from Greg as he drawled, "Wrong play, partner."

Turning back to the game, Kelsey didn't say or do anything

to retaliate as he sank two balls, tied up the score then missed the eleven. Desperate to deny her the winning shot, he leaned on his cue stick and tried to catch her off guard and ease his conscience by stating, "It's nothing personal you know, my reasons for wanting to keep my distance."

She jerked and glared at him. "I never said it was. Trust me, I don't want to be here anymore than you want the responsibility of having me around." As if that statement bothered her more than it did him, she bent and made a clean shot, nicely sinking the last ball and then, without flaw, pocketed the eight.

---

AFTER DECIDING it was no fun pursuing or even teasing a man who made it clear he had no interest in having her around, Kelsey pouted and stayed away from both men for the next few days. It wasn't worth the frustration and hurt to continue flirting and poking at either Greg or Devin when neither shied away from telling her exactly how they felt about her presence. Granted, Greg had been friendly and welcoming, at least ten times more so than Devin, but it wasn't enough to ease her unhappiness over being here in the first place, or to assuage her hurt feelings. When not working, she found little to occupy her time since nothing about the ranch appealed to her except the owners.

*Quit being a wuss and get over it already.* Switching gears, she focused on her work and the two new clients her boss had sent her this morning. Along with the fresh breeze wafting in from the open window, the faint echo of lowing cattle, occasional high pitch of a neighing horse and voices of camping guests rousing themselves reached her ears. The sounds were vastly different from the constant busy clatter of her downtown office and loud bustling activity and traffic from the streets of Philly that filtered through the closed windows, but they didn't bother her as much as earlier in the week. Sometime in the past six days she seemed to have acclimated herself to her surroundings, if not to her hosts. Host, she corrected. As far as she knew, Devin was still none too happy about Greg's decision to agree to Jordan's request to offer her a temporary haven while they continued to investigate the man who attacked her.

When her attention wandered to the activities outside for the third time, Kelsey blew out a frustrated breath and pushed away from the desk. Maybe a sandwich and walk would clear her head and help keep her focused when she returned. Padding into the kitchen, she tried not to take the silence of the huge house to heart as she rummaged in the refrigerator for fixings for a sandwich. For four days she had stayed to herself, keeping to her room until she saw through the window both men leaving the house to attend to their agenda for the day. She'd taken advantage of Greg's offer to raid the kitchen any time she didn't want the buffet and had gotten by with making sandwiches or eggs once they were gone. Each night, Greg had rapped on her door when he'd come in, asking if she was okay or needed anything before calling out goodnight. Both men seemed content with her staying to herself.

"I don't care," she muttered as she slapped together a ham sandwich, grabbed a bottle of water and stepped outside. Settling in a rocker on the porch, she watched guests gather around the largest corral as Devin opened the gate and Greg herded a young calf inside. Eating her sandwich, she watched as Greg loosened a coiled rope, controlling his horse with his heavy thighs and knees. She envied the ease with which he sat the stallion and was surprised by the desire to master the feat of riding that well herself.

"Oh!" Kelsey sat up as Greg twirled the noosed end of the rope over his head while chasing the calf around until he got close enough to rope him. She groaned around a bite and then gulped a long drink of cold water as her needy body got all pumped up watching his agile leap off Cherokee. He controlled the bawling, none-too-happy calf by maintaining a tight, two-handed grip on the rope that emphasized the strength of his arms and legs. Devin entered to lend him a hand and she tried not to drool at the way their chaps framed their pelvises, the sexy leather wear drawing her eyes to their crotches and butts, depending on which way they turned.

*I need to get laid, scratch this itch that started when I was dumb enough to venture out on that balcony and got stirred up from the eyeful I got. Just eyeing her reluctant hosts proved to be enough to keep it going.* Padding back inside, she figured her prospects of getting her lust sated were slim to none.

Kelsey worked the rest of the afternoon and then went for a walk after telling Tom where she was headed. She stayed gone a little longer than usual and by the time she came strolling out of the woods, the evening dinner buffet had opened and she saw several people strolling toward the social hall laughing, their faces flushed from whatever activities they'd participated in and enjoyed that day. The appeal of this place still eluded her, and even though she wouldn't mind hanging out with others tonight, she trotted up the steps to the house to spend another evening feeling sorry for herself. There were times, like this, when her stubbornness irritated even her. Still, if her self-imposed solitude made Greg and Devin feel bad, it might be worth it.

When she wasn't tired by nine-thirty, she slipped on her silky, comfortable nightshirt, pulled her hair up in a sloppy ponytail, donned her magnetic blue-framed reading glasses and settled in front of the computer to work on her new accounts. Neither client had kept detailed books when they'd started their small business and going through the numbers was proving to be a tedious task.

It was still shy of ten o'clock when Kelsey heard the guys come in, their deep voices drawing goosebumps on her arms and distracting her from the notes she was jotting down. Instead of hearing them say goodnight to each other within a few minutes of entering the house, their low murmurs resonated down the hall from the den. Curiosity as well as annoyance that they seemed content with letting her be, prompted her to check out what was keeping them up later tonight. Slipping her pencil behind her ear, she rose and tiptoed down the hall, pausing around the corner to stay out of sight, but close enough now to listen in on the conversation. Devin's irritated voice reached her first, his words increasing her interest.

"Won't Jed be here? And she seems content staying to herself."

"That's bothering you, too, isn't it?" Greg drawled.

"Nope," he denied so fast Kelsey winced. "It's what I wanted from the start. I'm glad she reneged on the bet, too."

"Uh, huh, sure you are. Cut her some slack, Dev. She's not happy being away from everything she's known her whole life. I told you, I set her straight on the consequences for pushing us and she's been fine ever since."

"You didn't see her eating the other night," Devin muttered. Her lips curled at his disgruntled tone. "I bet she's plotting."

"And I bet you want her to keep her distance because you're worried you won't be able to resist her."

Greg's remark perked her up until Devin delivered his succinct reply with a derisive scoff. "There's not a woman out there I can't resist."

"If you say so. Anyway, Jed's brother fell and he's already left for the weekend. I said I would stay home. Go on to the club, if you want," Greg urged.

*Club?* The word renewed her inquisitiveness in their conversation and she halted in turning to go back to her room to listen further.

"And come home to you brooding because you were stuck babysitting? No thanks. The Barn will be there next week, along with all the willing submissives."

Kelsey gritted her teeth at the term 'babysitting' but her irritation took a backseat to the quick leap in her pulse upon hearing the term 'submissive'. Were they talking about a kink club, like Dominion? Before she could give in to the temptation to come around the corner and ask them point blank what they meant, Greg sighed and called out in a louder tone, "What are you doing, Kelsey?"

"Eavesdropping," she answered without hesitation, choosing honesty as she strolled into the den heedless of her skimpy nightshirt until both men's eyes zeroed in on her bare legs. A thrill whipped through her system as they eyed the outline of her turgid nipples pressing against the silky material. She twiddled her thumbs, standing in indecision as their slow perusal set up a low hum of arousal between her legs. Heat flared in their eyes as they reached her face, making her wonder if those hot looks stemmed from the view her see-through, thigh-skimming sheath offered or if they got off on the disheveled, geeky accountant appearance. She was more than willing to accept either explanation.

"What's The Barn?" she managed to ask as her toes curled into the thick, braided area rug.

Devin's dark brows snapped down in a frown. "None of your business. Go to bed."

That got her dander back up. Placing her fists on her hips, she narrowed her eyes. "I'm not a child to be sent to bed because the grownups have secrets."

"Then don't act like one by listening in on conversations and you won't be treated like one," Devin countered with a cool gaze.

Ignoring him, Kelsey took a step toward Greg, who was seated opposite Devin on the matching sofa. "I'm going bonkers here. Is this club in town? Can I go?"

"No."

"I'm not talking to you," she retorted without looking around at Devin.

"No. The Barn isn't a place for you, little bit. Behave and I'll take you into Billings on Sunday. Most of this week's guests are checking out in the morning and the new ones won't start arriving until Sunday afternoon." His green eyes slid around her to his partner. "Devin can stay here and welcome them without me."

"Or, you can let me come with you to this club and I'll help greet your new guests on Sunday." Considering their dominant personalities, those swats Greg had given her and the term 'submissives' she'd heard, Kelsey took a stab in the dark and surprised them by fudging the truth and saying with a shrug, "What's the big deal? I've been in clubs before, including ones that cater to submissives." Turning her head, she leveled a pointed glare on Devin.

The two of them shared a startled look before Devin's jaw went taut and his midnight eyes bored into her. "You have sexually submissive experience?"

His soft tone held a hint of menace that elicited a cold shiver and Kelsey hoped she wasn't biting off more than she could handle. It was obvious the McAllisters had left off telling them what she'd been doing when the assault had taken place, maybe even the type of establishment she'd been hired to work for that night. She saw this as an opportunity to not only alleviate her boredom, but possibly get this itch scratched her hosts were responsible for. If neither man wanted her, maybe she could hook up with someone who did, someone willing to answer the questions that had started that fateful night and had increased since finding herself drawn to these two virtual strangers. And then she might make it through the next three weeks without going stir crazy or lust crazy.

"Not much, but some," she hedged, thinking observing should count for something.

"How much is some?" Greg wanted to know.

Devin saved her from lying again by coming to his feet, exclaiming, "You're not seriously thinking of agreeing, are you?"

Greg stood, his eyes going from Devin to Kelsey. "Go on to bed, Kelsey. We'll let you know in the morning what we decide."

Thinking she better not push her luck, she nodded, pivoted and returned to her room. The pool of nervous sweat at the base of her spine dried as she slid into bed with different sexual scenarios flitting through her head, all of them with her paired with either Greg or Devin at a kink club similar to Dominion.

---

"NO FUCKING WAY," Devin snapped as soon as Kelsey left the room.

Greg was reluctant to grant Kelsey's wish, but not dead set against it. The girl pulled at something inside him, and he suspected it was the same for Devin. The sadness in her eyes when she'd asked him why Devin didn't like her still bothered him, and the taunting grin and comeback she'd given his partner when he tried to distract her at pool still drew his smile. He thought his cock would burst through his zipper when she came around the corner wearing nothing but that peach slip of a nightie and a pair of bright blue glasses. With her hair pulled up and that pencil nestled behind her ear, the fantasies rushing through his mind couldn't be stopped. Still, taking her up on her teasing, sexual innuendos wouldn't be wise. Desirable, hell yes, but not a good idea.

"Why? I saw a hint of submissiveness when I swatted her ass, but didn't want to acknowledge it, let alone mention it to you. If she's been to a club, nothing at The Barn will surprise her. She can come as a guest, just to hang out, not play, and it'll get her away from here for a few hours and hopefully appease her for a while."

Devin shook his head. "It's a risk. One, I'm not willing to take."

"What risk?" Greg returned, exasperated with the rigid line in the sand Devin had drawn over Kelsey's presence at the ranch. "We'll be right there, with friends. No one at the club would hurt her, and she'll be so happy she's going, she'll behave and not risk our wrath, or retaliation by not abiding by the rules."

"You don't believe that any more than I do. She didn't even blush standing in front of us with her hard nipples on display," Devin retorted.

A slow grin curved his lips and Greg couldn't resist nettling him. "Don't forget the cute, sexy accountant look. I loved the glasses."

Devin shrugged but Greg caught the twitch of his mouth before he stopped himself and said, "I like your first idea better. Take her into Billings on Sunday. I'll handle the tour group checking in." Kicking back the last swallow of his beer, Devin walked past him without another word.

Greg waited until he tossed his empty bottle into the recycle bin and started toward the stairs before risking his long-time friend's anger by announcing, "I'm going to let her come along. Deal with it." Devin's curses followed him as Greg went into his room praying Kelsey didn't give his partner cause to say I told you so.

## Chapter 6

*I'm a lousy judge of men.* The heated interest Kelsey thought she detected last night must have been an illusion because tonight, neither Greg nor Devin demonstrated an ounce of interest in her, not even a hint of male appreciation or lust. But she refused to allow their indifference to ruin her fun, or her plans for tonight. Just because their nonstop lecture during the first fifteen minutes of the drive left her ears ringing from all the rules they'd laid out for her to follow proved they harbored no lust for her whatsoever, didn't mean she couldn't enjoy tonight. If they didn't want her, she intended to hook up with someone who did, regardless of their number one rule – she was a guest, allowed to observe and nothing more. She refrained from glaring at either man each time one added a stipulation to the evening. Hell, if she abided by their list she might as well have stayed at the house. She didn't say that though, or grumble or complain. Nope, she sat docilely between the two men in the front of Greg's truck, dwarfed by their size and loving it, and kept her mouth shut except to answer 'I understand' when asked.

Every time one of them shifted his denim-clad leg alongside hers, her pussy clenched, the response irritating her. The slutty bitch needed to focus on something else, maybe someone else soon or she would go nuts. When the lectures stopped, she looked up at Devin and asked about the club's rule limiting everyone to two drinks, wishing his bulging bicep wasn't resting against her arm. It was hard enough to keep focused being sandwiched between their wide shoulders encased in tightly stretched T-shirts that emphasized their thick muscles. "Why do they limit everyone's drinking? Doesn't the club make a large profit off alcohol sales like other clubs?" She realized her mistake when he frowned and a suspicious look entered his dark eyes.

"That's standard practice for any gathering of BDSM players. Didn't your introduction to the club you went to cover that?"

"Yes." She twirled her thumbs and gazed out the windshield. "I forgot is all. The first time was so overwhelming, I confess I didn't pay much attention to the rules." That, at least, was the truth.

"Just make sure you do tonight," Greg stated as he turned off the highway onto a narrow, tree-lined bumpy road. "I don't want to regret giving in to you and give Devin a reason to say 'I told you so'."

"No," she murmured, "I wouldn't want that either."

Greg sighed and squeezed her thigh. "Relax. The Barn's rules don't require high protocol, such as addressing every Dom with Master or Sir, but there are a few who will insist. Since you don't know anyone, play it safe and be respectful to everyone."

"Got it. This road is kind of spooky." The headlights offered the only illumination until they came to a clearing and outdoor floodlights lit the double-door entry to the two-story converted barn. The wide upper window above the doors glowed in a dimmer, amber shade.

Greg rolled to a stop in the already crowded gravel parking lot and Devin opened his door, his tone dry, as he glanced back at her as he got out, "Maybe you'll find what's inside spooky as well and won't want to return." Shutting the door, he strolled inside, not bothering to wait for them.

Kelsey couldn't hide the hurt in her voice as she whispered, "He really doesn't like me, does he?"

Shaking his head, Greg squeezed her bare thigh, his calloused, warm touch sending a delightful ripple of pleasure up her inner leg. "That's the problem, little bit. He *does* like you. Come on. And don't worry. I won't abandon you until I introduce you to a few women you can visit with and get to know."

She didn't want him to abandon her at all but wasn't sure if it was because of nervousness over hedging on the truth of her experience that turned her palms sweaty as he lifted her down from the truck or because of the tightness around her chest at the thought of either man hooking up with someone else. Either way, she needed to get her act together before they got inside.

Greg pulled open the front door and ushered her into the foyer with a hand on her lower back. The music seeping through another set of double doors across the wood floor hit her first. The low sultry voice drew a wave of sensual awareness that put all her senses on high alert and pulled her nipples into taut pinpoints.

Placing his hat on a hook next to a row of other Stetsons, Greg nodded toward the wall of small cubbies, most holding a pair of shoes. "Pick one, and store your shoes before we go in. I phoned Master Caden and let him know you were coming tonight. He, his brother and the Willow Springs sheriff own the club."

Picking up her sandals, Kelsey slid them inside a cubby, tossing Greg a grin over her shoulder. "Does that mean naughty subs run the risk of getting handcuffed and arrested?"

His eyes warmed as he returned her teasing smile. "Maybe not arrested, but handcuffed is always a possibility, and punishment is a given. Ready?" He reached for the door and pulled it open.

At first glance, the large, high-ceilinged space appeared much the same as any club with tables and chairs scattered around a bar, music pumping in the background and a group of people swaying close together on a small dance floor. But as he led her through the room, the two women she spotted strapped over padded benches across from the dancers dispelled that notion right away. Kelsey winced at viewing their side-by-side, bright red butts even as her own buttocks clenched and her pussy went damp. *Get a grip, girl*, she told herself as Greg reached out with one finger and pressed under her lower jaw, urging her to close her mouth.

With a questioning glance, he inquired, "Surely you've seen a spanking bench in use before?"

"Oh, yes, of course. I... well, considering the bar and tables, I assumed they'd be in another room." *Oh, shit*. From the way he narrowed his eyes and those green orbs turned suspicious, she knew that excuse sounded as lame to him as it did to her. Thinking to divert his attention, she cast a quick glance around and saw an open shower in use. Luckily, she managed to swallow her gasp of surprise and cover her ineptness with both honesty and interest in the display. "Now, that I've never seen."

Greg switched his gaze to the couple in the shower, the woman bent at the waist, her hands braced on a tiled seat, her body jerking with each forceful thrust from the man behind her gripping her hips. Water streaming from four showerheads sluiced over their naked bodies, adding to the sheer eroticism of the scene. "That's Sue Ellen and Master Brett. I'll introduce you later. I see Tamara and Sydney at the bar."

Even though Kelsey's black skirt came to mid-thigh and her button-up gray silk blouse was the sexiest top she owned, her outfit was still modest and boring compared to what she saw as soon as she'd stepped into the cavernous room. The women they passed wearing anything at all still revealed more of their bodies than her one-piece bathing suit, and from their looks, appeared to enjoy the eyes on them. When Greg guided her over to a short redhead and a slender, black-haired girl perched on bar stools, she found herself envying their lingerie, and the ease with which they sat there wearing next to nothing. How on earth did she think she could pull this off?

"They're friends of yours?" she asked him before they were within hearing distance of the two women. The frisson of envy sneaking past her guard needed to be tucked away, and fast.

"Yes, and wives of the Dunbar brothers and owners, Caden and Connor. Relax. You'll like them." Greg prodded her forward with a press on her lower back.

Kelsey thought it might be best if he took off sooner rather than later if he was that astute at reading her. As much as she'd wanted to come tonight, she didn't want to get on Greg's bad side too. Dealing with Devin's constant annoyance with her was difficult enough. "I'm not tense, just taking everything in. This place is a lot different from the club I visited." She looked up at a soft cry echoing from the upper level and this time wasn't shocked or surprised at what she saw. The equipment she could see from this far away and shrouded in dim lighting seemed much the same as at Dominion, and the sounds emanating from the loft were just as similar.

"If you say so," he replied in a skeptical tone before greeting his friends. "Tamara, Sydney, this is my guest, Kelsey. She's visiting the ranch for a few weeks."

"Welcome to The Barn, Kelsey. I'm Sydney." The redhead held out her hand and Kelsey returned her friendly smile.

"Thank you. This place is bigger than it looked from outside." She sucked in a breath as Greg grasped her waist and lifted her onto a barstool, the heat of his hands seeping through her blouse. To cover the longing that simple touch stirred up, she flicked him an irritated look. "I'm perfectly capable of seating myself."

"I didn't say you weren't." He pinched her chin and

reminded her, "That's Sir or Master Greg. Remember that if another Dom talks to you."

"Like me. I'm Master Caden, Kelsey. Welcome to my club." The tall man with piercing blue eyes standing behind the bar held out a large hand that engulfed her much smaller one when she shook it.

"Nice to meet you, Sir. Thank you for having me." *Okay, that wasn't so hard*, she admitted.

He nodded and then told Greg, "Devin just went upstairs to monitor. Your slot is next. Does that work?"

"Sure. If you ladies don't mind keeping Kelsey company, I'll head up and assist my partner."

"Leave, Master Greg. We'll take good care of her." The gray-eyed girl leaned around Sydney and finger-waved to Kelsey. "I'm Tamara. My husband will be late, so stick with me and I'll be happy to show you around."

"Good enough." He hesitated and then yanked on Kelsey's long hair hard enough to tug on her scalp and gain her undivided attention. "Behave and remember the rules. We'll come find you in a little while."

A hot flash of anger tightened her muscles and it took supreme effort to keep from lashing out at him. It seemed he and Devin thought nothing of trotting off to have fun with someone else while ordering her to stay put and twiddle her thumbs. She was damn tired of people telling her what to do, of controlling her life even if they said it's for her own good and safety. Remembering his disconcerting perceptiveness, Kelsey reined in the urge to argue, and instead put on her sweet, eager to comply face.

"Of course. I'm looking forward to getting to know your friends."

Kelsey held her breath as his eyes bored into hers, as if gauging her sincerity. She didn't know what he saw but breathed easier when he huffed, spun on his heel and headed toward the stairs.

"Oh, wow, you seem to have gotten under his skin. You will definitely have to tell us how." Sydney mumbled in awe.

Caden reached across the bar top and flicked her bare shoulder. "Or, you could mind your own business, darlin'. Kelsey, what can I get you?"

"I'd love a rum and coke, if that's okay."

"Coming right up."

Sydney leaned over to whisper, "Okay, quick, tell," as Tamara hopped off her stool to take the one on the other side of Kelsey with an excited gleam in her eyes.

Kelsey tried not to envy how comfortable the two women appeared wearing eye-drawing silk teddies that left their braless breasts easily visible. She wished she had the freedom to indulge in wearing fetish wear and to explore the cravings that started two weeks ago, yearnings that had only escalated since staying with two of the hottest men here.

With a shrug to disguise her disgruntlement with her current situation and the guys, she replied, "I hate to burst your bubble, but I don't know what you're talking about. What makes you think I've made any kind of impression on Master Greg?" Oh, it was scary how easy that title rolled off her tongue, and alarming at how much she enjoyed saying it here.

"Because between him and Master Devin, he's the easier going of the two, and I've never seen him look at a sub here the way he did you," Tamara said, fanning herself.

Both girls straightened up as Master Caden returned with her drink. "Here you go. When you're ready for your second drink, just stop by."

"Thank you."

He eyed her for a moment, one of those silent, probing looks that made her fidget before he said, "Greg mentioned you had experience as a submissive."

Kelsey didn't know if he wanted details or was just curious and grew nervous under his stare. "I do, Sir, but not much.

There's a lot that's still new." She found it much easier to lie when there was a thread of truth to what she said.

He nodded, as if her answer satisfied an uncertainty he had about her. "In that case we can cut you a little slack." A call from the end of the bar put him back to work and Tamara and Sydney took advantage of his distraction to resituate at a nearby table.

"You're the first guest Masters Greg and Devin have brought to the club. You have to give us the juicy details on what's going on between you three," Sydney insisted as soon as they sat down.

Kelsey became too distracted watching the man at the next table reach inside the corset of the woman perched on his lap and scoop out her breast without pausing in his conversation with the other couple to heed Sydney's comment right away. The arousing scene drew an acute awareness of the constant tingles racing over her bare labia with every move she made. On one hand, it was nice to know her responses to kink were the same as the first glimpse she'd gotten inside a club, but on the other, they made for a long, frustrating evening if she abided by Greg and Devin's rules.

Tamara's giggle pulled her eyes off the man's hand and the woman's flushed face from the tight grip of his fingers squeezing her nipple. "What? Oh, sorry. Um, no, there's nothing going on between us." Kelsey scowled as she spoke as openly as Sydney. "Not for my lack of trying though." Since it didn't sound as if the guys had revealed the reason for her stay with them, she kept that little tidbit to herself. "It seems they don't cross that line with their guests. Bummer, huh?"

"Oh, that really sucks." Sydney sighed. "My Caden was just as rigid when I came to work for him. I sympathize with your frustration."

"Me, too," Tamara added, taking a sip of her beer. "Connor's stubbornness over not risking our friendship with sex drove me bonkers."

"But it worked out, for both of you?" They looked happy, and Master Caden's blue eyes had held an enviable gleam of love and lust as he'd gazed at his wife.

Tamara's mouth twisted into a wry grimace. "Eventually. Have you met anyone else yet?"

Shaking her head, she took a sip of the sweet rum and coke before saying, "No. Master Greg pointed out the couple in the shower before nudging me toward the bar, but I'm terrible with names, so don't expect me to remember anyone for one night."

Sydney's face fell. "Will you only be at the ranch for a week then?"

"No, closer to a month, but I had enough of a time finagling an invitation tonight, so I don't know if I'll be back." And just in case that happened, she intended to go through with the plan that had been flitting through her head all day. Despite the guys' friggin' rules, if someone showed an interest in her tonight, she would use this chance to explore her newfound interest and end the needy ache that had taken up permanent residence in her body lately.

"Since you've been left to your own devices and I'm on my own for about another hour, why don't I give you a tour, or did Master Greg already show you enough?" Tamara asked.

"No, I'd love to look around." Her palms grew damp with nervousness and excitement. "Thanks."

"In that case, let's go upstairs. That's where most of the bondage equipment is. Or, if you'd rather, we can step out back and enjoy the hot tub."

"I'd love that, but I didn't bring a swimsuit." Once again, Kelsey could have kicked herself as soon as she spoke, the amused expressions on the two women's faces adding to her annoyance with herself for making such a stupid statement.

"You really are new at this, aren't you?" Sydney teased. "Relax. Yes, we usually get in the hot tub naked, but that doesn't mean everyone here is comfortable stripping bare. There are a few who prefer the secluded corners for a scene or leaving something on while playing. Caden is signaling me, so I gotta go. Nice meeting you, Kelsey. I hope you come back."

"Thanks, Sydney."

"You haven't seen the loft yet, right?" Tamara slid off the stool.

Kelsey shook her head and cast a look up to the second floor. "No, Greg, Master Greg just mentioned it."

"Come on. The wooden A frame is new and the Wheel of Misfortune is unique. When you return to your club, you can tell them about it."

With a wince at Tamara's false assumption due to her lie, Kelsey rose, curious about both apparatus. But as they reached the stairs next to the dance floor, she paused as she realized one or both of the guys might already be involved with someone. Did she really want to see either man she'd been fantasizing about with his hands all over someone else? She didn't welcome the prick of jealousy responsible for the tight clutch of her abdomen, but also didn't want the image of either Greg or Devin with one of these experienced, eager submissives popping into her head over the next few weeks.

Before she could say anything, Tamara turned on the first step, a smile spreading across her face as she looked over Kelsey's head. Glancing around, she saw two tall men coming toward them, the one with blue eyes just like Sydney's husband holding out his hand toward Tamara.

"You made it back early." Tamara melted against the cowboy's lean body as he hauled her against him and swooped down to take her mouth in a kiss that had Kelsey shuffling her feet in response.

The dark haired man with him cocked his head and winked one, just as dark eye at her, holding out his hand. "I'm Master Kurt, the new Dom."

What the heck was it about the men in this state? She'd yet to meet one who didn't tower over her and couldn't melt the panties off a nun with one piercing look. Kelsey took his hand with a wry grin, happy with the diversion from pining for attention from either of her hosts. "I'm Kelsey, and I'm also new."

"New to The Barn or new to the lifestyle?" he asked, squeezing her hand.

"Both." She breathed a sigh of relief she could answer one question honestly.

"Oh!" Tamara gasped. "Sorry, Kelsey, this is my husband, Master Connor." She turned toward Kurt, adding, "Nice to see you again, Sir."

"Kelsey, welcome to The Barn." Tamara's sexy husband reached out and squeezed her shoulder with a warm look. Why couldn't Greg or Devin be as pleased to have her here?

"Thank you. It's nice to meet everyone."

"I'm up at the bar," Connor said. "Tam can keep you company until I'm done, if you wish."

"No need," Kurt interjected. "I'm free and wouldn't mind continuing Kelsey's education, if you're interested?"

Kelsey took one second to consider the number one rule the guys left her with – she was here to observe, not play – and another second to realize this might be the perfect opportunity to banish the constant fantasies and cravings for Greg and Devin from her head. "I am, very much so, Sir." Maybe that title didn't roll off her tongue as easily or feel as right as when she applied it to Greg earlier, but she refused to let that minor detail detour her from accepting his offer. "Thank you." Taking Master Kurt's hand again, she turned to Tamara. "Thanks. I hope we can visit again later."

"Me too." She finger waved as Master Connor tugged her after him.

Master Kurt didn't waste any time taking charge, for which Kelsey was grateful as he led her onto the dance floor. "Do you have your own safeword or would you prefer using the club standard?" he asked, pulling her against him as the music changed to a slower tune.

She wasn't sure what he was talking about but since she wasn't playing this safe by accepting his invitation, she decided she didn't need to risk asking. "The standard is easy to remember," she answered, liking the ripple of his muscles against her as they swayed. She'd never been much of a dancer, but he made it easy by leading and moving her body with seamless effort the way he wanted her to go. There was definitely something to be said for turning over control for a short time.

"You are a little thing, aren't you?" Master Kurt slid a hand between them and cupped her breast, warming her with his touch and next words. "But I've found good things can come in small packages. Nice." His thumb brushed her nipple and she leaned into his touch even though she couldn't keep from casting a self-conscious look around.

"I honestly don't know what to say to that. No one's said such a thing to me." And how pathetic was that admission? Her previous lovers had a lot more to answer for than not sticking around, she decided.

"Then you've been with the wrong men." He shifted the arm wrapped around her back downward, using his hand against her butt to urge her against the slow swaying of his pelvis against hers. "You look willing but uncomfortable. Am I right?"

Kelsey blew out a small breath. "You're really good at this, aren't you?"

"Yes. Would you rather we take this to the secluded nook for more privacy?"

Before she could think it through, or worry about the ramifications, she nodded and let Master Kurt escort her toward the front of the room with her heart beating in a rapid, staccato rhythm. The girls and slutty bitch were dancing for joy, but a part of her, a big part, couldn't help wishing it was Greg, or even cranky Devin leading her into a small alcove against the wall.

Enclosed on two of the sides by a short, half wall topped with bright green plants, the cozy space sporting one small sofa offered the most seclusion in this place.

"Better?" he asked, taking a seat and tugging her onto his lap.

"Yes, thank you. I'm still…" Pausing, she considered how to phrase her explanation then said, "Wrapping my head around a few things."

"Understood, so use the safeword if you become too uncomfortable, but try to push yourself. It's the only way to find out what works for you. Now, put your hands behind your back, lace your fingers together and keep them there."

He slid his arm down to her hips to leave room for her clasped hands. This left her leaning against the high arm of the sofa with her legs draped sideways over his thighs. Tightening the hand cupping her hip, he distracted her from the awkwardness of the position by popping open the top button of her blouse.

"You have an attractive, tight little body I wish to see more of," Master Kurt stated, his black eyes boring into hers as he flicked open several more buttons.

A small shudder went through her and Kelsey gripped her hands tighter behind her back as he spread her top open, baring both breasts to his eyes and the cooler air. She liked having his eyes on her, and the simmering arousal as he circled one turgid tip with his finger, his gaze shifting from her flushed face to her breasts and then back up. One thing dominant men seemed to have in common was a focused, intent way of watching their partner, a trait that made her wonder what her expression might be revealing. Right now, she hoped he couldn't read her thoughts, which kept straying to two other men, or see how much she wished it was either Greg or even Devin holding her, touching her.

"Very pretty." He plumped her small mound and then plucked at her nipple, tightening his fingers by slow degrees. "Tell me, do you like a touch of pain as well as bondage?"

"What makes you think I like bondage?" she asked, avoiding the question as his grip drew tiny pinpricks around her nipple.

"You're leaving your hands behind you, not even thinking about releasing them. Answer my question. Are you accepting of light pain?" He emphasized that order with a tighter pinch to her tender bud, the discomfort prompting her to press her thighs closer together to stop the answering quiver of her pussy muscles.

Her response reminded Kelsey of the arousing flush she'd experienced from Greg's light smacks on her butt. The squeezes Master Kurt kept up on her nipple elicited close to the same heated reaction but something was missing this time, something she couldn't, or didn't want to put a finger on. It was upsetting on several levels to discover her initial enthusiasm for accepting his offer was ebbing instead of escalating.

"I don't know, Sir," she replied, tacking on the title when he tightened the hand on her hip in warning.

"You're about to find out," a deep, gravelly voice growled from the alcove's opening.

Kelsey jerked, her startled gaze flying towards Devin's dark, disapproving face as he stood there glowering with booted feet apart and muscled arms crossed. "Uh, oh," she muttered, thinking maybe it had been ill-advised to break his and Greg's number one rule in agreeing to let her come tonight.

Master Kurt squeezed her breast and hip tighter and looked at Devin. "Problem?" he drawled with a lift of one brow.

"Tell Master Kurt, Kelsey," Devin commanded.

Kelsey's annoyance with him and their rules rose to the surface, propelling her off Kurt's lap as she yanked her blouse closed. "That was an unfair rule, and you know it, Devin." The stormy look swirling in his dark blue eyes proved she was playing with fire, but some untapped perverse part of her flat-out didn't care.

Kurt came to his feet, his glower matching Devin's and causing her to take a hasty step back. "I'll leave it to you to take her to task for whatever infraction she has incurred, Master Devin. I apologize if I crossed a line here."

"You didn't, Kurt, but Kelsey was allowed to attend tonight as our guest to socialize, and that's all, a small fact I'm sure she neglected to mention."

He sent her a cold glare and then nodded at Devin, walking out without another look at her, leaving her with a man who didn't want her to come tonight in the first place, let alone be a guest at his ranch for a few weeks. Why couldn't it have been Greg who had discovered her with Master Kurt?

## Chapter 7

Devin kept Kelsey pinned in place with his glare as he struggled to get himself under control. He didn't know what pissed him off most, her blatant, unrepentant disregard for his and Greg's orders or the obvious reluctance on her face as she sat on Kurt's lap and let him touch her. He'd caught a glimpse of something in her eyes he'd only seen on the faces of newbies, a hint of unease from girls who were exploring the lifestyle for the first time and were unsure about what they were doing and feeling.

Which meant she had lied about her experience. *Damn it, I knew she was trouble.* The problem was, that small package of trouble had caused a clutch in his abdomen the moment he'd seen someone else's hands on her, something he'd never felt with another woman. He swore Greg would pay for this, one way or another. In the meantime, as opposed as he was to getting involved with her in any way, he'd never shirked his duties as a Dom and wouldn't start now. Taking slow steps toward her, his lips curled in a taunting grin as the defiance sparking in those bright blue eyes switched to wariness.

"I believe *Master* Greg mentioned consequences for bad

behavior," he reminded her as he reached for the hand not clutching her blouse. The look he'd gotten of her small, soft breasts tipped with pale pink nipples had been enough to stir his cock into an uncomfortable, semi-erection pressing against his zipper, enough to irritate him with how badly he wanted to shove Kurt's hand aside and replace it with his own — something else she needed to answer for.

"I thought you didn't want anything to do with me," she stated, the slight tremor in her voice telling him she wasn't as sure of herself as she was trying to portray.

"I don't, but all Masters here at The Barn have a duty to enforce the rules, and that includes the orders we gave you earlier." Keeping a firm grip on her hand, he took a seat on the sofa and tugged her to stand between his spread thighs. "Did it not once occur to you there might be reasons, damn good ones, for Master Greg and me telling you not to get involved with anyone tonight?" He continued to emphasize their titles so she knew she wasn't dealing with her hosts here at the club.

Whatever intimidation he'd inspired in her a moment ago disappeared as she narrowed her eyes and tightened her hand on her blouse. "Did it not occur to either of you I'm a grown woman who is capable of making my own decisions?"

"I don't appreciate your smart-aleck reply any more than my suspicions you lied about your experience in submitting and with the BDSM lifestyle. Even someone who has spent minimal time at a club and is still learning the rules, knows not to talk back, and definitely wouldn't dare disobey a direct order, as you have. You've been here an hour and have one — lied, and two — disobeyed our instructions." Kelsey's face flushed as he ticked off her transgressions, but she didn't try to pull away from him. If he wasn't mistaken, the gleam in her eyes and the press of her turgid nipples against her top suggested she wasn't afraid of what he would do. A part of Devin admired her gumption and another part craved to see just how far her bravado would extend.

"Did you even bother to negotiate a safeword with Master Kurt?"

The look of guilt crossing her face stirred his anger anew, especially when she tried hiding it with an evasive answer. "I agreed to the standard word."

"And that would be?" When she bit her lip and shuffled her bare feet, the force of his ire made him take a deep breath before giving her the answer. "Red, damn it. Yet another infraction you're going to answer for."

With a hard yank and no warning, Devin pulled her over his left thigh, lifting his right leg to pin her flailing legs down. Kelsey's surprise cost her the hold on her blouse, the sides flying open again as she went down. Shackling her wrists together in his left hand, he held her arms pinned against her lower back as he flipped her skirt up and smacked her panty-covered, wriggling ass.

He didn't tell her green meant continue and yellow pause as he didn't consider those choices an option with this woman. It would either be continue as he saw fit or stop altogether. "Let's discuss why you were given orders to keep to socializing tonight." He cracked his palm against her soft buttocks again, enjoying their jiggle. And her gasp. "Since we know little to nothing about you or your experience, it would have been irresponsible to turn you loose and allow you to fend for yourself." *Smack!* "What if you had lied to one of the stricter Doms and he pushed you too far? Would you have been able to stop him before he traumatized you? I think not." *Smack!*

"I'm sorry," she choked, shifting her hips as he swatted her two more times before resting his hand on her warm butt. The thin panties offered little protection in hiding her quivering heat.

"That's a start, but not good enough, baby." With a quick shove, he lowered her panties to mid-thigh, his mouth watering at the sight of her small, pink-tinged, round buttocks, his hand itching to feel her bare flesh heating up even more. "You lied, and then set out to deliberately go against our wishes after we were nice enough to give in to your insistence to come out with us tonight." Lifting his arm he delivered a volley of bare-assed spanks, each one a little harder. After five, he paused and caressed her burning backside, the sheen coating her pussy slit drawing his eyes and his frustration. *Fuck*, how could he continue to resist her if she was going to get aroused from the hot pain he was heaping upon her?

And then she whipped her tear-streaked, red face around and gazed at him with remorse shining in her damp eyes. "I... I never thought about that." She hiccupped and his hardened resolve to remain aloof crumbled a little more. "You're right." With a nod, she turned her head back down and lifted her hips. "You shouldn't stop yet, Sir. Please."

*Well, son-of-a-bitch. Now what?*

---

KELSEY'S BACKSIDE throbbed and ached, the discomfort contrasting with the damp heat building deep inside her pussy or adding to it. She wasn't sure which. The urge to cringe and shift away in mortification battled with the need to arch for more. She found Master Devin's powerful hold on her wrists and legs a comforting embrace against the storm of sensations flooding her system. A sob burst from her throat as he struck in the center of both burning cheeks, and yet she never thought to call a stop to the blistering torment by saying red. His litany of berating words brought tears to her eyes and she knew she deserved the stinging pain. What she couldn't wrap her mind around was the slow build-up of arousal spreading inside her swelling core. That was just wrong on so many levels she couldn't count. Wasn't it?

"When I think about the trouble you could have caused, the precarious position you could have put both yourself and a Dom in with your hedging lies, I want to shake you." She caught her breath as he raised the leg under her hips, tilting her forward, and landed several swats on the sensitive areas below her buttocks. "Safewords are just that, words to ensure your safety, and not meant to be taken lightly, or," he smacked her thigh, "lied about knowing."

*Okay, I get it, I screwed up.* Kelsey didn't mind admitting when she was wrong, but that one word kept repeating itself over and over in head, stopping her from showing *too* much remorse. *More, more, more.* Considering how much she hurt, she wondered if she'd lost her sanity as well as all control over her body.

"I said I was sorry," Kelsey reminded him as he tempered the last few slaps. She shuddered on a low groan when he switched to light, titillating caresses over her pulsating flesh, the soothing strokes helping her to relax as she absorbed the myriad of sensations encompassing her entire lower body.

Master Devin squeezed one throbbing cheek, his thumb sneaking between her buttocks to coast back and forth over her anus. She stiffened, the surprising pleasurable tingles of that taboo touch catching her off guard. "It was your bad luck I'm the one who came downstairs first and discovered what you were up to. Master Greg probably would have gone easier on you."

"I wouldn't bet on it."

Kelsey jerked at hearing Greg's disgruntled voice behind her. Picturing his view of her exposed, red butt and the placement of his friend's thumb brought on a wave of excitement that left her shaken in a whole new way as she thrilled to being the object of both men's attention. Granted, it was angry notice they were giving her, but she would take what she could get if these rioting sensations were her reward.

Devin released her and helped her sit up on his lap. Her blouse gaped open and both men's eyes moved to her bare, hard-tipped breasts. Kelsey relished their heated gazes so much she made no move to cover herself but couldn't help wincing as she adjusted her position and her tender skin scraped over rough denim.

"How long have you been standing there?" Devin's thighs tightened under Kelsey and Greg's jaw went taut, reminding her to tack on, "Sir."

"Long enough." Greg's green gaze slid to Devin. "What did she do?"

Devin grunted. "What didn't she do? I told you this was a mistake."

Why was it these two could stir up her horny juices with just a look and then irritate the hell out of her with a few words? Whatever the reason they both pulled such strong yet opposite reactions from her, she'd had enough of this talking over her head. Squirming off Devin's lap, she pulled up her panties and worked on buttoning her blouse as she snapped, "I'm right here, in case you failed to notice."

"Oh, I noticed, little bit," Greg drawled with a return of warmth to his eyes. "Now, go find a seat and wait for me. Without arguing." He jerked his head, indicating the main room outside the secluded nook.

"Fine." She huffed in exasperation. "But if you keep insisting on stifling me with your friggin' rules, I'm going home, regardless of what Jordan and Theresa want." With a glare toward them both, she stomped out as best she could in bare feet and with her body trembling on the brink of a much-needed orgasm. She could feel their eyes following her as she found an empty table and sat down, the return of pressure on her sore butt doing nothing to cool her overheated senses.

After a few minutes of twiddling her thumbs, Kelsey stood and padded over to the bar, noticing there was another man tending it, one who looked as dark and forbidding as Devin. Sliding onto a stool next to a brunette wearing large, black-framed glasses and a silky sheath, she noted the possessive gleam in the gray/green eyes beneath the new bartender's Stetson. One thing positive she had to say about the men in this state, they were all drool-worthy.

Nudging his hat back with a thumb, he talked around the toothpick in his mouth. "You must be Kelsey, Devin and Greg's guest. I'm Master Grayson and this is my wife, Avery. Do you have your drink card?"

"Yes, right here. I'd like a rum and coke, please." She fished it out of her skirt pocket and handed it over, turning a smile on Avery as she took her hand.

"Hi, Kelsey. Are you having a good time?"

Her grin turned rueful. "Honestly? I'm not sure." Shifting on the seat reignited the soreness covering both cheeks and the tingles around her rear orifice, sending a shiver down her back. "I'm reserving judgment since it's all so new."

Avery's face showed empathy as she leaned closer and asked, "Did you get in trouble already?"

*Already? I've been in trouble since I met those two.* Kelsey didn't want to admit that but figured the other trouble she had landed herself into tonight, as well as the consequences wouldn't surprise Avery, or anyone else here. "Yes, much to my discomfort." Not to mention the arousal still humming through her veins. "It seems I didn't take a few rules serious enough."

Grayson set her drink in front of her with an inquisitive look. "I thought Greg and Devin said you attended a club before."

"She wasn't truthful about that important tidbit," Greg stated from behind her as he dropped a hard hand on her shoulder and kept her in place with his grip.

Master Grayson's face darkened and Avery winced, flicking her another look of pity. "Uh, that probably wasn't a good idea."

"Yeah, I found that out." Kelsey twisted, craning her head up to give Greg a cheeky grin. "I'm still debating whether it was worth it or not."

Greg couldn't stop his lips from twitching but managed to remain stern as he replied, "For God's sake, don't let Master

Devin hear you say that. I'm still trying to smooth his ruffled feathers." *And keep him from saying I told you so.* He didn't need his partner telling him that agreeing to Jordan's request had been a mistake. He was having enough trouble keeping his hands off Kelsey after seeing her heart shaped ass cherry red and the swollen, slick proof of how her first hard spanking affected her. There was no doubt he wanted her sandwiched between him and Devin, and from the look on his friend's face when he'd held her quivering on his lap, he was no longer immune to the idea. Greg knew he was in for a lecture when they returned home.

"When I leave he'll be back to his happy self," she said, reminding him of her earlier threat.

Grayson gazed at Greg over Kelsey's bright blonde head, one black brow lifted as he waited for his answer to that remark. With his engorged cock pressing against his zipper, his reaction upon hearing her first threaten to return home had been relief followed by an alarming sense of panic. Now, his only response was determination not to end up responsible for another attack on her, or worse. Regardless of her irritation with him and Devin, and of his escalating lust, he refused to let her go until the McAllisters gave them the all clear.

"We will discuss all this tomorrow, but you know as well as I, you won't go against your foster parents' wishes when they're only thinking of your safety."

"Anything I need to know about?" Grayson asked sharply. As the county sheriff, their ranch fell under his jurisdiction.

"No, but I'll be sure to let you know if that changes. Master Grayson is the sheriff, Kelsey."

Avery laughed at Kelsey's piqued expression. "Give it up, Kelsey. In case you haven't figured it out yet in your time at the ranch, when these guys get into protective mode, there's no talking them out of it."

"I think I just found that out. You call it protective, but I call it over-bearing." She turned toward him and asked, "Is there anything I *can* do tonight?"

"We'll see." Greg caught the hopeful expression on Kelsey's face and the remainder of his anger with her slipped away. It was obvious she wouldn't be opposed to exploring some of what she was feeling with him, and it was much harder to turn her down now that he'd seen her indisputable streak of submissiveness. Before he crossed the line he and Devin had agreed upon, he needed to speak with his partner. The two of them didn't always share a sub when playing, but he respected Devin's opinion and sensibilities on the subject of getting involved with a woman under their protection. Even though Devin had left anything to do with agreeing to the McAllisters' request to shelter Kelsey for a few weeks up to him, Greg saw the look in his eyes as he'd held her shuddering, aroused body on his lap. He wanted to help her explore her new desires as much as Greg did, he just didn't want to admit it.

Kelsey's eyes widened and her face flushed as she looked over Greg's shoulder. Turning to see what snagged her attention, he grinned as Dan joined them, Nan's hand clutched in his, the tips of her full breasts now pierced with attached chains clipped to the D ring in the center of her collar. "Aren't you a pretty sight, Nan?"

"I think so." Dan reached up and flicked one nipple.

"Thank you, Sirs." Her golden eyes swiveled toward Kelsey. "You must be Master Greg's guest. I'm Nan."

"Nice to meet you."

Greg spotted Devin heading their way and lifted Kelsey off the stool, liking the way she leaned into him. Glancing from Grayson to Dan, he said, "With your permission, I think Kelsey might benefit from some girl talk in the hot tub."

"I'll be here for another forty minutes, so go ahead Avery," Grayson replied with a nod.

"Your girl does look as if she has questions." Dan winked at

Kelsey then took Nan's mouth in a deep, possessive kiss before releasing her with a nudge toward the other two. "Have fun."

"I'll come out and get you shortly," Greg told Kelsey. "Don't go wandering off."

"Of course not."

She turned to follow Avery and Nan but not before he caught the roll of her eyes, a gesture prompting him to address with a quick, physical reprimand. The swat he delivered on her sore ass drew a sharp inhale and forced her hand behind her to cover the offended area. "Careful," he warned when she turned and glared at him.

Grayson grinned, watching the three girls walk out back. "She's not shy, is she?"

"If you're talking about Kelsey, the answer's no," Devin remarked as he slid onto the stool next to the one Greg took a seat on.

Dan sent him a quizzical glance. "You don't sound happy about having her around."

"I'm not." His gaze slid toward the back glass slider and he narrowed his eyes.

Greg looked out and saw Kelsey's bare breasts jiggle as she shimmied out of her skirt. Taking a half step around, she bent slowly and picked up her top and skirt and laid them on a deck chair.

Devin turned his dark look on Greg. "She did that on purpose."

Amused by both Kelsey and his friend, he drawled, "So don't watch," his remark drawing a chuckle from Grayson and Dan.

"I always enjoy a teasing striptease, especially one that gives me a lovely look at a new sub." Dan smirked as he brought his beer bottle to his lips.

"I do believe that's the first complaint over a sub revealing herself I've heard from you, Fisher." Grayson handed him a brew. "Here. Chill."

For the first time since he'd picked up Kelsey over a week ago, Greg saw Devin's tense shoulders relax and a rueful grin pull at the corners of his mouth.

---

KELSEY SHUDDERED, the hot, bubbling water doing little to prevent the chill hearing about Nan's horrendous ordeal caused. "And Greg and Devin didn't know about what happened during those three days that asshole kept you locked down there?" She couldn't help but admire the strength it took for Nan to return home and work to get her life back after being kidnapped by a sadist and left locked in a dark cellar room after he'd taken a whip to her.

Nan sank lower on the seat until the water rose to her nipples, sighing in enviable pleasure. "No, that was another mistake I made, thinking I could just jump back into a scene after everything he put me through. They were as ticked off at me as Master Dan when I freaked out."

"But look on the bright side," Avery said, slowly kicking her legs back and forth under the water. "You and Master Dan realized how deep your feelings ran and now you're living together and getting married."

"Congratulations," Kelsey returned, wondering if she would ever be so lucky. "Please tell me that jerk paid for what he did to you."

"He's sitting in prison right now, thank God," Nan answered. "That's something Avery and I have in common. We both got to put away some really bad people."

Kelsey resisted taking another peek toward the glass doors to see what Greg and Devin might be doing, giving her full attention to Avery. "You too? Tell me, please."

Nan smirked, turning her head to the side to look at Avery. "She's just using us to distract her from Masters Devin and Greg.

I can tell you now, Kelsey, it won't work," she warned, shifting her gaze across the tub toward her.

"Hey, I *am* interested in hearing about your ordeals, and how they landed you here, but maybe you could enlighten me on why I can't think about anything except getting one of them to relieve this ache that started with a really painful spanking." She shifted on the seat, and yeah, the slutty bitch still spasmed in response to the lingering soreness.

Avery giggled. "I was as confused and aroused as you when I got my first spanking. But, wow, the orgasms an intense punishment can lead to will have you begging for another one."

Kelsey sighed in relief. "So this feeling is normal. That helps to know."

"The key to learning what works for you, to discovering whether you prefer a Master's dominance for a fun bout of kinky sex or because his control settles something deeper inside you is exploring with the right person." Nan looked through the glass doors at Greg and Devin, who still sat at the bar. "Or with two right men."

Listening to Nan confirmed one suspicion hovering in Kelsey's mind tonight – her temporary hosts were into ménage. Imagining herself with both men ignited a heated rush though her veins that matched the hot temperature of the swirling water. Too bad Devin didn't even like her, let alone want her staying in their home for a few more weeks. His attitude toward her before tonight, and when he'd flipped her over his lap, didn't jive with the tender, comforting way he'd held her after blistering her butt for her transgressions. Through the roaring in her head and the fast, escalating gush of arousal his painful punishment ignited, she managed to hear the concern in his voice as he had berated her and explained why her disobedience could have landed her and Master Kurt in an untenable situation.

Hearing Greg's voice, realizing he was looking at her bare, chastised butt and likely noticing her seeping juices, and then seeing anger toward her reflected in those green eyes for the first time left her as shaken as Devin's hard hand. She tightened her legs, wishing it could be that easy to still the need still quaking deep inside her pussy since she doubted she could entice either man into educating her further during the next few weeks, or talk one into allowing her to return to The Barn after her behavior.

"What's wrong?" Without her glasses, it was easy to see the compassion reflected in Avery's eyes.

"I doubt I'll get the chance to do any more exploring after tonight, at least not here, and not with either Master Greg or Master Devin." Damn it, it shouldn't be that easy to say their titles, not after they'd made it clear how unhappy they were with her.

Nan scowled and shook her head. "If they won't invite you back, call one of us. If need be, I'll drive out to the ranch and pick you up and then you can stay the night with us, at Dan's place."

Her offer pleased Kelsey, warming her where the guy's displeasure left her cold, as did Avery's adamant head nod in agreement. Sadly, her body didn't appear to want anyone right now except one, or heck, maybe both of her hosts. Add that irritating admittance to the fact Greg, for sure, wouldn't go back on his promise to watch over her until the McAllisters gave the all clear made for a bleak picture for the rest of her stay in Montana.

"Thanks, but Greg made a promise to stick close regarding my stay with them." She went on to give them a quick rundown of why she was at the Wild Horse Dude Ranch, staying in their house in the first place.

"Oh, wow, I hate to say it, but you might be right. Like I said before, if there's one thing I know for sure it's these guys take protecting us seriously," Avery said.

All three girls heard the slider open and looked over to see Master Greg stepping outside, his Stetson returned to his head.

But it was Kelsey he zeroed in on, her nipples that puckered under his heated gaze as he eyed her breasts bobbing just above the water. Snatching a towel off a bench, he flipped it over his shoulder, strode over to the hot tub and reached in to grasp her upper arms. Lifting her out as if she weighed nothing, Kelsey was happy to have his hands on her. Her heart went pitter-patter and her abdomen clenched as she pressed her wet body against him and gazed up into his rugged face beneath the lowered brim of his hat.

"Time to leave, little bit," he stated, nudging her back to whip the towel around her. With brisk rubs over her back, buttocks and down her legs, her body went noodle-soft, her eyes blinking in drowsy pleasure.

"*Mmm*, that feels good." She sighed, closing her eyes as he moved up the inside of her legs, kneaded her thighs and then cupped a towel-covered hand over her pulsing crotch.

"I bet that feels even better," Nan called out from behind her, amusement lacing her voice.

Kelsey opened her eyes as Master Greg rubbed her bare folds with the nubby cloth. The swift, stimulating pressure back and forth over that sensitive flesh started a tingling that spread up her core. "God, yes," she moaned before injecting a note of warning in her voice as she added, "You better not be toying with me."

"Uh, oh."

Avery's whisper reached Kelsey as Greg narrowed his eyes, dragged the towel up to dry her torso and then looped it around her neck to draw her up on her toes against him. "You're forgetting your place, and the rules again."

For a split second she thought he would kiss her, but disappointment swamped her as he released the ends of the towel, tossed it over the deck rail and handed her her clothes. "Get dressed and meet me in the foyer. Goodnight, ladies." With a nod to Avery and Nan, he turned his back on Kelsey and sauntered inside without another word.

Tiredness and a wave of depression settled on Kelsey's shoulders as she dressed. If orders and touches that never led where she wanted to go were all either man was willing to give her, she planned to call Jordan and Theresa first thing in the morning. While it appeared she was a glutton for erotic punishment, she wasn't one for self-abuse, which is what staying much longer in Greg and Devin's house would amount to.

"It was nice meeting you, and everyone else. Thank you for hanging out with me." She buttoned her blouse without looking at the two women still lounging in the hot tub.

"Since you don't have your phone on you, one of us can call the ranch and get a hold of you this week," Nan offered. "Don't fret, Kelsey, they're all reluctant in the beginning."

She smiled and waved with a nod as she turned to go inside, hoping the McAllisters wouldn't still insist on her staying. A girl could only take so much, after all.

## Chapter 8

"We need to talk," Greg whispered as his eyes flicked from Kelsey's sleeping face to Devin before he shifted his gaze back out the windshield. He was tired and edgy but felt this couldn't wait. Not after the stunt Kelsey had pulled tonight. Her lie about how much experience in the lifestyle she had, followed by the way she disregarded their orders to jump into a scene with someone she knew nothing about, proved how troubled and uncertain she was over the McAllisters leaving her with him. As irate as her actions made him, he could still feel for the girl who had been trying so hard this past week to use him as a diversion from her insecurities.

"You've changed your mind about getting involved, haven't you?" Devin's quiet voice held more resignation than annoyance.

"I don't like to see her hurting." He could just make out Devin's derisive look in the dark truck cab as they drove down the highway. "Okay, let me rephrase if you're going to be obtuse. I don't like to see her struggling so hard with the emotional upheaval of her life that she's willing to pull stunts like the ones tonight. As you know, I'm on board with dishing out both punishing and stimulating pain. You saw her response to your spanking as well as I," Greg reminded him. It was not only the slick puffiness of Kelsey's enticing folds that had snagged his attention off her bright red, rounded buttocks that prompted him to reconsider getting physically involved with her. The way she hadn't shied away from his presence and the glazed look in her damp blue eyes when Devin had flipped her over was a combination he was hard pressed to ignore.

Kelsey took that moment to slowly slide sideways, her head coming to rest on Devin's upper arm. With a low curse followed by a deep sigh, he wrapped his arm around her, snuggling her against his side. Greg chuckled when her arm fell forward, her hand landing on Devin's upper thigh.

"Shit. As if this whole night wasn't frustrating and long enough already," Devin grumbled.

Greg's smile stayed in place as he made the turn onto the narrower, rougher road that led to the ranch. "Come on," he coaxed his friend. "Admit she's gotten under your skin just enough that you want to tutor her as much as I do. It'll only be for a few weeks, and even if Jordan calls with proof she's at risk, she's safer and out of harm's way at the ranch than anywhere else."

Greg always did have a way of pointing out facts that made them sound more reasonable than Devin wanted to admit. One week, he thought in disgust. How had the little minx managed to put a chink in his resolve never to get physically involved with a victim again, or in her case, a possible victim? Yeah, the risk to her was not determined at this point, but he still suffered nightmares over their last assignment. If that were to happen again, he didn't know if he'd survive it.

"You're thinking too hard, like always," Greg stated as he pulled in front of their sprawling cabin home. "All I'm asking is you give it some thought, like I am."

Devin looked at the welcoming home he'd found peace in, at the shrouded shapes of barns, stables and cabins that made up their dude ranch, an enterprise he'd discovered to his surprise suited his thirst for adventure and outdoorsmanship. Then he glanced down at the white blonde head resting against him, the fey appearance Kelsey's small features lent her, and remembered her drenched blue eyes filled with need as he'd held her quaking body on his lap. The vivid recall of her soft skin heating under his punishing hand, the bounce of her surprisingly plump mounds, the glistening sheen coating her pussy lips and her soft, melodious cries that never included her safeword tugged at his cock, and his conscience.

They'd left her dangling unfulfilled on purpose, neither willing to reward her behavior no matter how tempted they both were to delve between those bare folds. She likely didn't understand that was part of her punishment, and that was just one thing they needed to address even if Devin didn't agree to cave the way Greg already had.

"You'll take her on even if I don't, won't you? Is it that easy for you to forget what happened the last time?"

"Fuck, Dev, you know that's not the case. But Jordan's right. We did everything we could to first protect Catherine and then to save her." Greg shrugged, unrepentant. "To answer your first question, I probably will."

"Since I don't like that idea any more than entering into a short-term D/s relationship, do you mind giving me another day to decide before talking to her?"

"Not at all." Opening his door, Greg slid out and turned around to look back at him. "But just so you know, I don't plan to do a lot of talking at first. She's pushed this. Now she needs to know just what she's been asking for."

"I can get on board with that if I join you. Right now, I guess we better get her to bed. She's not budging." Devin lifted Kelsey onto his lap as Greg came around and opened the passenger side door. Carrying his small burden up the steps and into the house, they both went to her bedroom where Greg flung the covers back on the bed before he laid her down.

Without waking, she mumbled and rolled on her side, pulling her knees up. "She'll sleep better out of those clothes," Devin whispered, reaching for the side zipper on her skirt.

It wasn't the first time they'd stripped a girl without a word passing between them. In less than thirty seconds, they had her divested of both the skirt and blouse and tucked under the covers, sound asleep as they tiptoed out.

Kelsey waited until Greg and Devin closed the door and she heard their booted footsteps receding down the hall before blinking her eyes open. Their voices had been vague murmurs all the way back to the ranch as she succumbed to the exhaustion pulling at her. It wasn't until Devin cradled her in his arms and carried her inside that she roused enough to heed their surroundings and what they were saying. She wasn't dumb enough to let them know she was awake once Devin mentioned removing her clothes. She'd wanted their hands on her from the first day but hadn't pined for both of them together until tonight.

Drowsiness pulled her back under, the faint echo of their deep voices murmuring as they'd undressed her following her into sleep, her skin still warm and tingly from the light grazes of their rough fingers.

---

"IF YOU CAN'T FIND a connection by now, there isn't one." Kelsey vibrated with frustration as she held the phone to her ear, gazing out the bedroom window, her eyes glued to Greg and Devin.

Jordan's long pause on the other end of the line drew her suspicions, but, like always, he had a ready reply. "Not necessarily. It just means the man who assaulted you was good at hiding his tracks. We have found solid proof he was hired to do a job, just not what that job was."

"How about if I come back and stay with you?" she asked, hoping he didn't hear the note of desperation in her voice.

"What's wrong, Kels? Has Greg or Devin done something to upset you?"

*Just stirred up my neglected libido and left me hanging with no relief in sight.* She might be a grown woman pushing thirty, but she still thought of both McAllisters as parental elders and couldn't imagine Jordan's reaction if she were to answer that honestly. "No, they've been very… accommodating," she replied for lack of a better word. "It's this place, it's just not my thing, you know?"

"I'm sorry, but try to make the best of it, okay? I promise, Theresa and I are working hard to figure out why he was at Dominion. Given the seclusion of the club's locale and his rap sheet, no one believes it was a random break-in. We're unearthing more and more every day, so give us the full month, please."

He would have to go and utter that one word, wouldn't he? Helpless against the plea and worry in Jordan's voice, Kelsey sighed and leaned her forehead on the window. "Okay, I'll hang out here a little longer. But, Jordan, hurry up and clear me, would you? I want to come home."

"And we want you back here. I'll have Theresa give you a call this evening. Thank you, honey."

"Yeah, yeah. Talk to you soon. Bye." She clicked off wondering how she would make it over two more weeks without going stir wacko or lust crazy.

The quiet this morning got to her first upon awakening. With all the guests except the sweet older men, Otis and Silas, having checked out yesterday and the employees taking off, the ranch appeared more desolate and foreign to her than ever. Except for her two reluctant hosts. She watched Greg smile wide enough to reveal a row of white teeth as he slapped Devin on the back before the two strode into the stable. Her gaze slid to their tight butts showcased in snug, worn denim and she released another sigh that fogged the window. Hot didn't begin to describe those two and lust was too mild a term for what they conjured up deep inside her every time she looked at them.

Kelsey wasn't sure how much of their conversation on the way home last night she heard, but a few words had filtered through her subconscious, 'tutor' being one. She didn't know what all that entailed, or if they were discussing her, but given Devin's reticence and how much she still craved them, it wasn't wise to read anything promising into the tidbits she recalled. *Their. Them.* Just one night of seeing them together in that sex-charged atmosphere and it was already so easy to pair them together.

She straightened and her heart set up a rapid tattoo as they strolled out of the stable leading their saddled horses and Cleo. When Devin tethered Thor to the rail, turned and strode toward the house with long, ground-eating strides and a determined set to his rugged jaw, her palms grew damp. Stepping away from the window, she quickly slid her feet into her sneakers, thankful she had put on jeans this morning instead of shorts despite the warmer temperature forecasted for today. The simple, light blue summer top was thin and tight enough to mold to the turgid outline of her nipples, and that was just from the thought of going riding with them.

"Kelsey!" Devin called out as soon as she heard the front door open.

Dashing out of the bedroom and down the hall, she tried and failed not to appear too eager for any amount of time either chose to spend with her. So she was a pathetic, desperate mess. They could deal with it.

"I'm ready. We're going riding, right?"

For the first time since meeting him, his tough as leather face softened as he nodded. "Yes. We have a few hours before the tour bus arrives with guests, and Greg and I thought it a good time to show you around more of our property. Come on, let's get going."

She liked the impatience shimmering in his eyes as he raked her from head to toe with a look she couldn't decipher. With a spring in her step and a beaming smile, she hurried forward to take his outstretched hand.

"I should ask if you're good to ride this morning. No lingering side effects after last night?"

"Not enough to keep me sitting around all day twiddling my thumbs." In fact, the vague soreness she awoke with was just enough to keep her stirred up, to remind her of that painful, but mind-opening experience.

"From what I've noticed, you twiddle your thumbs out of habit, not boredom." He brushed the pad of her thumb with his before releasing her hand. "Mount up and stay between us."

She was beginning to think that's exactly where she wanted to be. Turning to Greg who already sat astride Cherokee, she looked up into his less intimidating face. "Good morning. Thanks for taking me out."

"You're welcome, little bit. How are you this morning?"

*Shivery. Hot. Giddy.* "Good, thanks." She stroked Cleo's shoulder before swinging up into the saddle, glad she was such a small horse. "And even better now that you're luring me away from work." A look passed between the two that drew a delicate ripple of awareness along her arms as they turned the horses, putting her in the middle before setting out.

As soon as they entered the wide-open prairie, Devin said, "Tap her sides with your heels and we'll trot over toward the tree line. Keep your grip tight on the reins but don't pull unless you need to slow down. Move your body with the horse. Ready?"

"As I'll ever be." She would rather be sitting with one of

them for a faster ride but refused to let her unease show. If they thought she could handle this, then she would.

"We'll stay right with you, Kelsey." Greg nodded, waiting for her to make the first move.

It didn't take much, a slight nudge against the little mare's sides and she picked up the pace as if eager to get going. Bouncing on the saddle without a lap to cushion her butt and distract her was more jarring, but also offered an exhilarating sense of freedom she'd never experienced before. Eyeing her escorts, she tried to mimic the smooth up and down movements of their bodies and soon got into the rhythm that eased the discomfort. With a shake of her head that sent her long hair flying around her, she laughed in sheer pleasure.

"You and Tom were right," Devin called over to Greg. "She is a natural."

"See?" Greg sent Kelsey a wink. "You're not all city girl."

*Oh, yes, I am.* But she could take this for a short time, especially if these two kept giving her such positive signs they were mellowing toward her. She didn't expect much more than that from Devin, but a little went a long way toward easing her dispirit over being sent here.

"One ride doesn't make me a country hick, cowboy." She sent him a taunting grin.

He smiled, looking over her head. "Hear that, Dev? She thinks we're hicks."

"You would think she'd be more careful with what she says around us after last night. Pull up, Kelsey."

She caught her breath as they slowed to a walk and then halted altogether. Following the point of Devin's finger, she saw a huge moose standing near the trees. "Crap, those things are freaking big." A thought came to her and she swung an accusing look toward Devin and then Greg. "I swear, if I see that animal's head on any walls I'll come after you with a hunting rifle." She liked animals, especially dogs, even though she'd never owned one. Every so often something would trigger a vague memory clip of a small, black puppy, but with it always came a frisson of unease. Her unknown roots never bothered her unless that tidbit from her early childhood popped up.

Greg lifted his hat and ran a hand through his sweat-dampened hair, saying, "I don't hunt. That's Devin's thing."

Her mind quickly switched gears and slipped into the gutter because she thought that habit of his was sexy, but that didn't stop her from turning an accusing gaze on Devin. Holding up a hand, he drawled, "I only hunt what can be put on the table. Mary is a whiz at coming up with wildlife recipes. Later this afternoon, we'll be barbequing pheasant and venison along with beef and chicken for a cookout with the new guests coming in."

Devin shook his head as Kelsey wrinkled her nose. "Yuck."

Nudging Thor close enough their lower legs brushed, Devin pinned Kelsey with his dark blue gaze. "You don't know what you'll like until you try it."

Okay, there was definitely a hint of double meaning to that remark, backed by another shared look between the two, and for the life of her, she couldn't figure out what they were up to. "Meaning?" she asked point blank.

"Meaning let's take our ride through the woods. That path is just one of the ones we take on trail rides." Greg nodded toward the wide break in the trees and then led the way toward it.

"It's so much cooler in here," she commented as they walked the horses single file along the rugged trail. That was something she already knew from her walks but couldn't think of anything else to say since she didn't know what they were up to. "How far are we going? I've hiked to the creek and back, but that's it."

"We plan to go swimming on horseback next week since the weather is predicted to be warmer than usual for September. We'll follow the creek until it opens up into a small lake deep enough for the horses to swim. They love it." Devin parted

Thor's neck. It wasn't lost on Kelsey he didn't answer her question but instead diverted her from it with that bit of information.

"Am I good enough to go?"

Greg twisted around and eyed her relaxed seat. "If not by then, you can ride with me. Turn here."

Kelsey pulled the reins to the right, following him down a narrower path for a short distance and then looked around in pleasant surprise as they came to a small copse. Sporting a bed of moss green ground cover and long logs squared off around a fire pit, she could see the gurgling stream just beyond the trees. "Oh, this is a great spot."

"We like it for the seclusion." Devin dismounted and before she could follow suit, he came around and plucked her from the saddle, making no move to step back once her feet hit the ground.

Whether by a silent command or on her own, Cleo deserted her for the company of the two larger males a few feet away, leaving Kelsey standing with Devin's large hands still holding onto her waist as Greg came up behind her. Her breathing quickened as they both stepped close enough their warm breath wafted along her neck as they bent their heads. She slammed her eyes closed against the rapid rise of her senses their nearness evoked.

"Uh, not that I'm complaining, but what's going on?" she whispered, sucking in a gulp of air as two pairs of lips ghosted over the tender skin of her neck, the teasing kisses and nibbles bringing about a spate of goosebumps.

"You've been very clear about wanting what we can give you. You saw enough last night to know what we're into, and what we expect in return while satisfying more of your curiosity. All that's left is for you to agree." Greg nipped her earlobe hard enough for the pleasure-producing sting to pull her nipples into taut buds.

Kelsey's eyes flew open and she gazed in surprise up into

Devin's sun-weathered face and dark eyes. "But…" Her voice stuttered along with her heart. "You don't even like me!"

"You're a pesky handful," he stated, fisting one hand in her hair and pulling her head back. "But I like you just fine."

Not exactly a compliment, she thought as his hot mouth covered hers, but she'd take it if it meant putting an end to the rioting sensations plaguing her nonstop. He eased up on her mouth to sink his teeth into her lower lip, her gasp giving him an opening to delve inside with his tongue. Kelsey leaned against his hard frame with a moan of eager surrender, his hands tightening on her hair and hip as her insides heated with each stroke over her tongue. The leisurely exploration along with the smooth glide of their damp lips pressing together got her fired up on all cylinders until the press of Greg's body against her back reminded her of the one word she hadn't acknowledged or addressed. *We*

"Does this mean yes, little bit?" Greg whispered in her ear before dipping his tongue inside to tease the sensitive dips and canals.

Shivers racked Kelsey's body as she pulled her mouth from Devin's to answer. "I can't think. What do you mean by 'we'?"

Devin slid his hand from her hip to grip one butt cheek while Greg reached in front of her to palm her right breast and reply, "Just this, both of us most of the time, separate on occasion. Trust us, we know what we're doing."

"Here's a hint, cowboy." She groaned, quivering inside as she imagined more of these heady feelings from being sandwiched between the two. "Mentioning your past experience is a mood killer."

"But if we didn't have experience, we wouldn't be good at our job as Doms." Devin squeezed her buttock. "Yes or no, baby?"

She'd always hated it when other guys called her baby, but every time she heard the generic pet name resonating in Devin's deep, slow drawl, she wanted to melt in a puddle at his feet.

"Yes," she agreed in a breathless rush. She might be unsure about taking on both at the same time, but she was also glad she didn't have to choose one. "But don't blame me if you're disappointed. Unlike you, this is new to me and I was pushing to enlist just one of you to entertain me while I'm here, not both." She felt it only fair to warn them of her inexperience in this area, but damn, it was hard to think with them so close and touching her.

"We haven't disappointed anyone or been disappointed by a newbie before, but why don't we give you an example of what we can do together?" Greg released her breast to pinch her chin and turn her face up to his descending mouth. Devin tugged on her hair again, angling her head just right and holding her there. Between their dual grips, Kelsey had no choice but to open to Greg, and bask in that loss of control.

With a low moan of surrender, she welcomed the invasion of his tongue as she clung to his lips. Lost in their dual possession, she didn't notice their free hands were on the move until a rough palm slid under her top, up her bare abdomen and quick, deft fingers flicked open her bra. She whimpered, a needy whine as Greg released her mouth, stroked over her still throbbing lower lip and cupped one naked breast.

"Soft, and the perfect handful." He released her chin to slip that hand under her shirt and cover her other breast.

"*Oh, God.*" Kelsey couldn't think of anything else to say as the slight breeze wafted over her exposed lower half when Devin shoved down her jeans and panties to rest at mid-thigh. Her buttocks clenched and her pussy swelled, slickened and grew heavy with need.

For the first time, his lips spread in a full-fledged grin as he pressed his hand between her legs, the scratchy callouses scraping over the tender, delicate skin of her labia. "And just think, this is only a prelude to what we can, and will do to you." Keeping his eyes on her face, he released her hair and gripped one buttock while slowly working two fingers inside her.

Kelsey shuddered, leaned her head back against Greg's chest and clutched his thick forearms in a panicked attempt to stay upright. The intoxicating experience of being semi-naked outdoors for the first time, of standing sandwiched between two men for the first time and of enjoying the touch of four hands on her for the first time drove her to the cusp of orgasm within moments. Heat consumed her body as fingers gripped her nipples and tightened while more fingers continued to press deeper and deeper inside her pussy, slowly stretching muscles too tight from neglect. She squeezed her inner walls as he started to pull back, desperate to keep those digits right where they were.

"Loosen up, baby," Devin growled, the sharp pinch to her butt distracting her from holding the grip. "There you go."

Basking in Devin's warm approval, Kelsey arched her neck to give Greg easy access for his nibbling mouth. "That's a girl," he murmured in a deep rumble she felt clear to her toes. "Give yourself to us and we'll take you places you've never been before."

A sharp cry spilled from her throat as Devin pinched her aching clit the same moment Greg added pressure to her already throbbing tips. The tight squeezes switched to light plucks on the three most responsive parts of every woman's body, that sole focus sending her on an upward spiral of consuming lust that exploded in a mind-numbing orgasm. She tried arching her hips forward, into Devin's now plunging hand and Greg's kneading grips, but Devin's hold on her buttock tightened, shackling her in place for their dual assault. Colors exploded behind her eyes as her body quaked and broke out in a light sheen of perspiration

Before the smaller contractions ending her climax had abated, Greg released her breasts and Devin pulled his fingers from her still clutching pussy. Moving so fast she couldn't quite take it in, they formed a bar by clasping each other's forearms and then pushed her over it. With a squeal, she latched onto their thighs to anchor herself as they began smacking her cheeks in a simultaneous, steady rhythm. The resonating echo of repetitive, bare-flesh slapping bounced around the copse as heat blossomed across her backside, aided and abetted by the brush of warm air and their deep murmurs.

"Don't stop, Kelsey. Keep coming for us." Devin slid his hand between her abused, pulsing cheeks to dampen her back entrance with slick fingers.

"One more, little bit." Greg followed that command by delving inside her pussy with a forceful, three fingered thrust, the barrage of pummeling strokes stretching and filling her long-neglected sheath almost to the point of discomfort.

"I don't know…" she gasped and stumbled to a stop as Devin breached her anus and screwed one finger inside that virgin orifice.

"Then trust us to know," he returned, pushing harder and deeper as Greg plundered her soaking depths with breath-robbing jabs aimed right over her clit.

The ground below her started to blur as Kelsey's entire body convulsed in another climax. Praying they wouldn't let her fall, she rode the waves of ecstasy until she lay shuddering in a quivering heap over their linked arms.

## Chapter 9

Devin cut another quick glance toward Kelsey where she slouched sidesaddle in front of Greg. Her rosy, sated appearance hadn't lessened any in the last fifteen minutes during their ride back. Even with her bright blue eyes closed and her body soft and lax, she still tempted him more than anyone who had come before her, and how fucked up was that? He'd barely made it a week after vowing not to get involved with her and here he was, unable to keep his eyes off her. He could still feel the way her slick vaginal muscles had gripped his fingers, soaking them with her creamy climax, and how she shook lying over their arms as they had swatted her ass and fingered her to orgasm number two after she protested she couldn't.

He'd awoken this morning willing to continue discussing the issue of getting personally involved with Kelsey. After tossing and turning all night with images of her sweet ass and even sweeter submission plaguing him, he'd conceded there was only one way to settle both his curiosity over how far they could take her and to calm the raging lust her every-day presence had conjured up. Even after her surprising embracement of his punishing hand last night, her eager responses to both of them today had taken him unawares. She'd been an enticing small bundle of accepting heat and mewling cries that had slipped past his guard and pissed him off when he found himself reluctant to let her go.

"Don't say it," he warned Greg when his friend who knew him too well caught his look.

"Say what?"

Kelsey's drowsy response went straight to Devin's cock and he responded by kicking Thor into a trot, leaving it up to Greg to answer her. He kept the stallion's gait slow enough little Cleo could follow alongside him in an easy trot as they covered the last quarter mile to the stable. Cherokee came thundering in behind them, the large red tossing his head, looking as exhilarated from that quick run as Kelsey. His growing interest in the girl left him unsettled and not happy about it.

Dismounting, he tossed Cleo's reins to Kelsey as Greg lifted her down, not bothering to curb his irritation when he snapped, "Now's as good a time as any to see to your own horse's care after a ride." The spasm of hurt that crossed her pixie face drew a pang of guilt, and Greg's frown didn't help. Just because he wasn't altogether pleased with himself didn't mean he should take his mood out on her, he admitted with a sigh, especially after just initiating her to the control of two men.

Stepping forward, he cupped her chin and tilted her face up, her jaw going rigid in his hand. Rubbing the pad of his thumb over her plump lower lip, he murmured, "Sorry. I can be a bastard. Are you doing okay?"

Kelsey rewarded his concern with a narrowing of those bright blue eyes, darting her tongue out to lick his thumb as he pulled her lip down and rubbed the soft dampness of the pink tissues. "Just fine, Sir," she drawled as he pulled his hand back as if burned. Greg chuckled and earned his glare.

"Good." Devin nodded and stepped back. "Loosen the strap and Greg will haul the saddle inside. I have to check the meat for the grill before the guests arrive." He went back to Thor and made short work of removing his saddle and turning him loose in the corral with a slap on the rump that reminded him how it felt smacking Kelsey's heart-shaped, malleable ass.

Greg knew his amusement with Devin was reflected on his face and didn't care. It was fun watching his best friend succumb to Kelsey's charms as he'd suspected he might. He unsaddled the horses and turned them loose in the corral before hefting Cleo's smaller saddle over his shoulder and gripping the pommel of Cherokee's.

"Devin is likely trying to work through your responses to that little scene as much as I imagine you are. I think you're not only a natural at riding, but at submitting to the right person, or people."

"Those being you and Devin?" she asked. Her large blue eyes remained steady on him even though a faint blush crept over her face.

"Yes, while you're here. Who knows? Maybe you can attend a club in Philly for real when you return and be much better prepared." An unaccustomed tightness squeezed his chest at the thought of her going home and hooking up with someone else. If Devin had a similar reaction it was no wonder he didn't want to linger upon their return.

"Maybe." She waved an airy hand toward him. "But right now, I think I'll concentrate on the present, and what you two are offering. Thanks for the ride and the orgasms. I need to get some work done."

His lips curled in amusement as she pivoted and practically skipped across the lawn and up the front steps to the house, his gaze on her twitching ass. She had spunk and sass, which he liked, but he still saw the shadow of insecurity in her eyes that never seemed to fade completely.

## Submitting to Two Doms

"HAVE YOU FOUND HER YET?" the impatient male voice demanded as soon as he answered the call.

"Not yet, but we have something to go on. If it pans out, it won't take long to make the arrangements to get to her. Give us a few more days." Soothing impatient clients might come with the territory when one hired themselves out to do the dirty work others were too squeamish to handle themselves, but he and his partner didn't have to like it. If this guy kept up with the nagging calls, he just might be tempted to take him out instead of the mark.

"That's what you said a few days ago. October second is only a few weeks away," the caller reminded him for about the tenth time.

"Calm down. I told you, once we secure her location we can move quickly. You know we're good at what we do, or you wouldn't have come to us and been willing to pay our fee."

"You damn well better be. I'm screwed if she's still breathing past the second."

The connection went dead and he tossed the phone down on the bed, glancing toward his partner. "The guy's a pain in the ass. Let's get back to digging so we can put this job behind us before I get mean."

A taunting smile and reply of, "No, we wouldn't want that," was the only response he got.

---

KELSEY SHIFTED on the chair and then swore at the warm, tingling reminder of what the two men she kept eying out the window had put her through earlier. That pesky word, *more*, continued to pop up no matter what either man subjected her to. She had a feeling now that they had agreed to 'entertain' her while she was their guest that they'd just begun demonstrating what had been missing from her previous affairs. If they continued to give her such off the chart orgasms, she could live with that. At least she would have some awesome memories to take home with her. Heck, if she continued to get into the whole submission/kinky sex thing, maybe she could join Dominion. Of course, she would have to talk the owner, Master Jared into forgiving her for disobeying his order the one time she was there, which resulted in her exile to this foreign land.

Her gaze slid out the bedroom window again, leaving the numbers lined up in neat columns she was supposed to be tallying. Who could concentrate on accounting when the deep, rumbling voices of two tall cowboys wearing those sexy leather chaps and Stetsons that were lowered just enough to shield their eyes kept intruding? Watching them on and off for the last several hours, she'd developed an appreciation for how hard they worked and how much they seemed to love what they do. With Tom and the Ingrams having the day off, it was left to them to sign in their guests and show them around. There weren't as many as last week, just twelve new people spending the next three days of their two-week tour here. By the time they were unloaded from the bus and shown to their cabins, the afternoon sun had dipped into dusk.

Despite how much she was looking forward to whatever Greg and Devin had in mind for her, Kelsey still couldn't understand the draw of this isolated, wilderness setting. She'd grown fond of the little mare, Cleo, and liked riding more than she'd imagined. Hanging out in the social hall in the evenings was enjoyable but a far cry from hitting the clubs with a few friends or co-workers. And she missed shopping, her favorite restaurants and the McAllisters.

Greg looked toward her window just then, the small smile curving his sexy mouth sending the girls and slutty bitch into a happy tizzy. At this point, she didn't know what she wanted most – more of him and Devin or to go home. Then he crooked his finger and Kelsey didn't give home another thought. Shutting down her work, she sprang up and hightailed it outside. With their guests now milling around and Devin starting up a huge grill, she knew she wouldn't get anything more than their company this evening, but somehow she was just as good with that as she'd been with both men's hands on her earlier.

"Okay, I concede you were right," Kelsey mumbled an hour later as she shoveled in another forkful of pheasant. "This bird is as good as chicken and turkey." Sitting between Greg and Devin, she'd found it difficult to concentrate on eating at first, but her hunger followed by enjoyment of new tastes soon worked to refocus her attention. "And this corn is awesome."

Devin yanked on her hair, the tug against her scalp having a ripple effect straight down to her toes. "You should have believed me when I told you corn on the cob is best cooked on the grill."

"Yeah, yeah, you're always right, I get it." She smirked up at him as she sank her teeth into the buttered sweet corn. They'd hauled platters of food straight off the grill into the social hall, the chore of feeding their guests falling to Greg and Devin with Mary and Les gone until morning. From the enthusiasm of the newcomers, they too enjoyed the wildlife cuisine of venison and wild birds.

"She learns fast," Greg said over her head before turning his heated green gaze on her. "That should work in your favor, and ours going forward."

Kelsey's pussy went damp as she recalled what she'd witnessed both at Dominion and at The Barn, making her wonder which scenes they would instigate with her, and when. "Are you going to tell me what you have in mind?"

"No," they returned at the same time.

Their implacable answer delivered in their sensuous tenors elicited delightful shivers up and down her body in an odd mixture of unease and excitement. She'd never imagined those two emotions combined could stall her breathing as well as stir the constant, low-simmering arousal she experienced whenever one or both men were near, or looked at her, or she heard their voice, or... *Hell, I've really got a bad case of the hots, don't I?* She blamed it on her dissatisfaction with her perfectly nice previous boyfriends, even if they did discard her as easily as the parents she didn't remember and the foster parents who came before the McAllisters. That remembrance always put her in the dumps, so she shoved those memories aside to concentrate on the very pleasant here and now.

"It's not nice to keep me guessing, you know."

Devin shrugged in that way of his that stated loud and clear 'too bad' without words. Greg gripped her thigh under the table and squeezed. "Careful, little bit. Your bravado may not hold up against some of the things we might do."

Her nipples puckered and she rubbed her arm over them to ease the ache, making sure she disguised the gesture as reaching over to place her hand on Greg's thick bicep. "I'm willing to risk it. Can we go play now?"

A laugh burst from Devin as Greg's eyes crinkled in amusement before they both responded with a resounding, "No," and then stood to mingle and converse with their guests. Kelsey sighed in unfulfilled longing and then concentrated on finishing a meal that was every bit as good as the food she'd dined on in some of Philly's best restaurants. By the time she was shoveling in the last bite, Otis and Silas were strolling over and filling the guy's seats.

"Are you attending the horse clinic tomorrow, Kelsey?" Otis asked.

"I planned to check it out. You've probably been coming here long enough you already know what they'll be teaching."

"That and we're getting too old to be on those critters," Silas replied. "We wanted to let you know we plan on spending the afternoon fishing, if you want to stop by. A girl needs to know how to toss a line."

"So you've been telling me for a week," she teased. The two

older men had taken a shine to her, one she found heartwarming and that she cherished. She'd never known grandparents, not that she remembered, and she liked the attention the two gave her. "I have to work, but if I get enough done, I'll hike up there. Thanks for the invite." She didn't have the heart to tell them she possessed no interest in the mindless sport. If it meant bringing a smile to their lined faces, she would suffer through an hour of boredom, but she would not handle those slimy, wriggling things.

"If you catch anything, the guys or Mary will cook it up for you. There's nothing like fresh-caught trout or bass. Silas likes whitefish," Otis said.

Kelsey wrinkled her nose. "I like fish I don't have to handle while still alive."

Both men chuckled as they stood and Silas warned her, "Don't get attached to any of the cattle around here, then. See you tomorrow, hon."

---

*BE careful what you wish for*. That was Kelsey's first thought the next morning as she opened the bathroom door wearing nothing but a towel to see Greg standing in the hall holding a small package. The look in his eyes as he took his time inspecting her from head to toe initiated those tiny ripples of awareness again, the ones that slide just under the skin and then slithered downward to zip up between her suddenly weak legs.

Twiddling her thumbs, she hoped he didn't notice her curled toes as she greeted him with an inquiring tilt of her head. "Good morning."

"Morning, little bit." With his eyes on hers, he strode forward, grasped her hand and tugged her into the bedroom and over to the bed. Taking a seat, he laid the objects in his other hand next to his hip, tightening his grip as he reached up and whipped off her towel.

Kelsey didn't know what she liked more, what aroused her the most — his hot gaze or imagining where he planned to put the strange, bulbous object on the bed. When he pulled a tube of lube from his side pocket she had her answer, and interest turned to unease.

"Um, Greg…"

"Master Greg or Sir," he interrupted. "Know what I like best about your size?" He yanked on her hand and sent her face down over his muscled thighs. "It's so easy to position you where I want you. I've been wanting you like this since I saw you over Devin's lap, this little ass all rosy and soft. Nothing beats having such a soft, tempting ass to do with as I wish."

He squeezed her right buttock and she whipped her dangling head up with a shake to get her hair out of her eyes. "But, I haven't done anything." Familiar tingling warmth she'd only experienced from a swat covered her cheek and kept her protest from sounding like a complaint.

Greg smiled and rubbed. "Who says I'm going to punish you? I just want to play for a minute before I introduce you to the inflatable plug."

Intrigued, amused and aroused, Kelsey returned his teasing grin. "Oh, okay." Scooting forward, she braced her hands on the floor, wiggled her butt and called back, "Have fun then."

His laugh sounded like it burst from his throat as he traced circles over one buttock and then the other, his touch so light it tickled. "I like how you continue to surprise me. It makes me want to find ways to surprise you in return."

Greg played with her butt. That was the only way Kelsey could describe the way he kneaded her buttocks, squeezing the fleshy mounds then letting go to watch them jiggle. She squirmed in embarrassment as he pressed them together and then pried them apart, over and over. A pinch to her right cheek drew a startled yelp and a flutter deep inside her pussy.

"It's not nice to pinch girls," she admonished with a giggle as he tickled the sensitive corner between her buttock and thigh.

"I never claimed to be nice. For such a little thing, you have a nice, plump ass." He braced his arm over her thighs and then proceeded to pluck his way across both cheeks, alternating between tight pinches and taunting, little tweaks that heated her flesh in a different way than the spanking she'd expected.

Somehow, Kelsey wasn't surprised to find herself responding to his playful touches with as much enthusiasm and wet heat as she did to his harsher treatment of her backside. For a solid ten minutes, he kept her awash in a myriad of sensations, varying his softer touches and manipulations with harder squeezing and pressing of her malleable flesh. By the time he stopped and caressed her trembling buttocks, she lay like a limp, wet noodle, her pussy spasming in empty neediness. She was sure when she returned home and looked back on this moment, she would feel shameful of her current state considering he'd just been 'playing' with her. But that was later; this was now.

Greg jerked Kelsey from her fogged euphoria with the touch of his rough finger gliding between her buttocks. Tensing her cheeks, she whispered, "Sir?" as he breached her puckered hole with the lube's nozzle, a sudden cold ripple replacing the warmth she was just basking in.

"Playtime's over. You pushed both of us into this relationship, Kelsey, and now it's time for another lesson in what that means. This will be cool at first."

He was right. A squirt of ointment dampened and chilled her dark channel, but when he replaced the tube with the smooth, rounded tip of the plug while teasing the damp seam of her pussy lips, heat returned, blossoming deep inside her. "That feels funny, and good." She groaned as the soft oval object slid inside with ease until the only part left out was the short dangling cord with the small bulb on the end.

Greg tickled her clit with a teasing stroke as he said, "This will likely feel even stranger. Deep breath as I inflate the plug."

It took only a few pumps to fill enough air into the intruding toy to put pressure against the hidden, unbeknown nerve endings lining her rectum. Kelsey shook as she released her breath, Greg's soothing strokes over her buttocks and slow dips in and out of her sheath helping her adjust to the foreign sensations and slight discomfort that was already easing as he turned her over.

Rooting out her clit, he hugged her tight against him, demanding, "Come for me, Kelsey."

And just like that, she exploded in climax, grabbing his wrist to keep him from pulling all the way out of her gripping pussy. As pleasure engulfed her body, turning her nipples into stiff peaks and her vagina into a wet, clutching inferno, she marveled at how talented he was at using one digit to fragment her into a million vibrating pieces.

Greg marveled at Kelsey's response as he held her small, trembling body close, giving her a few seconds to come down from the orgasmic high before tipping up her chin and inspecting her face. He noted the blush that could have come from embarrassment, but after checking her eyes and seeing the sated bliss reflected in the bright blue depths, he figured it stemmed more from arousal. Fuck but he couldn't wait to get inside her. Not yet, but soon, he vowed.

"Good girl. I want you to leave the plug in for an hour and then remove it." Nudging her up, he stood and gave her a quick, hard kiss. "The clinic starts in ten minutes. Don't be late." He turned before letting go with a wide grin at the stunned look on her face as she realized he meant for her to attend part of the horse clinic with the plug still in place.

Devin was already in one corral with Thor, demonstrating the proper way to saddle and mount to the guests standing around at the rail. Tom was in the next enclosure with several horses, giving a few guests the chance to practice mounting and dismounting. He joined them on the sidelines, ready to answer questions as he kept an eye out for Kelsey. When he spotted her walking with hesitant steps toward them, he struggled to hold back his grin. She might question and think about balking, but damned if the girl didn't have grit and a cock gripping way of embracing new kinks.

She'd missed the first part of this morning's instructions, but since they had consisted of going over mostly safety tips she already knew, Greg didn't bother filling her in. He would rather stand there for the next thirty minutes watching the expressions cross her face every time she moved but as Devin wound down his instruction phase, he pivoted to go get Cherokee and take his turn at the helm.

Most of the group had ridden before, so they were able to wrap up the morning's instructions an hour later. Devin took names of those who wanted to go on the afternoon hike as Greg slid the saddle off his stallion and turned to put it over the rail. He checked the time as soon as he saw Kelsey still at the rail, now conversing with Otis and Silas who had just shown up. Lifting his hand, he snagged her attention, scowled and pointed to the house. She'd left the plug in too long, obviously unaware of the health risks that could impose. The fact she'd grown comfortable with the new toy boded well for her ability to take both him and Devin at the same time, a prospect that sent his blood on a torrential rush surging through his veins.

She returned his frown, her mouth tightening in irritation, but then said something to the older men who had taken a shine to her before stomping toward the front porch. She didn't like being bossed around, but she would learn there were times it was needed even if she wasn't in a scene with one or both of them.

---

KELSEY MARCHED INTO THE HOUSE, welcoming the cool air

against her heated face as she strode down the hall toward the bathroom. Pulling down her jeans, she deflated the plug and removed it, a shudder racking her body as the softened sides glided along the sensitive lining of her butt. By the time the guys had ended this morning's clinic session and she turned to greet Otis and Silas, she'd grown comfortable enough with the foreign object nestled inside her not to squirm. It had only taken one step to stir her arousal back to life.

Cupping a hand between her legs, seeping juices coated her palm as she glared at the slutty bitch and muttered, "Are you never satisfied?" Her answer was another drip of cream. With a mental headshake at her continued craving for more, she yanked up her jeans. Either her sex life before meeting Greg and Devin was even more lacking than she'd thought all this time or those two were more potent than she'd bargained for.

Greg's silent command outside had irritated her at first, but as she now found herself adjusting to the emptiness inside her butt as opposed to the unaccustomed fullness, her annoyance slipped away. Maybe he knew what he was doing after all and she should continue to go with the flow since their attention had perked up her stay here exponentially.

Things grew quieter outside as she settled down to work, most of the guests going on the afternoon hike with their hosts. Kelsey welcomed the silence as she pulled up the new accounts she had yet to get organized enough to send them back to the clients. Several hours later, her growling stomach and the return of the trail exploring party had her doing a quick check of her work. It surprised her to see how much she'd accomplished without even realizing how fast and accurately she'd made more sense of the numbers sent to her.

Kelsey refused to delve too deeply into why it pleased her so much when Devin and Greg took seats on either side of her at dinner a short time later. Just because she enjoyed their attention even when they weren't tormenting her butt or giving her a mind-blowing orgasm didn't mean anything other than she liked them. Nothing wrong with that she kept telling herself as they urged her to socialize with the guests along with them. Greg challenged her to a game of pool as the hour grew late and Devin joined a poker game with Tom, Les and a few others. After she insisted she let Greg win, she helped Mary in the kitchen until the motherly woman noticed the tiredness pulling at her and sent her back to the house.

Since her bossiness felt more like caring, she caved and fell asleep as soon as she crawled under the covers to the sound of the guys coming in for the night.

The next morning, Kelsey didn't have to wait to open the bathroom door to see Devin; he stood leaning against the counter as she stepped out of the shower, the towel now out of her reach. Pushing her wet hair off her face, she stood still under his blatant perusal of her dripping naked body, those dark eyes heating her more than the steam from the hot shower.

"Don't either of you ever knock?" she asked with a breathless catch as he slid his eyes up to her face.

"Sure, on each other's doors. Not yours. Bend over the counter," he instructed.

"Why?" The question came automatically, as did the thrill skating down her spine. That was until his jaw went rigid and a flame leapt to life in his eyes as he reached for her.

With a push between her shoulders, he bent her at the hips as Kelsey caught him picking up her brush from her sideview. "That answer reminds me about your lie. Any woman who spent time in a club would know to either reply with a color or obey."

He brought the flat side of the wooden brush down on first her right buttock and then the left, the two swats fast and painful enough to draw a screech. Kelsey reached behind her to rub her aching backside but before she reached her goal, Devin had her hands shackled together in one large hand at her back.

"I didn't give you permission to touch yourself. Hold still. It's time for your plug."

A groan spilled from Kelsey's throat as she lay with her breasts and cheek pressed against the granite counter while he worked the greased, deflated toy past her tight sphincter and into her butt. What did it say about her she found his heavy-handedness as appealing as Greg's lighter approach yesterday, or about the welcome sigh that slipped out of her mouth as he inflated the plug one extra pump more than last time? She couldn't stop from wiggling her hips as she adjusted to the fullness again, but then he had the gall to spread her labia and slowly twist the wooden brush handle into her pussy.

"*Shit!*" She craned her head up to glare back at him despite the copious wetness that greeted the handle's insertion, her stomach and thighs trembling in reaction. "Are you really using my *brush*?"

He taunted her with a sardonic curl of his lips as he drawled, "I really am. Your pussy doesn't seem to mind." With another slow turn, the embedded handle widened her slick walls, adding to the overcrowded stuffy sensation now encompassing her entire lower half.

"My body's a traitorous bitch." Kelsey didn't think he could shock her further, but then, she never imagined he would pull her lips open with his free hand, expose her clit and pull the handle out to deliver a swat right on that tender nub of swollen flesh.

Her startled scream echoed in the small space, followed by pathetic whimpering as an explosion of pussy and butt-gripping pleasure darkened her vision. She came down from the exalted high to the clatter of the brush landing on the counter in front of her, the glistening handle proof of the decadent level she had sunk to. Nothing could have pleased her more at that moment than Devin assisting her up and pulling her into a snuggling embrace. Panting, she huddled against his thick chest, the steady thump of his heart and soothing back rub calming her shell-shocked senses.

"There you go," he whispered as her body went lax. Dipping his head, he met her rising mouth and kissed her, just a soft brush of his lips over hers, but it was enough. "Are you good now?"

"Oh, yeah." Moving back from the embrace that moved her as much as his actions, she reassured him by adding, "Real good, Sir," with a cheeky grin.

"That's a girl. No more than an hour with the plug." He turned, pausing at the door to toss back with a wave of his hand toward the brush, "You might want to wash that before using it again."

Kelsey reddened, thinking she might have bitten off more than she was prepared to handle. Then again, she was only here for a short time, so why not indulge every fantasy to help make the best of it?

## Chapter 10

"We've verified her identity and will have the job completed by this time next week."

Sven Lindgren breathed his first sigh of relief in over a year. "Call me when it's done."

He hung up, swiveled his chair to gaze out the window at the snow-capped peaks of the Alps, a view he never tired of looking at. He still couldn't believe his partner gave this up for a woman. Twenty-five years, he thought in disgust, and that son-of-a-bitch was still screwing with him. Everything would have stayed perfect if Fiske hadn't made that trip to the states and met Sharon Lewinsky at a New York art show. His lip curled as he recalled Fiske claiming he was in love and planned to expand their lucrative, and illegal business of money laundering to the other side of the Atlantic. As if it hadn't been difficult enough to stay out from under the watchful eye of the Swedish authorities.

For five years they had argued back and forth, long after Sharon's death in childbirth. Sven couldn't then nor now understand Fiske's obsession with the kid, or his determination to raise her in her mother's country. He'd had no idea the girl was in the next room when he'd flown over there to finally discuss their rift face to face with Fiske. He'd planned that confrontation for when she was supposed to be spending the weekend with her maternal grandmother. After their fight got out of hand and Sven reacted without thinking by snatching a knife sitting on the kitchen table, he'd fled the bloody corpse of his long-time friend and cohort in crime to hide out in his hotel until catching a morning flight out.

His hand shook as he reached for the glass of whiskey on his desk. He'd been in a frenzy after reading about Fiske's death in the paper and then spotting an article right below about a young blonde girl found wandering alone a block away. He recognized her picture and still broke out in a cold sweat whenever he thought about the kid witnessing what he'd done. After two failed attempts to take her out in the first five years, he'd figured he was safe enough and had let it go.

And then the huge, prestigious law firm of Lewis, Miller, Huffington and Clark had contacted him. The sweat started rolling all over again with their inquiries about Fiske's daughter's whereabouts and learning they were holding her inheritance, which would come to her on her thirtieth birthday. There was no telling what was in that lockbox, but given Fiske's admission he'd covered his ass and would take him down if they were to part ways, he couldn't risk the girl getting hold of those contents. His partner had been meticulous about keeping detailed records of their illicit activities, damn it.

Sven gulped down the last of his drink, enjoying the distraction of the fiery burn. The odds of the lawyers tracking her down before his goon took her out were now much slimmer. Soon, and with a small amount of time to spare, this would be over. He was starting to feel better, so optimistic in fact, he thought of giving his hired mercenaries a raise and then quickly changed his mind. They deserved no tips after stressing him with the long wait.

WEDNESDAY MORNING KELSEY emerged from the bathroom expecting, even hoping to see either Greg or Devin waiting to insert the butt plug again. After using the toy twice, she'd gotten used to the snug fit and had come to terms with the unexpected sensations that orifice could produce. Disappointment swamped her upon seeing the empty hallway, her first thought an irritated *don't they know I only have a short time to get all I can out of them*? As busy as they were, she supposed she should be more grateful for the time they had given her. By the time she'd pulled on her jeans and a loose tank top, the extra lining allowing her to go braless without visible notice, the silence of the house was grating on her nerves. Weird, she thought, just plain weird. She lived alone and was used to long stretches of silence in the mornings and evenings.

Maybe it was the nightmares from causing a man's death that wouldn't let up and kept disturbing her sleep that brought about these unexplainable emotions. Waking every morning with guilt dragging her down didn't improve her mood and reminded her how much she wanted the uncertainty over that man's attack settled once and for all so she could go home.

By that evening, Kelsey decided her plan to soak up as much of Greg and Devin's attention while she could wasn't going as well as she desired. Both men had been so busy running the clinic and entertaining their guests, the only time she'd spent with them other than the fifteen minutes the previous two mornings had been for dinner at the social hall. With everyone else around. With no privacy, time or freedom to indulge in her newfound joy of kinky sex. With *two* dominant guys. They returned to the house long after she had gone to bed and worked all day doing activities with the guests.

It wasn't right, she grumbled to herself as she compared the sums on the debit and credit columns listed on the computer screen. After finally agreeing to a short, physical relationship, it was just plain inconsiderate to leave her hanging after showing her how she got off on their heavy-handed dominance. She'd shaved again that morning, and as she squirmed in her seat at the desk all day, the newly bared, sensitive skin prickled with each slide of her silky panties. The teasing distraction both titillated and annoyed her.

To divert her mind from the constant hum of neediness those two men were responsible for, she thought of home, wondering if any of her friends missed her. Jordan had insisted she refrain from contacting anyone except her boss and him and Theresa until she returned to Philly. Because she liked that they cared so much, she'd agreed to all their terms since that awful night and suffered their restrictions in silence.

She missed home, yearned for the familiarity of her surroundings, friends and co-workers. She never did well with change, which, she knew, was one of the McAllisters' chief concerns over insisting she come to Montana. In an effort not to cause them grief, she'd been trying to make the best of this trip. But it hadn't been easy. Her unhappiness with the whole situation had driven her to pursue her hot hosts. When they'd given her the attention she craved, she thought she had it made until she went home, but no, here she was today, spending the day alone while they lavished all their attention on everyone else.

*Their* paying *guests, you moron*. Her cranky annoyance made no sense and with a disgusted sigh aimed at herself, Kelsey finished her work and shut down her accounts for the day. It was too early for dinner, but maybe Mary could use some help. Shoving back from the desk, she stood and left the house only to stop on the porch when she spotted Greg and Devin standing around outside the far barn with Tom and Otis and Silas. An irrational surge of resentment tightened her muscles. If they had time to stand around doing nothing, why couldn't they spend those moments with her? She knew her petty anger was out of place but couldn't seem to help herself.

Stomping down the steps, she stormed across the lawn,

returning Otis and Silas's greeting with an absent wave as they passed her heading toward the social hall. She didn't catch their questioning looks as she halted in front of the other three. Placing her fists on her hips, Kelsey glared at Greg and Devin, disregarding Tom's presence. "You've been gone all day," she snapped, ignoring the way both men narrowed their eyes at her accusatory tone.

"Tom was around. What did you need?" Devin asked coolly.

*You.* Taken aback by the first answer that popped into her head, Kelsey went cold then hot. Flustered, she pivoted, tossing back in irritation, "Nothing. Just forget it." Striding toward the social hall, she berated herself for acting like an idiot and for the pathetic need she seemed to have developed for not one, but both men.

---

"SOMEONE'S HAD A BAD DAY." Tom smiled at Greg and Devin. "I have a few things to finish up." He nodded toward Kelsey's stiff, retreating back. "Good luck with that."

Greg eyed the sway of Kelsey's near-white hair as her small frame all but vibrated with tension. When Jordan had introduced her at the airport, he'd caught his first glimpse of uncertainty flickering in her expressive eyes that didn't match the brazen attitude she'd given them since. That look kept popping up, and he intended to ask Jordan more about her past, and their relationship with her, the next time he called. He waited until Tom was out of earshot before murmuring, "I wonder if our girl missed us today or what we've introduced her to."

Devin's glare didn't surprise Greg, nor did his answer. "She's not *our* girl. I agreed to indulge her for a short time, that's it."

"Okay." No sense in arguing with him, Greg thought. Since Kelsey would be leaving by the end of the month, he knew it wouldn't be wise to give in to the soft spot he'd developed for her or consider anything except a short-term liaison. But given the quick twist in his gut when he'd seen her stomping toward them with that glint of pain in her bright eyes, he feared it might be too late to keep from wishing she would hang around for a while. "But we shouldn't reward her for that pissy attitude."

"Oh, I'm sure we can find a way to deal with it, but not with another spanking. She likes that punishment too much. Tomorrow we'll have a short window of opportunity between the time this group checks out and the next reservations arrive."

Greg lifted his hat and brushed his hair back as they started walking toward the house to wash up for the evening. "At least we have an easier schedule over the next week. Tomorrow, the newlywed couple and the hunting party are the only new arrivals, and we're just providing cabins and food for the hunters. Our young lovebirds weren't interested in the day consuming group activities, just in hiking and a trail ride or swimming with the horses, if the weather holds out."

Devin tossed his hat on a hook just inside the front door as they entered. "That just leaves the Kilpatricks to check in on Friday. They're wanting a few days of quiet and rest before driving back to Virginia, so it looks like we'll have an easier go of it over the weekend, until it picks up again next week. I'm more than ready to slow down and have the place to ourselves. We've been booked solid since May."

"Four months of working twelve to fourteen hour days is needed and worth it to take the winter months off. Quit complaining and go shower. I'm hungry." Greg veered down the hall to his bedroom as Devin took the stairs to his, his mind jumping to all the different ways they could torture Kelsey's delectable, petite body.

---

"WHAT ELSE CAN I help you with, Mary?" Kelsey returned the

tray she'd carried the desserts out to the buffet on to the kitchen counter, refusing to give in to the urge to look towards the front doors. She didn't care if those two were speculating on her attitude. Let them wonder. She was *so* ready to get out of this backwoods place and back home. If she didn't know better, she would swear it was that time of month, given her mood swings all day.

Mary proved to be as shrewd as Greg and Devin when she glanced around from pulling a large pan out of the oven, frowned and asked, "Something bothering you, hon?"

Tears pricked her eyes and she turned her head as she answered, "No, just at odds with myself all day, and missing home."

"You're not used to traveling?" Mary set the pan down and pulled off the foil cover. Kelsey's stomach rumbled as she caught a whiff of the bubbling lasagna.

"Not alone." And the guys had eased her loneliness the last few days, until today. Surely, she couldn't have become addicted to their attention in such a short time. If so, she was in trouble when she returned home. "My foster parents took me on a few short trips when I was a teenager, but we never left Pennsylvania. They thought I would like a change when I mentioned planning a vacation." The lie they had come up with to give the ranch employees didn't sit well with her. Mary and Les, as well as Tom had been good to her. Even though she understood the need to keep the real reason she was hanging around here between her and Greg and Devin, she didn't have to like it.

"Aren't you enjoying yourself, then?"

Mary looked upset at the thought of her not having fun and Kelsey couldn't stand to worry the motherly woman. It wouldn't be right to take out her lousy mood on her when she'd been so nice. To reveal she'd spent the day pining for Greg and Devin's attention sounded petty and selfish even to her.

"I am, Mary. In fact, tomorrow afternoon, Otis and Silas are going to take me fishing. I'm not sure I'll like it, but I've never shied away from trying something at least once."

"Good to know, Kelsey."

Kelsey jumped upon hearing Devin's slow drawl behind her followed by his large hand landing on her shoulder. He squeezed, and she sucked in a deep breath as that simple touch filled her with warmth.

"Quit teasing the girl and carry this out to the buffet, Devin," Mary told him with a twinkle in her eyes.

"Lasagna? Mary, sweetheart, you know me too well." Dropping his hand, he stepped around her and picked up the hot pads before reaching for the large pan. "God, this looks good. I'm going to fill my plate before anyone else gets in line." He turned, his midnight gaze landing on Kelsey before he walked out without another word, leaving her to wonder what he meant by that remark.

"Go on, hon. Everything's done for now. I appreciate your help."

"Okay. It sounds like I better get in line behind Devin if I want a taste of your lasagna."

Thinking it best to stay away from her hosts until she got herself under control, Kelsey joined Otis and Silas for dinner. They must not have cared since they both seemed content to dine and spend the evening with their other guests. She tried not to let their indifference rub her wrong; after all, she chose to socialize tonight with everyone but them too. But that small corner of her brain reserved just for them didn't like it.

Kelsey managed to dump her unexplainable bad mood while sitting down to eat with Silas and Otis. She'd grown fond of them, enjoying the way they bickered back and forth and liked to tease her. After beating them both at pool, she followed Tom and a few others out to the fire pit to roast marshmallows and listen to him play the guitar. By the time she fell into bed, she was tired enough to make it almost to morning without being disturbed by the memory of a man falling over a rail to his death.

After a successful morning of getting caught up with her work, Kelsey ventured outside the next day in a better mood. The tour bus was loaded and pulling out, which meant the ranch would be quiet for a few hours before the next guests checked in. And that meant Greg and Devin wouldn't be as busy. She hoped they would carve out time to treat her to a few more of those powerful orgasms they were so good at giving her. She didn't have nearly enough yet to get her by after she left. What she craved most was their full possession. They'd shown her what they could do with fingers and mouths. Now she wanted more.

A delicate shiver crawled up her spine as Kelsey watched them stride into the stables, wondering if their cock size was as big as the rest of them. She'd never given much thought to that until now, but then, her previous boyfriends were average in build. They came out of the stable astride their stallions and took off at a gallop toward a small herd of black cattle.

*They have chores to do, animals that needed tending, you moron.* The silent lecture worked to dispel the grip of disappointment clogging her throat. After grabbing a bottled water, she found Tom and told him she would be at the creek with Otis and Silas and then took off down the forested path she'd come to know so well. Even learning how to reel in a slimy, squirming fish was better than spending the afternoon alone.

---

"THERE YOU ARE. Where have you been?" Devin eyed Kelsey's flushed face and bright eyes as she entered the house, his gut clenching when she broke out into a beaming smile.

"I caught a fish! It was kind of gross, and I refused to touch the slimy thing, but I caught it all by myself!"

"Proud of yourself, are you?" He didn't know if she knew it, but she exhibited the same enthusiasm whenever she took Cleo out and attempted a new maneuver. "It seems you're turning into a regular outdoorsman."

She wrinkled her nose in that way he found so cute and he had to take a mental step back. One of them showing signs of attachment to a girl who was only a temporary guest in their home was bad enough.

"I don't think so." She shrugged and looked away from him. "Just entertaining myself with what's available."

He caught the slight accusation in her light tone and softened a tad more toward her. Greg had been right; she wanted more of what they'd introduced her to. That fit in well with their plans before they had to prepare for two more arrivals shortly.

He crooked his finger. "Come with me."

Kelsey started to twiddle her thumbs, suspicion clouding her eyes as her brows dipped in a frown. "Why?"

Devin spun on his heel, his tone taking on a darker edge with his answer. "Because I said to." The thrill of satisfaction running through him when she padded behind him without complaint shouldn't feel so good, and he refused to read anything more into it than a sub pleasing him with her obedience. Her sudden, indrawn breath told him the moment she spotted Greg standing by the sofa in the den, holding a silicone hand paddle down at his side.

"Little bit, we're not happy with you," Greg said as soon as she reached him, Devin moving to flank her on the other side. "Strip."

She stiffened, but there was no denying the pucker of her nipples under the thin tee shirt. "Is this because I was in a bad mood yesterday, because if so…"

Devin held up a hand and she clamped her lips together, the spark of irritation in her wide eyes at odds with the twirling of her thumbs. "We're going to address the reason for your pissy mood. You were put out because we didn't take the time to explore more of your interest in the lifestyle, but just like at the club, you never considered we might have had a reason for stepping back for a day, did you?"

Kelsey bit her lip, a look of chagrin crossing her face as she flicked a wary glance from him to Greg before muttering a lame defense. "I figured you were too busy working."

"Well, you figured wrong. I don't like to repeat an order twice, but given you're still a newbie, I'll make one exception. Strip." Greg snapped the red hand-shaped rubber end of the paddle against his thigh.

*She's so small*, Devin thought, watching her pull her top off and then shimmy out of her tight jeans. They didn't fuck all the women they shared at the same time, reserving that pleasure for the few who showed an interest in double penetration. Neither of them could tell if Kelsey was interested in going that far, but if she was, they would have to give it careful consideration before indulging her. Her size alone might make it impossible. He admitted he wouldn't mind pinning that petite, soft body under him for a long ride between her thighs. But it was how badly he'd been aching to do so ever since he'd felt her tight, slick muscles squeezing his fingers that needed examining. That was why he'd used the hairbrush on her; he hadn't been sure he could hold back if he felt her wet heat again. That was a hard truth to admit since he'd fought against welcoming her here and was also why he'd come up with this scene for today. He knew his best friend too well to tell Greg that.

Greg moved behind her as he stepped forward and cupped her nape, tilting her head back. "In case you haven't figured it out, *Master* Greg and I have been Doms a long time and, believe it or not, we know what we're doing. You're not only a newbie, but you have a small, tight body. Neither of us would risk causing you physical damage by pushing too hard too fast, hence, the day off to give you time to both mentally and physically adjust to our preferences."

"Oh." A quick, teasing grin lit up her face as she leaned into Devin. "Does this mean my reprieve is over?"

"It means," Greg stated, snapping the spanker on her right buttock, "that you have another lesson coming. You already know to say red to put a halt on what we're doing. But if you're unsure, say yellow and we'll pause to address your concerns. If you're good and we ask for a color, give us the green light for continue. Got it?" He swatted her other cheek and she yelped in surprise.

"Yes, yes, I got it." Her rushed tone changed to wariness as Devin released her nape and pulled the small vial of peppermint oil from his pocket.

"Some women like this, some find it too intense. You will let us know if that's the case with you." After rubbing the oil into both nipples and feeling them grow taut under his finger, he handed the bottle to Greg. "It's time for you to make up to your Doms for your lack of trust." With a quick, hard kiss, he lowered his zipper and released his cock into his hand before taking a seat on the sofa. He waited until Greg stuck one booted foot between her feet and nudged them further apart before ordering, "Spread your pussy open for Master Greg, baby."

Kelsey gulped as she dropped her hands to her labia. She should feel bad for not trusting in their experience more but was too excited about the prospect of taking that beautiful cock in her mouth. Fellatio had always been a tit for tat part of sex for her; if her partner was willing to go down on her, she was happy to reciprocate. But for the first time, she wanted to put her mouth on a man's straining erection for no other reason than to please him. That in itself gave her a pleasurable vibe that popped up goosebumps along her arms.

Her nipples warmed and tingled from the oil. She was already damp, her thumbs sliding along her labia as she tried to get enough traction to push the puffy folds apart. She was both mortified and aroused by Devin's dark eyes pinned to her crotch and Greg's oily fingers gliding between her cheeks, over her anus on their way to her pussy from behind, the chaotic responses spiking her pulse and snagging her breath.

"Oh, God," Kelsey choked as Greg went right for her clit as soon as she managed to spread her slick lips. The brush of oil on the sensitive bundle of already swollen nerves worked as diabolically there as it did on her nipples. But they didn't give her time to adjust to the arousing stimulation as Greg palmed her shoulders and pushed her to her knees between Devin's spread thighs.

Leaning over her, he whispered in her ear, "Take him in your mouth, Kelsey. Let me watch you please my friend."

She could no more turn away from his dark commanding voice than she could resist the temptation to taste the pearl droplet seeping from Devin's smooth cock head. As soon as her knees hit the braided rug, she bent forward and wrapped her lips around his crown. With one swipe of her tongue, she tasted his essence and basked in the low groan rumbling from his chest above her. Her nipples and clit throbbed and heated even more, the targeted sensations distracting her from her duty until the sharp slap of the spanker hit the under curve of one cheek.

"Focus, little bit." Greg swatted her other side, the dual stings working to center her.

Kelsey pushed at Devin's hand still wrapped around the wide width of his length, pleased when he let go and let her take his place. So hard, so hot, a rod of silk covered steel. His cock seared her palm where she could feel his blood pumping through the thick veins. Closing her eyes, she dipped down, tightened her lips and took long, slow licks around and up and down his rigid length. Hard, calloused hands cupped her breasts, fingers tugged on her engorged, burning clit and steady swats of that small rubber hand covered her quivering backside.

The stinging taps peppering her buttocks spurred her on, the one landing between her legs, on the tender skin of her labia, shook her to the core. Through the storm of sensations battering her body, she worked his straining shaft. Tight suctions as she pulled up, light tongue swirls as she descended. Devin jerked in her mouth as she pressed her tongue under the rim of his mushroom cap, his low curse forcing her eyes open.

"Breathe, baby," he instructed, releasing one breast to tug on her hair and pull her off him.

Shaking with the deep breath she took, Kelsey glanced up at Greg as he caressed her buttocks with the spanker. The lust she saw swirling in his green gaze begged for release. She tightened her hand on Devin as she reached out and tried to tug Greg's zipper down. "Shit. You'll have to help or risk getting pinched."

"Wouldn't want that. Are you sure, Kelsey?" he asked, covering her hand with his.

She replied without hesitation. "Green. How's that for an answer?"

Devin pinched her nipple with a warning. "Don't get cheeky. We have to be sure."

*Damn, this strict protocol shit can be cool, but it can also be a pain.* Of course, she didn't say that aloud, just smiled sweetly and replied, "Sorry, Sir."

Greg shook his head and freed his erection into her waiting hand. Pumping Devin's cock, she dipped her head over Greg's shaft, his girth and length filling and stretching her mouth every bit as much as Devin's had. Moving back and forth between the two, she pumped and sucked, stroked and squeezed, loving their hands running all over her, wherever they could reach. Her breathing quickened along with theirs as she found pleasure in arousing them. Greg jumped in her hand with a deep groan as Devin did the same in her mouth. Lifting her head, she licked her lips as she jerked on both cocks until they spewed their releases onto her hands. She'd been so intent on pleasing them, she'd forgotten about her own burning need until she saw Devin reach across to the end table and grab a handful of wipes.

"What are you doing?" she gasped as he handed some to Greg who used his to cleanse the oil from her nipples.

Devin cleaned her hands as he answered, "Did you think you would get rewarded with an orgasm for not trusting us? That's not the way this works, Kelsey."

Shaking in disbelief as Greg gave her one of his wicked grins and swiped up between her labia, it took every ounce of Kelsey's control to keep from screaming in frustration. Even after Greg finished, her nipples and clit still ached with soft pulses of arousal. "You're not serious, are you?" From the looks on their faces as Devin stood and they both tucked their sated members back into their jeans, she knew they were. Any other time, she might enjoy being on her knees naked between them, but not with her body clamoring for relief.

"As a heart attack. But because you are a newbie and still learning, we won't forbid you from getting yourself off." With a playful yank on her hair, Greg winked and walked toward the front door.

"See you at dinner." Devin chucked her under the chin and left with Greg, neither man looking back.

Pushing to her feet, Kelsey padded down the hall to the bathroom. She hadn't minded masturbating before meeting those two, but now the prospect wasn't as appealing. Stepping into the shower under the hot spray, she leaned against the wall and dipped one finger inside her pussy, going straight for her clit. Her still damp muscles fluttered as she milked the swollen nub for a quick release. Within seconds, an orgasm clutched around her invading digit, a pleasant, brief euphoria that fell far short of what Greg and Devin could deliver, either separately or together. God, she hoped in her pursuit of a pleasant distraction during these few weeks she hadn't doomed any future relationships once she returned home. Wouldn't that suck above all else?

## Chapter 11

Greg twisted in the saddle to check on Kelsey for about the fifth time since heading out an hour ago. The Kilpatricks had arrived first thing that morning, just in time to enjoy a big breakfast with everyone. Otis and Silas hadn't wasted any time taking off for the creek right after eating and he'd left Devin behind to outfit the hunting group with mounts before leading them west to get an early start on grouse hunting since the birds were more active in the early morning cooler hours. He would only go so far with the group as they were familiar with Montana's hunting ranges, miles away from the ranch's hiking and riding trails, making it safe to shoot hunting rifles. After testing the young newlyweds and the fifty-something Kilpatricks on their proclaimed riding skills, Greg had started the long, scenic trail ride up the hills, leaving the quicker, shorter route for the return trip down. Once Devin made sure the hunters were acclimated, he planned to meet up with Greg, Kelsey and the two couples on the flattops for a picnic lunch before making the ride back down off the hills with them.

He didn't know what was bugging him today, but some sixth sense kept prodding Greg into keeping an even closer eye on

Kelsey. There was no physical reason why he should feel that urge; she appeared fine. For the first time, she had ventured over to the social hall for breakfast that morning and greeted everyone with her usual cheeky flare, putting her work off to join them. He and Devin had checked on her last night before turning in, only to find her snuggled comfortably in bed, sleeping peacefully. Their scene yesterday must have agreed with her even though she hadn't looked happy about having to see to her own release. He still found her surprised, disgruntled glare amusing.

But an itch had settled between his shoulders as soon as they hit the trails, an unsettling case of the jitters he hadn't experienced since leaving the FBI. If it kept up, he planned to call Jordan this evening to see if there was any new information about the man who had attacked Kelsey. Seated on Cleo with a contented smile, her head cocked as she listened to something the Kilpatricks were saying, she appeared at ease. She looked up just then, her cheeks taking on a rosy hue he suspected had nothing to do with the unseasonable, mid-eighties temperature as they attempted to assess each other with their eyes. The girl was definitely not a twenty-four-seven submissive, which suited him just fine, or would if she weren't returning home soon.

"We'll be happy to change places with her," Vickie drawled. The young bride's mouth curled in a knowing smile.

Greg tipped his hat lower and shook his head. "No need, just making sure everyone's still with us and not having a problem with their mount. Look there, through the trees." Pulling to a halt, he pointed toward the mountain goat gingerly making its way down the hillside. He took a few moments to relate some facts about the habitat and other animals to watch for before moving again.

They emerged from the forested trail onto the flattop thirty minutes later to find Devin with his binoculars out, already scouting for wildlife sightings. "This is almost barren compared to the mountainside trek we just took," Mr. Kilpatrick commented as he dismounted and lifted his arms to assist his wife. She didn't need the help – both of them had proved to be excellent horsemen – but her smile as she slid into his arms indicated she enjoyed her husband's chivalry.

"It has its own beauty." Devin lowered the binoculars and handed them to Kelsey as the others stretched their legs. "Just be sure you stay several feet back from the ledges. Look north. That's a herd of mule deer."

Devin's face softened as Kelsey looked through the glasses and said, "Hey, they're kind of cool." With a grin, she handed the binoculars to the newlyweds.

"So, there *are* some things you find entertaining around here," Greg whispered in her ear. He didn't have long to wait for the now familiar teasing look she slid from him to Devin, the one that caused a strange clutch in his chest and sent blood pumping downward to his cock.

"I've discovered a couple of fun things that help pass the time. Are we eating lunch over there?" She nodded toward the covered picnic area he and Devin had built, complete with a barbeque pit and two long tables with benches.

"Shortly. Devin and I have to play guide first." Pointing to the lookout post, he said, "The scopes will give you an even closer view for miles." He squeezed her shoulder and then nodded at Devin to follow him as the small group walked over to the telescopes.

As soon as Kelsey joined them and was out of earshot on the other side of the hilltop, Devin asked, "What's up? I know that look. Something's bugging you."

Greg shook his head as he kept his eyes on Kelsey. "Fuck if I know. I can't shake an uneasy feeling and it's irritating the hell out of me."

"Neither of us has discounted the occasional odd sensation before, so we won't start now, but our guests seem fine, and pleased with this outing. And Kelsey's speaking to us, so she must not be too put out over yesterday's punishment." Devin scanned the group with a careful eye.

With a derisive look, Greg scoffed, "It wasn't much of a punishment. Are we getting soft in our old age?"

"No, and I'm not old so neither are you. But I agree. I'm not sure we did her any favors going easy. She might not get that consideration if she joins a club back home." Devin's gaze turned brooding as her laugh resonated around the hilltop.

Greg knew better than to mention Devin's softening toward the girl. Regardless of caring for her, Kelsey had made it clear from day one she didn't want to be here and had no intentions of returning after she left. Going back to their discussion about his unexplainable sixth sense kicking in, he said, "The hunting group checked out, their licenses were in order and other than for dinner and breakfast, I doubt we see much of them. They're seasoned outdoorsmen, so they know how to take care of themselves and I'm not worried about them."

"No use in standing here fretting over nothing tangible then. Let's go do our jobs and stick a little closer to everyone until we get back to the cabins."

They spent close to two hours walking the flattop and viewing the wide expanse of prairie and distant mountains through the binoculars and telescopes. The group was excited to spot a cougar, a mama bear and her two cubs and a herd of caribou. Greg and Devin had made this trip so many times, the information they relayed about each sighting, whether it was fauna or flora, rolled easily off their tongues. They took time out to eat the sack lunches Mary and Les had put together before giving them another fifteen minutes to explore while they readied the horses for the return trip down.

---

KELSEY TURNED from her last look out the telescope and

wasn't surprised to see Devin's dark gaze on her. She loved having both men's eyes on her when she stood before them naked, but could do without the hovering and ever watchful looks they'd been subjecting her to all day. Unless they knew something she didn't, and that would piss her off. As much as she was reaping the rewards of submitting to their sexual demands, she still didn't want to be here and intended to hold Jordan and Theresa to their promise and hightail it home in ten days. She had no doubt the cramp in her abdomen when she thought of saying goodbye to her hosts would disappear as soon as she got back to Philly.

"This has been fun, hasn't it, dear?" Mrs. Kilpatrick smiled as the five of them strolled toward the horses upon Greg's wave.

"It has, although my butt might be saddle weary by the time we get back down." The slight soreness Kelsey already felt was nothing like the pleasant ache from a spanking. She gave a mental headshake at the wayward thought. *I really need to quit with those comparisons.*

"Greg mentioned taking a shortcut back down." Jeffrey Sorenson glanced around from in front of her and the Kilpatricks as he swung his wife's hand.

Kelsey found the young couple cute. "I won't complain about that. You guys must have more experience than me." Last week the only guests she spent much time with were Otis and Silas, but she was glad she played hooky from work today to join this outing. Any time she could spend with Greg and Devin would mean more memories to take home with her. The bad part of that would come when she compared every guy she met with them, as she knew she would.

"It's been a while since I've been on a horse, but it was like riding a bike. Some things you never forget how to do." Mr. Kilpatrick winked at his wife over Kelsey's head.

It was obvious how close the two couples were, and as she stepped away from them when they reached the horses, Kelsey wondered if she would ever be that lucky. She doubted it, considering how easily the men in her past relationships had walked away. Sadness pulled her shoulders down as she patted Cleo's soft neck, wishing she knew why no one cared enough about her to stick around. Except for Jordan and Theresa, whose closeness she cherished.

Kelsey was so immersed in her thoughts and not paying attention to anyone else that Cleo's sudden high-pitched whinny and agitation caught her unprepared. The usually quiet, docile mare reared up, pawing the air and shaking her head hard enough to yank the reins out of her hand and send her stumbling back to avoid her thrashing hooves. Fear of the unknown prodded her to keep shuffling out of harm's way, heedless of Greg's warning shout to stop. Her foot caught on a protrusion and sent her sprawling backward to land on her side right on the edge of the hill. With a startled cry, she tumbled over the side, rolled twice and came to a jarring stop in the brush alongside the hill.

"Kelsey!"

Pushing her hair back with a trembling hand, she looked up the few feet to the ledge to see both Greg and Devin lying on their stomachs with their hands stretched out toward her.

"If you're not hurt, lift your arms so we can help you up," Devin ordered, his voice calm compared to Greg's strident tone when he called out for her to halt.

She sucked in a deep breath and crawled upward. "I'm fine," she assured them, raising first her right arm and waiting until Greg gripped her forearm before giving Devin her left. With an effortless tug, they hauled her up, pulling her away from the ground so as not to scrape her body against the rugged terrain. If she weren't so rattled, Kelsey might have found that quick soaring lift fun. Falling against Devin as soon as her feet were on the ground, she leaned against his rigid body, trying to dislodge her heart from her throat as her breathing continued to stutter in and out. Everything had happened so fast that she found the whole episode a bit surreal as she stood there shaking.

Greg placed his hand on her lower back, rubbing in soothing circles as he leaned down and whispered, "Are you sure you're okay? Nothing hurts?"

She shook her head, wishing he would kiss her, not caring the other guests were gawking. Pulling back with a deep breath, she held up her scratched arms. "Just some cuts. What... what happened with Cleo?"

"I'll check her while Devin puts something on those." With an abruptness he'd never exhibited toward her, Greg spun around and strode toward the young mare that now stood quivering and pawing the ground.

"Are you all right?" Vickie rushed forward as Devin wrapped his arm around her waist and led her toward Thor.

"Just shook up, not harmed." And embarrassed, but Kelsey couldn't hide that from the concerned looks on the other's faces. "It's not the first time I've tripped over my own feet while here. Right, Devin?"

He didn't return her smile, just looked her over with a critical eye before pulling a first-aid kit from his saddlebag. "I'll dab some antibiotic ointment on those cuts and scrapes and then you'll ride back down with me. If the rest of you would mount up, we can get going in a few minutes."

For the first time, she didn't take umbrage with his commanding tone. At this point, she would even walk down the hill rather than get on Cleo. "Ow," she muttered as Devin first cleaned the reddened gashes and then blotted them with ointment.

His hand tightened on her wrist as he held her arm up. "It could have been so much worse."

Kelsey winced as he gently applied cream to a tender cut. "But it wasn't. I'm likely to be sorer from riding than that tumble."

"A hot soak in the tub when we get back will go a long way to ease those aches. Any place I missed?"

She wished she could see more of his face, but he kept his hat lowered and head angled away. "No. Thank you."

"Devin, bring me that cream when you're done," Greg called out, one hand running in soothing circles on Cleo's flank.

"Wait here, then." Carrying the tube of ointment, he left her to walk over to Greg and Cleo.

The stinging in her arms started to ease as she watched the two men conversing in hushed tones while tending to something Greg spotted on Cleo, and a few minutes later, curiosity propelled her forward. As soon as she saw the trickle of blood on Cleo's hip, she dashed to her side, her fear forgotten in her concern.

"Poor baby. What happened?"

"Most likely a female horse fly or deer fly. Their bite is extremely painful and will draw blood, but even so, her reaction was extreme." Greg tended the oozing sore with gentle fingers, Devin moving to the horse's head to keep her as still as possible.

"So she was hurt, and scared?" Reaching out a tentative hand, Kelsey felt delicate shuddering ripples running under the smooth coat.

"Yes, but like I said, she never should have reacted that way. I'll examine the bite more closely when the swelling goes down." Capping the ointment, Greg cupped her jaw and tilted her head up. "You're okay?"

"Yes, so you can quit asking. Devin wants me to ride down with him, but maybe…"

"No," they interrupted at the same time. Greg grasped her shoulders and turned her toward Thor. Sliding his hands down to her waist, he lifted her up and Devin swung her in front of him.

"You two handle me like I weigh ten pounds," she huffed, settling back against him.

"That's the best part about your size." Devin tightened his arm around her waist and turned Thor to lead the riders down the hill.

---

HE ENTERED THE RUSTIC CABIN, shut the door and leaned against it. A rare smile curved his mouth as he gazed at his partner lounging in front of the fireplace. "That was quick thinking up there, digging your nail into that bug bite."

"It was, wasn't it?" She sighed, irritation flitting across her face. "Too bad it didn't give us better results. I was hoping she would at least end up hurt bad enough to lay her up at the house. It would have made getting to her with no one else around easier."

"Maybe, maybe not. Young and Fisher seem damned protective of her when we were told no one knows about the contract." Walking over, he threw himself onto the sofa next to her and propped his feet on the coffee table. "I'm thinking arranging an accident isn't going to work."

"You give in too easily," she retorted. "We're here until Tuesday. If an opportunity doesn't present itself by then, we'll leave and sneak back to finish the job. It won't be the first time we've trekked through woods at night."

"True, but if I have to go through that much trouble and risk, that impatient asshole is paying more."

She patted his arm. "I always did say good things come to those who wait."

---

"THERE'S MORE irritation here than a fly bite." Tom eyed the puffy sore on Cleo's hip with a skeptical look. "They hurt, but I agree with you, she shouldn't have reacted like that. I'll keep an eye on it, and her."

Devin stroked the mare's nose, glad to see she'd settled down and her gentle nature was once more shining through. "I was on the other side of Thor, so couldn't see her clearly. Everyone was gathered around behind the horses, getting ready to mount. With only a few other horses bedded down inside tonight, she'll rest quietly and maybe we can get a better look at it in the morning."

He would never forget the surge of gut-clenching panic he experienced when Cleo's thrashing hooves missed Kelsey's face by inches, or the anxiety that had propelled him forward as she rolled down the hillside. Thank God, she hadn't slid too far and they were able to bring her up with little effort. His throat constricted every time he imagined all the ways she could have ended up hurt much worse. And wouldn't his best friend just love to know the extent of his worry and concern over the girl?

With a last pat to Cleo's shoulder, Devin followed Tom out of the stall and caught Greg talking into his phone as he signaled to him from the front of the stables. "See you in a few minutes at the hall," he told his manager, leaving Tom to scoop grain into Cleo's feeder to see what Greg wanted.

"Hold on, Jordan. Devin's here and we're taking this outside." Jerking his head toward the doors, Greg said, "McAllister needs to talk to both of us about Kelsey."

From the urgency in Greg's voice, Devin figured this wasn't Kelsey's foster parent just checking in. As soon as they stepped out into the night-fallen cooler air and verified no one else was around, Greg switched his cell to speaker and Jordan's voice rang with sharp concern.

"You stay glued to Kelsey if you have to handcuff her to your side."

"You found out something." Greg's knuckles went white as he held the phone between them.

With everyone except Tom and Kelsey already at the social

hall for dinner, the only sounds in the yard were the night life stirring in the woods and McAllister's voice. Jordan paused, as if weighing his words then replied, "Yes, and it goes back to Kelsey's childhood, to when she was five and found alone several blocks from the house where it was later discovered her father had been murdered."

"Son-of-a-bitch, you knew that all this time, didn't you?" Devin snapped, pissed off at their deceit in keeping Kelsey's past from them.

"DNA proved she was related to Fiske Olssen, a Swede with dual citizenship. It wasn't until after we gave her a name and had her ensconced in foster care that we discovered her birth certificate. Her real name is Inga Olssen and her mother died in childbirth. At the time of his death, we had Olssen under surveillance for money-laundering and knew nothing about a daughter. He went to great efforts to keep her identity hidden."

Greg swore and narrowed his eyes. "She doesn't know any of this. I've heard her say she's a nobody when she's denying there's any threat against her."

Jordan's heavy sigh came through the line and they could hear Theresa sniffing in the background. "She wouldn't be a nobody even if she wasn't related to a murdered criminal. We knew at the time about Olssen's partner in Sweden and learned of an ongoing investigation over there that was at a standstill."

"Fine," Devin bit out, glaring at Greg for involving them in this mess. There was no way he would turn his back on Kelsey now. "Skip forward to now and tell us what you unearthed. Someone *is* after her, correct?"

"Yes. The authorities in Sweden referred a law firm searching for Inga Olssen to us since her father spent the last seven years of his life in the states. It appears he left her the contents of a lockbox to open upon her thirtieth birthday, which is coming up on October second. Both Sweden and we believe someone, likely Olssen's partner, Sven Lindgren is trying to stop her from inheriting. Authorities in Sweden are working on getting a court order to open the box without involving her."

Theresa's stern voice came on the line. "In the meantime, you don't let her out of your sight."

"Like you did the night she was assaulted? Where the hell was she that someone could get to her?" Devin growled.

"At a private club, miles from the city, with strict instructions to remain upstairs in the office. She had no business spying on the activities taking place downstairs but disobeying our orders as well as the club owners may have saved her life since her assailant is the one who ended up dead." Jordan's voice vibrated with tension.

"Are you talking about a BDSM club?" Greg looked at Devin and mouthed 'that explains a lot' when Jordan confirmed his suspicion.

"It wasn't my idea, but after I talked to her boss, which she doesn't know, I thought she would be as safe as she's been all these years. And yes, I know about your involvement in the lifestyle," he added in a dry tone.

"And you still trusted us with her. When do you plan to tell her all of this?" Greg asked as Devin started toward the house.

Jordan sighed. "You're going to insist on now, aren't you?"

"We won't keep her in the dark. You've done that long enough," Devin retorted, opening the front door. "We're headed over to dinner. Call her in two hours or we'll tell her." He pressed end before Greg had a chance to rebuke his statement.

"Don't worry," Greg returned, following him inside. "I agree with you. She has a right to know who she is. It won't be easy for her."

"I know." And Devin knew there was nothing they could do to change that.

*I WANTED THEIR ATTENTION, but this is ridiculous.* Kelsey sent Greg a questioning glance as he followed her to the buffet table, again. "What's with you?"

"Can't I get a dessert too?"

She snorted. "You can do whatever you want, but you know what I mean. Either you or Devin has been glued to my side since you walked in the door." She leaned closer, went up on her tiptoes and whispered in his ear as he bent down. "Since I know you don't intend to give me another lesson in submitting in front of your guests, back off."

Greg slid his hand under her hair and gripped her neck, his green eyes turning stormy as he sank his teeth into her lower lip, obviously not caring who saw. "We may not be in a scene but behave yourself anyway. I'll use any excuse to toss you over my knee."

For once, she wasn't put out with the girls and slutty bitch's quick, heated response to his dark tone and titillating threat. All too aware of how time was ticking away, she planned to get on board and stay there with whatever either of them wanted.

"I'll look forward to it," she returned, stepping back with a teasing grin. "But right now, I want a piece of that cherry pie."

"Then you better hurry," Mary quipped from behind her. "There's only one piece left."

"It's mine." Kelsey grabbed the plate before asking Mary, "Do you want some help cleaning up tonight?"

"No, thanks, dear. These hunters have almost cleaned out the buffet, so all Les and I have to do is load up the dishwasher. That's the best part about camp dining, everyone expects disposable dishes that can be tossed instead of washed. Go on, enjoy yourself."

Kelsey waited until Mary returned to the kitchen and Greg picked up a piece of chocolate cake and then placed his free hand on her lower back as they started back to their table before saying, "I hope this sudden hovering isn't because of my fall this afternoon. I told you I'm fine."

"Maybe we just want to make sure you don't have any more tripping accidents." He checked the time as they sat down, Devin and the two guests from the hunting party at their table having taken up a game of pool.

"Do you have a hot date later tonight? You keep checking the time." Devin had done the same thing while they ate.

"You know I don't. Besides, I'm a one-submissive-at-a-time Dom."

Greg winked at her and she let her misgivings about their odd behavior slide off in favor of basking in the rush of pleasure his statement produced.

Over the next ninety minutes, the guests trickled back to their cabins to turn in and Kelsey started feeling the effects of the long ride. By the time she waited for the social hall to clear so she could return to the house with Greg and Devin, the soothing relief from her long hot soak in the tub before dinner was gone. As they climbed the steps to the porch, her longing to crawl into bed was interrupted by the silent vibration of her phone.

"Who's calling this late?" she muttered, pausing on the porch to pull her cell out of her pocket. Seeing Jordan's number, she frowned, wondering why, given the even later time in Philly he hadn't waited until morning.

"Hey, Jordan, what's up?" A cold chill invaded her body as Greg and Devin each squeezed her shoulder and then stepped inside, leaving the door open as she stood on the porch listening to her foster parents' explanation for keeping her past a secret from her for twenty-five years.

## Chapter 12

Thirty minutes later, sobs tore through Kelsey's constricted throat as she hung up the phone and dashed inside. She didn't see Greg and Devin's concerned faces as she ran by them, slammed her bedroom door behind her and flung herself face down on the bed with uncontrollable tremors of scorching betrayal. *A lie. My whole life has been a lie.* No matter what Jordan or Theresa had said, they couldn't convince her she meant more to them than just being part of an unsolved case. As they had filled in the blank spots about whatever family she had come from, Kelsey still couldn't remember anything about her father or the night he'd been killed.

*Inga Olssen. Kelsey Hammond. Who am I?* She shuddered with the onslaught of fresh tears. Someone wanted her dead because of an inheritance she didn't even want. She couldn't wrap her mind around that revelation. All these years, the couple she thought had taken her in and kept her because they cared had only been doing their jobs. Jordan admitted he and Theresa had suspected the attempted kidnapping from a school outing when she'd been six and the break-in at her second foster home four years later weren't random incidents. When nothing else happened by the time she'd turned eighteen, they had figured she was safe from her father's enemies.

Until the assault at the club, Dominion.

If only they would have told her the truth from the beginning, or at least once they deemed she was no longer in danger. Then she wouldn't have woven fantasies around them caring for her as part of their family, she wouldn't have grown comfortable thinking of them as the parents she never knew or remembered. Like shattered glass, her emotions had splintered apart and fragmented the moment she heard Jordan's damning words and opened up a black chasm of nothingness when one thought worked its way to the forefront through her grief. *What now?*

As Kelsey lay on the bed, her body shaking from the gripping onslaught of her despair, she didn't hear the door open or the rustle of clothing. The covers were pushed out from under her and she didn't stop crying or lift her head. But when the bed dipped with Greg and Devin's weight and their naked, hot-as-a-furnace bodies pressed against her shivering form, their deep tenors finally penetrated the fog of heartache clouding her mind.

"Stop now, little bit, or you'll break my heart," Greg whispered in her ear as he untucked her shirt.

Devin's low, guttural demand came from her other side. "Enough, baby, before you hurt yourself."

She lifted and rolled at their urging, let them strip her clothes off and then sighed in blissful need as her bare flesh came into contact with all of those rippling muscles covered with smooth skin and hair-roughened limbs. Giving off as much heat as an Arizona desert, the coldness invading her body for the last hour slowly dissipated. A pent-up, convulsive sob broke through as they turned her on her side and swept their abrasive palms down her body, front and back. She moaned as they brought nerve endings to life with light grazes and hard squeezes, sweeping touches everywhere except where she needed them most.

"*Please*," she choked out, arching into their hands, shivering as hard, hot and heavy cocks brushed her stomach and pressed between her buttocks.

"Quiet, Kelsey. Don't talk, don't think. Just feel."

"No, sir, Master Greg. I need you. I need more." Kelsey didn't even wince at her whimpering, pleading tone; she was too far immersed in despair and aching need to care how desperate she sounded.

Devin's rare chuckle rumbled against her back. "While I like hearing our respected title coming out of your mouth, you're still not calling the shots."

A stinging slap landed on her right buttock, the burn sending her blood in a heated rush through her veins. She pressed closer to Greg only to have him work a hand between their sweat-dampened bodies and slide down to press up between her legs. Kelsey's frantic lust-induced state was fast reaching the boiling point, need for the sweet oblivion of a climax overruling everything else.

With a soft cry, she rolled on top of Greg, straddled his waist and rose above his straining erection. Reaching down, she gripped the pulsing shaft and pleaded with them again. *"Please."*

Their dual curses and quick fumbling over the side of the bed barely registered. A swath of moonlight streaming through the window above the bed bathed her body in a white glow as she held her breath waiting for Greg to sheath himself. Devin leaned up on an elbow and circled one turgid nipple with his finger before flicking the tender bud with a scrape of his nail.

*"Yes!"* Acceptance of the pinprick burst from her mouth as she arched back, thrusting her breasts forward. "More," she demanded as Greg gripped her hips and urged her down by slow increments, way too slow for the lust raging through her.

"No!" he snapped out when she tried taking all of him in at once. "I'm big and you're too fucking small." He tightened his hands on her hips. "I'll say how much, how fast."

Kelsey sucked in a deep breath as he worked his way inside

her, stretching muscles, scraping along sensitive, swollen tissues inch by slow, excruciating inch. She quivered and tightened around his steely girth as he bumped her womb. And then they took her over; Greg lifting her up, dragging her slick pussy along his rigid length before pummeling back up with a deep plunge while Devin made free with the rest of her bowing body. He plucked at her nipples and tickled her abdomen; traced along her sides and across her buttocks before pinching the fleshy globes.

The reality of Jordan's disclosures faded as raw sexual hunger invaded her body and took command of her senses. Her breath lodged in her throat, trapped so she couldn't breathe but for ragged gasps as they overwhelmed her with each forceful cock thrust and every hand sweep and finger tug on nipples, butt and everywhere in between. The orgasm hit her with hard waves of jolting pleasure as she rocked on Greg's lunging body and arched under Devin's marauding hand.

She was still trembling from the dichotomy of riotous sensations they had whipped up as they lowered her between them again. But Kelsey wasn't ready to deal with her past yet, not with that one word still echoing in her muddled head. *More.*

"We have more, baby, but you should be careful about insisting on what you want."

Kelsey didn't realize she'd spoken the word aloud until she heard Devin's growl in her ear and became smothered by his six-foot-two body covering her as he tucked her under him. "Being careful is your job," she panted, reaching between them, grabbing his sheathed cock and spreading her legs as she guided him into her still pulsating sheath. "Fuck me, *please*. I can think tomorrow."

Unable to resist, Devin powered into her, keeping his torso levered high enough for Greg to reach between them to pluck, pull and twist her nipples into reddened peaks. Kelsey's mewling cries and jerking hips egged him on, gave him permission to go deeper, ram faster, harder. Her slick pussy clenched around his dick as Greg elongated her nipples with fierce tugs and wedged his head between them to swallow her strident cry with the hard pressure of his mouth.

Lifting her legs around his back, her thighs tensed against his sides as he rode her with unrelenting, body-jarring, bed-creaking vigorous fucking. Her breathing grew as labored as his, those velvet soft muscles clamping around his thick length, tight as a vice as they massaged his girth with taut clutches, pumping his climax forward.

"Now, Kelsey," he ordered, unable to hold back from the heat of her spasming muscles. "Yeah, that's a girl." His groan of pleasure as she soaked him with her orgasm, her hips keeping up with his pounding rhythm, resonated around the room. Devin shook as orgasmic pulsations quivered up his shaft and spewed forth in a torrent of mindless pleasure that knocked him back a peg.

"Jesus," he panted, sliding out of her snug grip. Flicking Greg an accusing glare, he whispered above the small quaking body under him, "Now the fuck what?"

Greg reached over and swept Kelsey's damp hair off her neck and face, watching her eyelids drop closed with a small sigh of sated, exhausted contentment. "Now, we keep her safe."

"And then?" he persisted.

"And then she goes home. That's what she wants."

---

DEVIN TURNED from refilling the coffee pot when he heard Kelsey coming down the hall. His gut tightened as soon as she came around the corner and the anguish lurking in her puffy, red eyes changed to derision as soon as she saw him. Wearing nothing but the silky nightshirt she must have slipped on upon rising, her fey appearance and fragile demeanor drew him like a magnet, and he swore Greg would answer for that after she left.

As he'd been telling himself lately, just because he was drawn to her as a Dom didn't mean anything other than he wasn't entirely opposed to her presence anymore.

Sliding onto a stool at the counter, she cocked her head and said, "You must have drawn the short straw and gotten stuck with babysitting me first. Sucks to be you since you never wanted me here in the first place."

Leaning back against the counter, he crossed his arms and replied in a frigid tone, the pain in her eyes getting to him. "Knock it off, Kelsey. You're upset at what the McAllisters found out and kept from you. I get it. But don't put words in my mouth or make assumptions based on their actions. I was about to fix an omelet. Do you want one?"

"I'm not hungry."

She pouted and he suppressed the urge to order her to eat something. It would take time for her to reconcile with what she had learned about her past but he could push her along that path with a gentle nudge. Pouring her coffee, he added cream and handed it to her across the counter, not surprised when she questioned him.

"How did you know I take cream? You've never been here in the mornings when I've gotten up."

"Because I use cream also and Greg drinks his black. It was an easy deduction when I noticed how much was gone each morning. Don't go long without eating. You need to keep your strength up."

Her jaw tightened but she didn't say anything until she'd taken a few sips of coffee. When she did, he knew she was deliberately trying to piss him off. "Maybe you should be charging me like your other guests, or better yet, send a bill to the McAllisters. It was their idea for me to hole up with you."

Reaching across the counter, Devin gripped her chin and squeezed until he knew he had her focused attention. "I know you're upset with Jordan and Theresa but give them a break.

They were looking out for you and have had nothing but your best interests and safety at heart."

Tears filled her wide blue eyes until Kelsey wrenched away from his hold and blinked them away. "Thanks for the coffee. I need to get to work."

"Keep your curtains and window closed and leave the door open," he instructed as she hopped off the stool with mug in hand. "Greg's working the cattle today. When you're ready for a break, let me know and we can join him."

She waved her free hand. "Don't you have guest duties?"

He shook his head. "The hunting party left at dawn and won't return until tonight and our two couples are taking off on their own in their vehicles. The next group activity isn't until we swim with the horses, tomorrow."

"Lucky me then. I'll be your only obligation today."

Devin watched her walk down the hall, wishing he could erase the insecurity and despair that had returned to her wide blue eyes by telling her she wasn't an obligation. But just because he'd softened toward having her here and was determined to ensure she stayed safe now they knew the threat against her was real didn't mean she wasn't an obligation. He wouldn't lie and wouldn't say something he wasn't sure was true and add to her burden of coping with the two most important people in her life having already done that.

---

*I DON'T CARE, I don't care.* Honestly, why should it bother her Devin hadn't denied she was just an obligation, even after last night? It shouldn't upset Kelsey so much, just as learning the McAllisters had taken her in and kept such close tabs on her all these years because they felt duty bound shouldn't hurt. But it did.

Her phone buzzed as she reached her room, but when she

saw Theresa's name on the screen, she tossed it on the bed without answering. She didn't bother closing the door as she stripped off her nightgown, grabbed her jeans and a top and then padded naked into the hall toward the bathroom. Both Devin and Greg had seen and touched every inch of her body and knew where she was lacking, she mused, looking down at her small, B cup breasts. Losing herself in pleasure had been a welcome respite from the grief the McAllisters' revelations had unleashed and she didn't regret pleading for more from both men.

Three hours later, Kelsey shoved away from the computer with frustration crawling under her skin from the nonstop upsetting thoughts still plaguing her. All four of her previous break-ups combined didn't hurt her as much as the McAllisters' deception, but just like with those disappointments, she was determined to put it behind her and move on. After changing into shorts, she left her room in search of Devin.

She found him in their shared office, sitting behind the desk with a scowl on his face as he stared at the computer screen in front of him. Shoving aside the sudden longing for a comforting hug from him, she crossed her arms and stated, "I'm going to the creek to visit with Otis and Silas. Are you coming?"

*Crap. Why does that cool, appraising look get to me every time?* 'If you're leaving the house, so am I. Making sure you stay safe has to be easier than figuring out Greg's accounting."

She wasn't in the mood to be nice, so why did she find herself offering her services? "I can take a look at your books this afternoon, if you want." She shrugged, as if she didn't care if either he or Greg trusted her with their financial information.

"I would be forever grateful, and I know Greg would be too." Crossing the room, he surprised her by doing exactly what she wanted him to. Clasping her elbows, he hauled her against him and swooped down to take her lips in a searing kiss that brought her to her toes.

Kelsey forgot about her hurt feelings and pissy mood as Devin lifted her higher. On a low moan, she wrapped her legs around his waist, crossing her ankles against his back to secure her place as she rocked her crotch against his hard bulge. With one step, he had her pressed up against the wall, his mouth still moving with aggressive force over hers, his tongue never slowing in his invasive stroking inside her mouth. One hand shifted to her butt then under the loose leg of her shorts followed by a finger wedging inside her panties to tease her pussy lips.

She whimpered and tried to make it easier for him to slide that finger inside her. He did, just enough to rub her swollen clit and send her into the throes of a quick, gushing climax. Shaking from the sudden onslaught, she mewled as he released her lips and pulled out of her pussy at the same time.

"There. Feel better?" he asked as he moved back and she dropped her legs with a soft sigh.

Kelsey blinked several times to get her bearings while the last tremors of pleasure dwindled to small pulses. "I... why did you do that?"

"Because I wanted to, and you needed me to. Let's go. I could use a walk."

Devin held her hand and kept her at his side as they trekked through the woods to the creek. Kelsey remained quiet, telling herself that kiss and considerate orgasm meant nothing. As if knowing what was going on in her head, Devin gave her the silence, if not the space, she needed to come to terms with his about face toward her. As if she didn't have enough to muddle her thinking already.

"There you are." Silas waved them over as soon as they emerged from the trees.

Sinking down onto the ground by their camp chairs, she wrinkled her nose as Otis reeled in a wiggling trout. "I still don't get it, but hey, whatever floats your boat, guys."

"She's a city girl," Devin drawled, sitting next to her and taking the pole Otis handed him.

"And don't you forget it," she retorted.

He didn't look at her as he tossed the line and said, "No, baby, I won't."

*I'll miss the way he calls me baby in that slow drawl.* Just one more thing to fret over, she bemoaned.

They hung out for an hour, the guys tossing their catches into a bucket after Devin offered to grill them this evening. As he took her hand and led her back down the wooded path, Kelsey found herself reluctant for the other guests to return to the ranch. She rather enjoyed having Devin to herself. The only thing that could have made the afternoon better would have been Greg's presence too.

Halfway back to the ranch an uneasy feeling skittered down her back, turning her palms damp and lifting the tiny hairs on her arms. Casting a quick look through the dense foliage, an eerie, uncomfortable sense of being watched crept under her skin.

"What's wrong?" Devin moved closer, his body tense against hers as he looked around, his free hand inching around behind him.

"Just a funny feeling. Are you carrying a gun?" He nodded without taking his eyes off the woods. Instead of alarming her, knowing he was armed helped ease the trepidation alarming her. "Someone needs to neutralize this threat against me fast," she grumbled, picking up her step. "I'll be damned if I spend my last week here cowering in fear."

"Working on it," he assured her, both of them breathing easier once they emerged from the woods.

---

DEVIN KEPT hold of Kelsey's hand as he too had sensed someone, something sinister in the woods. Like Greg, he never discounted it as nothing when that sixth sense kicked in. Suspicion prompted him to make a mental note of the guests' who had returned as he steered her toward the corral where he spotted Greg and Tom. Both the Sorensons and Kilpatricks' vehicles were once again parked in front of their cabins and several members of the hunting party were mingling around the corral.

"What's up?" Greg asked as soon as they reached him, his voice low enough only Devin heard the underlying sharp edge of concern.

"Take over while I check something out," was all he said, knowing Greg would catch on. With a nod, Greg took Kelsey's hand from him.

Devin found what he was looking for ten minutes later. About ten yards from the trail in the woods, he came upon a spot where the foliage had been flattened, likely from someone lying prone for a while, as if in wait. It was too close to the cabins and too far from a designated hunting area for a hunting scout to be off track. It could be nothing, just coincidence, but neither he nor Greg would discount the disturbance just yet.

---

"HOW WAS YOUR WALK?" Greg left Tom visiting with a few of the hunters who had returned early as he escorted Kelsey to the smallest barn.

"Good, but I think Devin got the same queasy feeling of being watched right before we got back here. Where are we going?"

He picked up the pace, not one to ignore anyone who claimed to sense eyes on them, especially if that someone was Kelsey or Devin. "I'm sure if someone was lurking in the woods, for whatever reason, Devin will find evidence." Opening the barn door, he ushered her inside, both of them blinking to adjust going from bright sunshine into a darkened space. "This is where we bring livestock to give birth. The separation from the herd is less stressful for mama. This pair," he paused at the first stall, "will be turned back out to pasture today. The calf is two days old."

"Oh, he's so cute." She frowned, narrowing her eyes as she looked up at him. "I don't want to know what you breed them for, do I?"

"Probably not. Come over here." He tugged her over to the next stall, the need to erase the worry clouding her bright blue eyes taking hold as he tried not to think about how hard it was going to be to tell her goodbye. Pulling her in front of him, he braced his hands on the stall door, caging her in. "This little one is only two hours old."

Kelsey reached up and gripped the door, her hands appearing pale and small next to his much larger and darker ones. The growing compulsion to keep her close and ask her to stay rode him hard, but he had a lot of practice in putting his own needs second to those of the women he chose to get involved with.

He heard the awe in her voice as she whispered, "She can barely stand."

"It takes a few hours for them to steady themselves, but it's fun to watch them wobble around." Dropping his right hand, Greg slipped under her loose tee shirt and caressed the smooth, warm skin of her waist.

Her voice caught as she leaned into his touch. "It… must be hard to part with them. Don't you get attached?"

"Sometimes. But regardless of feelings, other priorities often take precedence. Tell me," he insisted in a harder tone as he unhooked the front clasp of her bra and filled his hand with her soft flesh, "any repercussions this morning from last night? It's not easy for a woman of your size to take two large men, one after the other."

She sucked in a deep breath as he rasped her nipple and bit her earlobe. "I woke up just fine, thank you. I'm not as delicate as I look."

"No, you're not. You've managed to surprise me at every turn." Greg plucked the distended bud, enjoying her quiver.

"Greg." He pinched her nipple and she gasped, "Sir, *please*." Arching her back, she pushed her breasts forward, the move smashing the one in his hand against his palm.

"I love hearing that breathless plea coming out of your mouth." Bringing his other hand under her top, he kneaded both mounds of pillow-soft flesh and then took hold of her nipples. "Ever climaxed from just nipple play?" he asked, putting pressure on the puckered tips.

Kelsey shook her head. "No. I don't think I can. Maybe if you…"

Greg spun her around, shoved the top up and lifted her to feast on her breasts. Her legs went around his waist and her arms around his head in a tight hold that smashed her breasts against his face. Gripping her ass, he licked, sucked and nipped her nipples, first one then the other. He didn't even pause for air before latching onto the opposite side. Opening his mouth, he engulfed as much of the small mass as he could before slowly pulling up, wrapping his lips around the nipple and tugging upward, elongating the tip and lifting her breast. With a sharper bite, he let go and was rewarded with her hand gripping his hair in a tight fist.

"Come for me, little bit," he ground out as he returned to the left. "Now." Using his teeth and lips, he latched onto the already reddened, stiff peak and brought her to a screaming orgasm.

Kelsey ground her pelvis against Greg's rock-hard abdomen as she splintered apart in a tumultuous climax. Riding the waves of pleasure pouring through her gyrating body, that one word she associated with him and Devin repeated itself yet again. *More, more, more...*

By the time Greg gently unlocked her arms from around his head and lowered her legs, the realization she had come from just nipple stimulation was working its way past the euphoria fogging her mind. Leaning against his comforting strength, the cute 'baby' bawl of the newborn calf behind her reached her ears and a giggle tickled her throat.

"Well, that was a first, and in a barn nonetheless." Kelsey looked up at him and couldn't resist clasping his whisker-roughed face, going up on her toes and giving him a soft kiss. "Thank you, cowboy."

"That's cowboy, sir." He swatted her butt with a crooked grin before leading her back outside. "Devin must be at the social hall with everyone else. I need to wash up before we head over."

And she needed a few minutes to compose herself, she thought as she went with him. Not that he gave her a choice. Between him and Devin, one of them remained at her side all day, their hovering nearness and ever-watchful looks a constant reminder of the now viable threat against her. By the time she finished wolfing down a plate of food, she realized how well the two of them had kept her distracted from fretting earlier with their single-minded, hot touches. But now, even surrounded by friendly people gathered for a good time, the despair from Jordan and Theresa's deception and fear of the unknown crept back up to tighten her chest.

She didn't want to think about the sudden changes affecting her life or where she would be with the McAllisters once they caught the person responsible. The only distraction that had succeeded in diverting her from the upheaval of her life since coming here was Devin and Greg's dominant control. She thought of the women she'd met at The Barn, the painful, frightening episodes in their lives they had overcome with help from their Doms and suddenly craved to be around the people who would understand the up and down emotions gripping her and the distracting pleasure of her two, temporary Doms focused attention in that sex-charged atmosphere.

Devin and Greg stood, each taking her hands, but as they started toward the group around the fireplace, she blurted in a tight whisper, "I want to go to the club."

They must have seen her desperation reflected on her face because instead of replying with an automatic denial, Devin cocked his head and asked, "Now?"

She nodded. "Yes, tonight. It's not too late, is it?"

"No, not at all." Greg glanced at Devin before saying, "I'll check with Tom, make sure he's good with seeing everyone back to their cabins."

## Chapter 13

Kelsey got the same electrically charged vibe entering The Barn as last week, confirming her reaction wasn't just a fluke. The low, sensuous beat of music blended with quiet voices and the occasional, high-pitched cry. She took a deep breath as Greg and Devin escorted her across the gleaming hard-wood floor, the mingling odors of sweet hay, exotic perfumes and musky sex assailing her senses.

"I think I could get used to this place," she murmured, her comment surprising her as much as them.

Devin's dark brows dipped down into a frown and his hand tightened around hers. "Since you're leaving soon, maybe you can return to the club in Philly."

"She'll need to heed the rules better. Why don't you give that some practice tonight?" Greg drawled, his green eyes lit with humor that countered the tight set to his jaw.

The problem was, other than not being able to figure these two out, the thought of going to any club like this without her two cowboys flanking her all night didn't appeal to her as much as it once had. Right now, with the McAllisters' betrayal and the threat against her verified causing her grief, all she could think about was how much she wanted them, and the sweet oblivion of those skyrocketing climaxes their dual touch could produce. The one time they'd gifted her with their bodies and she'd rolled off Greg and under Devin, would be forever seared into her mind as the most intense, sexual episode of her life. Unless she could push them into repeating it. As much as she appreciated their protective thoughtfulness in going slow and looking out for her well-being, like Devin said, she would be leaving soon. There would be plenty of time to recuperate from days of their dual possession once she left.

Kelsey halted a few feet from the table where Sydney and Tamara were waving her over to go up on her tiptoes and whisper, "I promise, I'll be on my best behavior if you two promise to quit treating me as if I'll break. I assure you, I'm not mentally or physically fragile."

Devin moved so fast, Kelsey didn't register what he was doing until his warm hand slid down the scooped neckline of her top and curled around her bare breast. "So, you're good with us ordering you to strip bare tonight?"

Embarrassment warred with lust as she cast a quick look around to see who might be watching. Last week, only Devin, Greg and Master Kurt had been privy to her bared breasts and butt in that secluded corner. "I didn't think of that," she admitted, unable to keep from leaning into his kneading squeezes. "So I don't honestly know."

"At least you're not lying. That's a good start." Greg kissed her, fast and hard as Devin removed his hand. When both men stepped back, the chill that replaced their heat left her as shaken as their touch. "You can think about how far you want us to take you tonight while we give you time to visit." Ushering her toward their table, Greg smiled at the girls he and Devin seemed to have a special fondness for. "Don't you two look pleased with yourselves?"

Sydney's small grin spread into a beaming smile. "We are,

Master Greg, but not as pleased as we've made our husbands." Tamara joined her in flicking Caden and Connor warm glances where they both stood behind the bar.

"Can we tell them, Master Connor?" Tamara's gray eyes gleamed with excitement.

"What's going on?" Devin looked from the girls to his friends, who seemed just as giddy as their wives.

Sydney and Tamara made the announcement together, their happy voices drawing attention from everyone around them. "We're pregnant!"

Kelsey stood to the side as everyone converged on the two couples, their happiness for them apparent in the sincerity of their well-wishes. She'd never felt more like an outsider and never craved friendship as much as in those few moments. She liked her friends and coworkers, but doubted if she'd feel as exuberant over the announcement of a baby, or if any of them would greet that news from her with such heartfelt enthusiasm. It was strange, and a little disheartening to discover there was something lacking in her life that she never realized before. This would be yet one more thing to cope with when she returned to Philly.

Damn, she really needed that temporary escape she'd been craving again from Greg and Devin. Even if it meant getting naked in front of others. She'd never see any of them again, which should make it easier.

"Sit down, Kelsey. Join us," Sydney insisted, glancing up at Greg and Devin. "If it's okay with you, Sirs."

"It is, and congratulations, you two." Devin bent and kissed each girl on the lips and then Greg followed suit. Their husbands' proud smiles hadn't slipped, so they were obviously good with the attention their expectant mothers were getting.

"Wow, that must be exciting, having your babies so close together." Kelsey sat down as the others strolled back to their tables and the guys took a seat at the bar. "One might think you planned it that way," she teased.

Tamara giggled. "We didn't, but people aren't going to believe us." She shrugged. "I don't care, I love the way it turned out. We're due just a few weeks apart."

"And now, the fun part will be seeing how the guys react if one or both of us has a girl." Sydney practically rubbed her hands together in anticipation of that possibility and all the fun she could have with Caden.

"As protective as I've noticed these guys are, I bet they would be as strict with a boy as a girl. I hope you'll send me a birth announcement." Kelsey would make sure she left them her contact information before leaving tonight.

Tamara's face fell. "Are you leaving soon? Will you come back?"

"I..." Would she? Kelsey eyed Greg and Devin and her heart executed a slow roll. She wanted them, she never denied that fact. And she acknowledged she would miss them, not just the awesome sexual experiences they'd given her, but *them*. But neither man had said a word about the future, nor hinted they would miss her. So, no, she wouldn't return just to go through the uncertainty of leaving again. "It's such a long way, and long-distance relationships don't fare well, so I doubt it. But I'd love to hear about your babies."

"Then we have to keep in touch," Sydney insisted.

---

"OKAY, WHAT GIVES?" Caden glanced from Devin to Greg, suspicion darkening his eyes and drawing his brother's attention.

Devin resisted the urge to look back at Kelsey, not surprised by his friend's quick observation. He waited until Greg gave him a nod in agreement before saying anything though. "We got word the threat against Kelsey is real. The FBI is on it, and moving on what they have as fast as they can. In the meantime, she doesn't make a move without one of us by her side."

"What can we do to help?" Connor asked, stepping forward with their beers.

Greg nodded his thanks, replying, "Nothing that we can think of right now, but the offer is appreciated. We have experience in protecting witnesses, and this situation amounts to taking the same precautions."

Devin tried not to think about how the last woman they'd sworn to protect had ended up. The scars from their bullet wounds weren't the only reminders of how they'd both failed. Greg had been right, they had done everything humanly possible to protect and shield Catherine, but that didn't negate the fact they'd rolled out of her bed in time to dress before all hell had broken loose, leaving him to always wonder if he'd been totally focused on the job. Greg continued to swear without hesitation he had been, but between the two of them, Devin remained the naysayer.

Caden thumbed his hat back. "Let Grayson know. He has law enforcement contacts, which might come in handy. I don't have to tell you how easy it would be for someone to sneak onto your property from the woods."

"No, you don't." Devin's gut cramped at the thought. "Which is why one or both of us will be with her at all times. With a large hunting party camping out on the ranch this week, the number of people coming and going will make it harder for a stranger to sneak in. And yes, we've already had Kelsey's foster parents run everyone's names through their system and they've cleared them."

"As far as they know," Greg added. "An experienced perp will have access to damned good aliases."

Connor's worried gaze swung to Kelsey. "Then let's hope your former boss is still good at his job."

It helped, Devin mused, to have friends who offered such

unconditional support. He turned to his best friend. "Shall we see how far we can push our girl?"

Greg smirked. "So, you're ready to admit she's our girl, now?"

"While she's here," he answered without inflection, sliding off the stool.

---

KELSEY'S PULSE kicked up a notch as she watched *Masters* Greg and Devin return to the table, their eyes resting on her face. Those deep, penetrating looks made it easy to remember their titles here at the club. She liked the contrast between their less formal but just as dominant at home persona and their sterner, more formal mien here at the club. She also liked how her body sat up and took notice the same, no matter where they were or which side of them she was facing. Was it any wonder she'd nicknamed her pussy 'slutty bitch'?

"What, pray tell, do you find so amusing?" Greg grasped her hand and pulled her up.

"Myself, and that's all I'm admitting. Where are we going?" She was proud of herself for not wincing at the breathless catch in her voice as she waved to Sydney and Tamara.

"To dance, for starters." Devin pulled her in front of him when they reached the dance floor, but it wasn't until Greg pressed against her back that she eased into the slow, pelvis-grinding movements they controlled with their hands on her hips.

She sighed, content to go where they led her. Here, she didn't have to think, make decisions or worry. Her heartache was forgotten with the tight grip of their hands, the press of those ripped abs and pectorals against her breasts and back and their thick thighs bunching against her legs with each sway of their bodies. Barefoot, she barely reached their chests, and for once she liked how her petite stature worked in her favor.

They didn't talk, just made free with her body as if they owned her. And she not only didn't care, but embraced each sweep of a calloused palm down her bare thighs, every light finger stroke up her bare arms, the tender kiss on the side of her neck, the sharp nip on her earlobe. Nestled between their tall, wide shoulders and long legs, it was easy to shut out the other people dancing so close, easy to forget it wasn't just the three of them in their own little world. Even when Greg unbuttoned her blouse down to her waist and Devin spread the sides open, baring her braless breasts, she found it easier not to shy away from the public exposure standing between the protective embrace of her two cowboys.

"There. Not so hard, is it?" Greg murmured in her ear as he slid a hand under her skirt and cupped one silk-covered buttock.

"Your bodies are shielding me." That was her excuse, and Kelsey felt more comfortable sticking to it than admitting to the decadent thrill of exhibitionism scorching her insides. She swallowed hard as Devin shifted just enough to allow the couple next to them to see her exposed state.

Cool air and the man's hot gaze hit her nipples, jolting her with lust. His slow wink sent a warm flush crawling up her neck, the heated buzz surging through her bloodstream potent enough to keep her on edge with wanting more. She whipped her eyes back up to Devin. "I haven't seen the upstairs yet." She prayed they took the hint without making her beg for what she wanted.

They exchanged that same look over her head she'd caught them doing several times before, a silent communication only the two of them could decipher. She didn't take offense, didn't care about how many times it had taken or with how many others they'd had to practice it on to perfect the technique of being able to read each other's thoughts and decisions when it came to dealing with a submissive's needs. She just wanted them to *act*.

Greg's hands tightened on her hip and butt as Devin's grip on her breasts switched to her nipple. "Little bit," Greg growled low, "you could try the patience of a saint. You're making it damn difficult to do what's right."

"Who cares about what's right?" *Jordan and Theresa certainly didn't. Neither has my father's partner and so-called friend.* Kelsey shoved aside the useless thoughts. "I'm leaving as soon as this guy is stopped. I don't have time for you to take things so slow."

Devin swore, stepped back and grabbed her hand. "I've warned you to be more careful about insisting on what you want. Let's go."

Her breasts swayed as they ushered her off the dance floor and toward the stairs. Kelsey bit her lip as Devin tugged her up behind him and Greg kept his hand on her lower back. The dimness of the loft did little to hide the scenes taking place at the different stations and apparatus, or to shield her bare breasts from appreciative glances as they took their time walking her around the upper floor.

She shook her head when they paused at a webbed, hanging swing, the woman occupying it with her legs bound in a wide V straining toward the man's hand pumping a large dildo in and out of her pussy. The padded cross looked interesting, but not the thin cane Master Dan was snapping across Nan's buttocks. The big, upright wagon wheel drew her curiosity until she read some of the possibilities spelled out on the smaller, spinning wheel. Wheel of Misfortune was an apt name for the contraption. When they walked over to a dangling chain with two cuffs attached on the end, her interest piqued along with her pulse.

"Okay, I'm good with giving this a try."

They smirked, the jerks, before Greg gave her one of his teasing grins. "Too bad. You don't get to call the shots. Haven't we mentioned that before?"

Devin steered her away from the chain station before she could reply. "We've already decided on a bench," he said.

"And you're the boss, right?" Kelsey meant to say that with sarcasm, but instead, her voice betrayed the sudden, breathless anticipation surging through her.

"Right." Greg slid her blouse off and laid it on a chair in the corner.

"Bend over, baby," Devin ordered, his tone steely soft, his hands on her shoulders, guiding her down, gentle. "No more talking unless we ask you a question or for a color."

She nodded before lying face down on the padded bench with a cutout for her nose and mouth. With her knees resting on the kneeler and her hips perched on the edge of the bench, the position was surprisingly comfortable. Until her arms were strapped down at her sides with a band over each wrist, followed by a wide strap tightening across her lower back. She yanked on the restraints, an automatic response to the ripple of unease that dulled her initial excitement. The instant anxiety over her helplessness changed with just as much speed to an arousing wave of heat, dispelling her cold panic as much as their deep voices rumbling in her ears.

"Deep breath, Kelsey. You're all right." Devin's no-nonsense order.

"We're right here, little bit. You're safe." Greg's warmer encouragement.

Hearing both men so close eased the last of her tension while ratcheting up her arousal. "Remember," Greg continued as she felt Devin move away, "you don't tell us, we tell you." He slid his hand down to her skirt and pulled it up. Cool air raised goosebumps across her buttocks as he lowered her panties, exposing her backside to whoever stood close enough to see. "Give me a color." His hand cracked on her right cheek.

"Green, Sir," she gasped, no longer caring if she had an audience. The only thing that mattered was having their hands and mouths on her again. As far as fucking in public, that was something she shied away from contemplating.

"Good girl. Keep your head down. Devin is returning with vibrating anal beads. You'll like those."

*Anal beads? Oh, dear. Just what have I gotten myself into this time?* They didn't give her time to wonder or fret. Fingers spread her cheeks and rubbed ointment around her puckered back entrance before pushing past the tight resistance to grease her insides. She shook as those thick digits pulled out of her and a row of cool, hard, round balls was pressed inside her.

"Relax, baby," Devin ordered as she tensed against the tight stretching and stuffed-full sensation encompassing her rectum. "Just two more."

Another push and the fourth smooth globe rolled inside her. Kelsey shook from the last insertion, exhaling her pent-up breath on a *whoosh* as soon as she adjusted to the foreign invasion. The next ten minutes passed in a blur of painful, stimulating swats delivered across both buttocks with a leather paddle as small pulsations erupted along the sensitive tissues lining her rear channel. Her tormentors' deep murmurs kept her on edge as effectively as the slow build-up of throbbing, heated pain.

"You pushed for our attention, and now you have it." Devin caressed one burning cheek.

"And you've thanked us for our thoughtfulness by complaining." She heard the paddle fall on the floor and assumed that was Greg's hand roaming over her other buttock.

*Be careful stating what you want.* Kelsey hadn't been, she knew that now, as she lay bound and at their mercy. She knew they wouldn't hurt her, and knowing the safeword gave her the courage not to use it as they released her wrists and the middle strap and then covered her eyes with a silk blindfold as she lifted her head.

"You'll do better and give us the response we want if you're not worrying over someone watching. This way," Greg said, turning her shoulders as Devin flipped her hips around, "you're free to just feel, and accept what we do or stop us."

Kelsey groaned as her sore backside pressed onto the bench, the ache emphasizing the steady ripples still wreaking havoc inside her butt. They were right. The darkness did work in her favor, ensuring all her other senses were heightened into full awareness as her wrists were again restrained and straps tightened across her spread thighs. Her skirt remained bunched around her waist and she wished it gone, yearned to offer her complete nudity for their pleasure. But she would take what she could get. Hadn't that been her motto since setting her sights on her two cowboys?

A rough palm covered her labia, an even rougher voice rumbled, "Nice. Already swollen and wet for us." Fingers slid between her folds as prickly stubble scratched her stomach and lips soothed the abrasion. Her toes curled with a deep, three-fingered thrust into her pussy and a hot mouth closing over her breast. A deep suction pulled the small mound upward, a deeper voice following the release. "So small and dainty, yet so damn fuckable."

"*Please.*" The plea spilled from Kelsey's lips as teeth and tongue replaced the fingers plummeting into her depths. The beads stilled and one plopped out with a tug that made her quiver from the desperate ache of arousal.

"No, not yet." Greg's tone bit as hard as his teeth on her nipple, shocking her with his harsh reply. She'd grown accustomed to Devin speaking with such a strong undertone, but not him.

"Okay. You don't have to get cranky." Silence greeted her complaint until Devin's voice reached her from between her legs.

"Fuck, but you're good at pushing buttons, baby." He sank his teeth into the soft flesh of her labia, the sharp, startling pain wrenching a cry from her. "Now, do we need to gag you?"

Kelsey shook her head, not liking that idea. "No, sir. I... *oh, God.*" Heat spiraled through her dripping pussy as he licked up her slit and then dipped between her folds to tongue her clit Greg stroked over each nipple and she strained to get closer to both mouths but met with the resistance of her bonds. Frustrated need tore through her but before she could complain, a click dropped her head backward. Devin wrapped his lips around the needy bundle of nerves and suckled, cutting off her alarmed cry by slowly withdrawing the beads from her ass.

Her mouth fell open on a gasp of skyrocketing pleasure only to get cut off by the press of Greg's smooth cock head between her lips and his voice coming from above her. "Good, because that doesn't fit into our plans."

Kelsey closed her mouth around Greg's flesh with a greedy groan. A soft ball was pressed into her right hand as Devin shifted his mouth off her saturated flesh. Desperation clawed at her insides as they left her hanging on the brink of orgasm and unable to do anything about it.

"Squeeze the ball if you can't handle this, us," Devin instructed as she felt his slick, latex-covered cock pushing against her rear entrance.

This time, when Kelsey's body quaked in need, she discovered a new ache, one to please the two men who, each in his own way, had been so good to her. Concentrating on the two invading cocks, she set aside her own lust to cater to theirs, and experienced a different kind of warm sensation making its way slowly through her body as she allowed them to use her as they wished. Tightening her lips around Greg's cock, she tried to relax as Devin breached her tight sphincter with a gentle but insistent push. She moaned at the stretch and burn then whimpered in frustration as they both pulled back.

Before she could voice an objection, they pressed forward again, dipping into her mouth and butt with careful thrusts, stopping with just their cock heads inside her. With well-orchestrated timing, they swirled and prodded, jabbing her orifices with strokes way too shallow and considerate for the fiery need coursing through her. She wanted them to slake their pleasure on her, to prove how much they lusted for her with uncontrollable, rapid thrusts. But, *oh, no*, she had to get saddled with not one, but two *considerate* Doms. What a bummer.

Some of Kelsey's frustration must have shown in her body language because Devin's irritated growl put her at ease. "You're so fucking tight, baby, I'm not going to last."

Greg's response also helped. "She's sucking me just as hard as I imagine her ass is gripping you. Ready?"

Their guttural rasps sent delightful shivers up and down her spine. Clamping her mouth around Greg's shaft, she strained toward Devin's muttered agreement. "Fuck, yes,"

"Damn it, Kelsey, loosen up," Greg ground out, his hands going to her tight jaw.

She shook her head, wishing she could look into his eyes and let him see what she wanted reflected in hers. All she could do was suck harder, press her tongue against that special spot nestled under the rim of his mushroom cap sure to send him over. The shallow plunges into her butt increased and went a little deeper, stretching her to take more. Both men groaned as their cocks jerked and then spewed, their climaxes thrilling Kelsey in a heady way she'd never imagined as she swallowed one down her throat and trembled around the other.

She sighed, her body going lax as they withdrew a few moments later. Another click brought her head back up and the blindfold was removed. She blinked until both their faces came into focus.

"Now it's your turn, little bit." Greg kissed her first, then Devin before dipping their heads to her breasts and releasing her wrists.

"Come for us, baby," Devin ordered in his no-nonsense way.

What choice did she have as the girls went ballistic from their dual suckling and the slutty bitch leapt for joy with the thrust of several fingers in both her pussy and rectum? She screamed, her orgasm breaking on waves of saturating pleasure that drenched her system and flooded her senses as her heart raced and her breathing stalled.

"Again," Greg insisted, nipping at one engorged tip.

Another climax rolled through her, as if her body decided it had no choice, no defense against those deep, commanding voices and deep-stroking fingers. The forgotten ball dropped from her nerveless fingers as she reached up and sank her fingers into their hair, holding them close until she could think straight again.

## Chapter 14

"We're ready to head out," Tom told Devin as his manager joined him at the head of the line of saddled horses.

Bracing one hand on Thor's saddle, Devin squinted, looking over the mounts they'd chosen to take the group on this ride to the lake. "More people signed up than Greg and I planned for," he murmured, his gaze swinging to the five young guys who had decided just that morning to ditch hunting for this excursion. Between them, the two couples and Otis and Silas' surprise sign-up, their group totaled fifteen. A number that made him uneasy considering the threat against Kelsey.

"You and I personally saddled the horses, so we know the cinches are secure, and these mounts have all made this ride before and enjoy the swim." Tom's eyes conveyed his curiosity as he looked at him. "What are you worried about?"

"There are always risks." They hadn't told any of their employees about Kelsey's troubles; she was their responsibility and one Devin was now embracing with every fiber of his being. Her submission this past week had reeled him in, hook, line and sinker, and he wouldn't breathe easy until the threat against her was removed, once and for all. "Let me check in with Greg and we'll get going."

Kelsey smiled at him as he strode down the line, taking time to say a word or two to the guests already mounted or standing by their horse. He would miss her, he thought as he searched for signs she wasn't dealing well with their scene last night. Sometimes, it was difficult to remember how new she was to their lifestyle. She'd fallen asleep on the long drive home last night, and just like last week, they'd carried her in, undressed her and put her to bed. Unlike last week, neither of them had been willing to leave her unprotected, not even in the safety of their locked, secure house, and they'd spent another cramped night squeezed together in the queen-sized bed.

Waking stiff and sore hadn't bothered him, nor had turning her over to Greg to escort her to breakfast while he grabbed a quick bite at home and met up with Tom to prepare for today's ride. What did rub Devin wrong was the thought of trying to keep her close with such a large group. If it wouldn't have meant taking a huge risk of losing the reputation they'd worked so hard to build up by refunding their fees and making up a lie to send them on their way, he would empty out the cabins today. Maybe not Otis and Silas, he mused as he waved to the older men who were beaming in fondness at Kelsey. They'd already cancelled the last, upcoming reservations before they shut down for the year.

"Hey, I'm ready to move." He drilled Greg with a piercing stare. "Everyone has been milling around the horses since Tom and I saddled them. Have you double checked Cleo?"

"No, but you obviously think we should," Greg returned, his green eyes darkening.

Kelsey's bright blue gaze swung from Greg to him, a small frown creasing her forehead. With her white/blonde hair pulled back in a high ponytail, she looked all of fifteen, and just as innocent, which accounted for the tight clench of Devin's abdomen.

"You saddled her yourself, Devin, so relax." She ran a hand

over Cleo's flank with a familiarity and fond look that proved how attached she'd become to the little mare.

"It never hurts to double check our work." Greg slipped between Cleo and Cherokee and flipped up the stirrup. A cold chill skated down Devin's spine when he heard Greg curse. "Fuck. It's loose, just enough the saddle could easily work itself sideways by the time we reach the lake." His icy gaze cut to Devin. "Someone was wily enough to do this with all these people around."

They both scanned their guests, most of whom had mounted and were sitting with eager anticipation etched on their faces as they bantered between each other. The likelihood one of them was the person hired to come after Kelsey couldn't be discounted, regardless of the background checks that cleared them. An impotent surge of rage gripped Devin. The incident with Cleo on the hilltop *could* have been an accident, but he had tightened that strap himself. It did not become loose without help. "I think it's best if we play it safe and…"

"No," Kelsey snapped, cutting him off and trying to squeeze past Greg to mount her horse. "I've been looking forward to this all week and I want to go." A wave of desperation tightened her entire body. She refused to give this person the satisfaction of seeing her cower and hide. She'd lost so much already; her trust in the McAllisters, her peace of mind and the freedom to come and go as she pleased, without fear. She wouldn't give up accumulating the memories she craved to take home with her. Looking up at Greg, who refused to budge, she reached up and pushed his hat back so she could see his eyes clearly. "Please. I want to do this and," she flicked her eyes back to Devin, "I trust you two to keep me safe."

She held her breath, waiting for their answer, and when it finally came, she went giddy with relief. Devin gave Greg a curt nod, spun around and strode to the front of the line as Greg lifted her into the saddle.

"I hope to God you don't make us regret this. I'll stay right behind you as we ride single file to the creek. Once there, we'll spread out a little, but *you will* remain glued to me or Devin, our horses neck to neck, our legs touching even in the lake."

"I will." She nodded and took the reins. "I promise." And she wasn't dumb enough to break that promise.

Cleo pranced as soon as her hooves splashed in the creek. The afternoon sun warmed Kelsey's head and shoulders as excited chatter from the other riders circled around her. Vicki turned in her saddle and looked back with a broad smile, the third time she'd done so since they'd started out.

"I thought the water would be too cold, but the light splashes feel good, don't they?" The younger woman's eyes bounced between Devin and Greg and then back to Kelsey.

Kelsey couldn't fault her for the glint of appreciation for her cowboys she didn't try to hide, but wondered why that light dimmed when the newlywed looked her way. Jealousy? That would be a first, she mused, and an ego-boosting thought. "Yeah, it does, but we might feel differently when we go deeper in the lake."

"It's not bad," Greg said. "Mountain lakes tend to be colder but the warmer temperature will make getting our legs wet comfortable." He pointed up ahead. "And here we are."

Kelsey noticed the stunning, picturesque view first as they waded through the gurgling creek right into the lake surrounded by majestic mountain rises and towering green pines. As the horses slowly moved into the deeper water, she took note of the way Greg and Devin kept constant watch on everyone while remaining close to her. If the reason for their over-protective diligence weren't so nerve-racking, she could learn to enjoy that side of them.

As soon as she felt the smooth glide of Cleo swimming under her, Kelsey shoved all worries aside to have fun. Nothing could have prepared her for the sheer enjoyment of floating through the water on horseback. Mr. Kilpatrick looked over and waved, eying her for a moment before calling out, "I figured a little thing like you would get swept off. Glad to see our hosts are making sure that doesn't happen."

"I'm stronger than I look," she returned with a smile. She still couldn't believe any of these people meant her harm and preferred thinking there had to be another explanation for the loosened strap after Devin had tightened it.

By the time they rode back to the corrals, still damp but exuberant over their outing, and nothing untoward had occurred, Kelsey was even more sure the strap had not been an intentional attempt to cause a mishap sometime during their ride. She didn't say that to the guys, however. One look at their set-in-stone faces as they dismounted and she knew they wouldn't lighten up.

---

"DID WE OVERREACT?" Greg stood in the den, ran a hand through his hair and around his neck as he watched Kelsey fix a cup of tea in the kitchen.

"Fuck, no," Devin retorted as he eyed her with a brooding look. "Do you honestly think we should let our guard down?"

"No, just wishing for her sake things were different. I don't like the shadows under her eyes."

"If there wasn't a threat, she wouldn't be here," Devin reminded him.

"Yeah, I guess," Greg agreed, sending him a shrewd look. "You've certainly done a one-eighty in the last week."

Devin shrugged. "She grew on me."

"I know what you mean. I'm going to have Jordan double check those names and get changed while you stay with her. I'll hurry to give you time before we start the barbeque. Did you get hold of that last reservation this morning?" With the hunting party checking out tomorrow and the two couples leaving Tuesday morning, they would have an easier time watching Kelsey. To play it safe, they'd decided to cancel the four upcoming reservations that were the last for the year, offering full refunds and a free, five-night stay next year for the inconvenience.

"Yes. He wasn't happy, but he was the only one to give me grief over it." Devin's tone indicated he didn't care and Greg agreed. One person's disgruntlement was worth the peace of mind in keeping Kelsey safe.

"Then let's get through the next thirty-six hours."

---

"THIS ISN'T WORKING," he said as soon as they entered the cabin. "We didn't factor in on Fisher and Young being glued to her hip." Frustration colored his tone and took a bite out of his usual calm manner.

"So we go to plan B. Check out at our scheduled time and back track at night. Instead of getting to her after an accident lays her up, we'll just take her out and run," his partner returned, stripping off her wet clothes.

"And her self-appointed bodyguards?"

She shrugged. "We'll do them for free just because they've foiled our plans and pissed me off."

---

"I'M GOING TO BED." Kelsey jumped up and looked at the two of them with hopeful expectation. Sitting nestled between her cowboys watching a movie without either man making a move to get under her clothes had added to her frustration of the past few days.

Yesterday, she'd stayed holed up in the house, working while

Greg and Devin took turns keeping guard and seeing the hunting party off. They'd disappointed her again by sharing her bed but not touching her. While she was grateful for their protection, she yearned to experience their full, dual possession before she went home. Now that the other guests were gone and the only ones left were Otis and Silas, whom she knew they trusted implicitly, there was no reason why they couldn't pick up where they'd left off Saturday night at the club. Jordan sent each of them a text that morning, letting them know the Swedish authorities were in possession of the lockbox she'd inherited. As soon as they verified the evidence her father hid in it, they would interrogate her father's partner and with luck, pull the identity of the hired thug from him so she could return home.

Greg stood and shook his head, hating to dim the light in her eyes, especially since he knew she wouldn't understand why neither of them intended to touch her again until they neutralized the threat to her safety. They wouldn't make that mistake again, and just because the guests had departed as of that morning didn't mean the hired perpetrator wouldn't double back. "Devin will stay with you in the bedroom. I'll be on watch out here."

Her eyes narrowed to blue slits as her gaze volleyed between the two of them. He knew the moment realization took hold and she took it about as well as he'd suspected. "Fine, but I want one kick at the bastard before you haul him off." She pivoted and all but stomped toward the hall.

Devin winced but Greg's lips twitched as he murmured, "I have no doubt where she'll aim that small foot or of its impact."

"Neither do I. I'll spell you in a few hours." Devin followed Kelsey to the bedroom as Greg settled back on the couch and put his feet up.

SILAS GLANCED at the bedside clock and finally gave up on getting to sleep. His insomnia had decided to kick his butt tonight and past experience told him he would continue fighting a losing battle just lying in bed. Grabbing his pants off the chair, he slipped them on and padded quietly out to the small living room. The tight space in the two-bedroom cabin didn't bother either him or Otis; they spent the month on the ranch for the fishing, peace and quiet and friendly socializing. Grabbing a can of pop from the mini refrigerator, he waited until he stepped outside and settled on the porch chair to pop it open and take a long, cold swig.

The star-studded night and fresh air calmed his annoyance over spending the last few hours tossing and turning while his best friend's light snores filtered through the walls. He envied Otis' restful sleep. His gaze swept the moon-lit yard as he brought the soda to his mouth again, every muscle tensing when he caught sight of two dark, hunkering shapes sneaking around behind their host's cabin. Nobody dressed in black clothing and ski masks ran around in a crouch on the ranch late at night, and given everyone except him and Otis had checked out that morning, his inner alarm went on high alert.

Dashing inside to get his phone and awaken Otis, he prayed he could reach either Devin or Greg.

---

GREG'S PHONE buzzed with a text, drawing his frown considering the late hour. He checked the sender and went taut with worry when he saw Silas' name. He and Otis were the only guests other than Kelsey they'd shared their private numbers with and neither man had ever had a need to use them. The 911 code that popped up followed by *two people sneaking behind your place* propelled him to his feet and storming down the hall with his gun in one hand and his other thumb texting Silas back. *On it, stay put.*

He entered the bedroom with a stealth he hadn't forgotten since retiring, but needn't have worried. Devin had already slid from the bed and clutched his piece as he rolled Kelsey off and bent to whisper in her ear. Bless her heart, she kept quiet, nodded and scooted under the bed without a word. Using hand signals, he informed his partner he was headed around back, leaving Devin to take the window.

Greg cursed under his breath as he inched around the rear of the house and saw both Otis and Silas creeping up behind the two perpetrators, one of whom was lifting a can of what looked like gasoline. The fuckers dared to force Kelsey out the front by setting fire under her window? He had no doubt their plan was to ambush her, Devin and him as they rushed out of the house.

Before he could take aim and fire, Otis ran forward, brandishing a large branch. Fear for the older man tightened his throat as he shouted, "Otis, stop!" Instead of backing off, Otis swung and knocked the can from the perp's hand just as the other would-be assailant pulled his own weapon. Greg didn't hesitate or flinch as he squeezed off two rounds and took the guy down; Devin's shot, coming from inside, hit the smaller person as Otis and Silas backed off and he swung out the window.

Greg and Devin kept their guns aimed at the downed invaders as they bent to check their pulses. "Is he still breathing?" Greg asked Devin after confirming the one he shot was dead.

"She." Devin whipped off the ski mask to reveal Mrs. Kilpatrick's sightless eyes staring up at him. "And I'm happy to say I'm still a damn good shot. She'll be joining her husband in Hell."

"Works for me." Greg looked toward Otis and Silas, who had crept up to join them. "What the hell were you thinking?"

Silas scowled. "You think we'd just sit on our porch while these two snuck up on you or that girl?"

Otis snorted. "Not likely."

Devin started to say something before his jaw went taut and

his gaze cut to behind Greg. Kelsey's wobbly voice whispered, "Is it over, then?"

"I told you to stay put," Devin snapped, his gut still cramped from the close call to her safety.

"You can ground me later, Dad," she returned sarcastically despite looking small, pale and shaken in the moonlight as she stood there in nothing but a short robe. "Are they…"

"Yes, they're dead. We made sure of it. Come on." Greg took her arm and nodded to the older men. "Thank you, both of you. You may as well come inside. The police will want your statements."

"I'll place the call and wait here." Devin spotted Tom standing several yards away, his rifle in his arms, his stance protective as he took in the scene. Fuck, but it was good to know their relationships with all three men went deeper than guests and hosts and employers and employee. He was also happy to breathe a sigh of relief the danger to Kelsey had been laid to rest once and for all. With the arrest of Sven Lindgren in Sweden, she could return home in a few days without fear.

The hard part, he was ready to admit, would be getting used to not having her around anymore.

---

IT WAS close to four in the morning by the time the Billings police had taken everyone's statements, talked to Jordan and left with the bodies of the Kilpatricks. Kelsey still couldn't believe the friendly couple had been hired to kill her. They'd seemed so nice. She'd refused to talk to either McAllister, but from what she heard, the Kilpatricks' alias had withstood the FBI's background search and more investigation would be needed before they could determine if the couple were professionals. If she weren't so tired, shell-shocked and despondent, that information would likely freak her out more. As it was, when Devin and Greg ordered her to bed, she didn't take umbrage at their bossiness and fell into an exhausted sleep as soon as she hit the mattress.

For the first time in days, Kelsey awoke alone in her bed, and she missed the presence of Greg or Devin. That didn't bode well for her return home, but she'd known the time would come when she'd have to go back to her less-than-satisfying sex life. Such were the woes of indulging in fantasies for a short time.

It felt strange to discover herself not only alone in bed but in the house as she padded into the kitchen. Like her first morning here, the coffee pot stood filled with her cup next to it. No note was needed as she knew where everything was now. She didn't know when the McAllisters would come get her, but she did remember today was the last day Mary and Les would be around until they returned in the spring. May seemed like such a long time away, she thought sadly, taking her mug with her as she left the house.

The ranch seemed so quiet and deserted without guests moving about or any activities taking place. Shielding her eyes with her hand, she peered out toward the pastures and could barely make out a handful of riders among the herd of cattle. Even with the distance though, she had no trouble zeroing in on Devin and Greg, the coldness that had gripped her since last night thawing as she drank in their tall frames, wide shoulders and the skill with which they maneuvered their horses among the herd. With a sigh of longing, she forced her feet to move, walking over to the social hall with a lump in her throat.

"My goodness, what a night you must have had." Mary came bustling over as soon as Kelsey entered, wrapping her soft arms around her in a motherly embrace that brought tears to her eyes.

"Now, Mary, the boys kept her safe, so don't fret. You'll upset the girl." Les put his arm around Kelsey's shoulders as soon as Mary released her and gave her a quick but tight hug.

"Thank you both." She smiled as she stepped back, needing

the space to get herself under control. "I know you're packing up for the winter. Is there anything I can do to help?"

"Aren't you a dear? Thank you, but no, we're about done. I do hope you'll come for a visit next year," Mary said.

"Oh, well, I don't know." She'd wanted to go home since she arrived, so she couldn't imagine wanting to return, at least not anytime soon. She would miss everyone, especially Greg and Devin, but the ache she experienced when she thought of not seeing them again would go away in time, wouldn't it? It was just the stress and unhappiness with her situation that brought them together and prompted her into going after them. How much longer could it last, anyway, when it was just sex? "If you're sure I can't be of help, I'll say goodbye."

"You take care," Les said, holding the door open for her.

*I always do, don't I?* Kelsey nodded, walked back out into the bright sun and spotted Cleo in the corral. Returning her cup to the house, she saddled the little mare, swung up and steered her toward the path that would take them to the creek. She had thanked Otis and Silas last night, but wouldn't mind wasting the afternoon riding solo and then visiting with them by the stream.

---

DEVIN AND GREG sat on the porch watching Kelsey gallop toward the stables, both admiring her skill in riding, the way her bright hair flew around her face and the sway of her small body. It had been Devin's idea to give her space today. He figured after having them hovering for days and insisting she stay close before the threat against her had been confirmed, she would appreciate the freedom to spend a few hours as she pleased. As she rode into the corral, he could see the rosy hue covering her cheeks, the blush of pleasure much easier to handle than seeing her pale features last night.

As if reading his thoughts, Greg said, "She held up good last night. Better than most would under the same circumstances."

"She did. Gotta admire the hell out of her for that," Devin murmured in agreement.

"Jordan called. They're upset she still won't speak to them. He said to tell her they'd be at the airport Friday morning to take her back."

"Yeah, I figured that from what I heard in the barn." And he'd been trying not to jump down his friend's throat for the twist in his gut when he thought of not having her around.

Greg snorted. "You're not fooling me. You're pissed, likely at me because you'll miss her as much I will." Pushing to his feet, he stretched, saying, "She still doesn't like it here and wants to go home. A sub's needs always come first."

Devin rose, his eyes on Kelsey as she as she strolled toward the porch. "Then I guess we should make the best of her last two days here."

## Chapter 15

Kelsey left the stable and started toward the house wondering what they would have for dinner. But when she spotted Devin and Greg waiting for her on the porch with muscled arms crossed, booted feet spread, their rugged, bristled jaws taut and their eyes shadowed by their lowered Stetsons, all thoughts of food fled as her pulse spiked and her palms turned clammy. Her whole body went on high alert, the girls and slutty bitch did their usual jig upon seeing them. With any luck, they were ready to sate a different kind of hunger in a way she'd been dreaming of for way too long.

"Did you enjoy your ride, little bit?" Greg took her hand as soon as she stepped onto the porch.

"Yes. I left Otis and Silas at the creek. They invited me to share their catches for dinner at their cabin, but I declined, hoping you had something in mind." She hadn't shied away from letting them know what she wanted and saw no reason to do so now. The slow curl to both men's lips warmed her from the inside out.

"Mary left a casserole and it's heating up now." Devin opened the door and pressed a hand against her butt to usher her inside. "I'll get it out of the oven while you get out of your clothes."

Stumbling to a stop inside the foyer, Kelsey gaped at him as Greg's hand tightened around hers. "You expect me to eat naked?"

"Yes. Got a problem with that?" Greg asked, the amusement in his tone curling her toes.

Her surprise changed to a familiar, illicit thrill and she shook her head with a wry grin. "Nope."

"Told you." Devin smirked at Greg before strolling into the kitchen.

Under Greg's watchful eye, she stripped off her jeans and top. "Be a good girl and go put your clothes in your room. But hurry, I'm hungry."

That was the start of the strangest, but most exhilarating evening she'd spent with them. They sat opposite her at the kitchen table, asking her what she'd like to do before she left Friday morning while her nipples puckered into tight, almost painful pinpoints under their heated gazes. At the mention of the McAllisters' arrival to take her home, her mood dropped from ecstatic to depressed. She should be happy her ordeal was finally over and she would be back in her own apartment by the weekend, right? The desperate clutch around her heart had to be because she would miss her cowboys. Home was where she wanted to be and within a few weeks, her time here would slip to the back of her mind with the other fond memories she'd kept of her previous relationships. Only none of those men had ever looked at her with such intense, focused gazes; had never put her needs or her safety above theirs and had never pulled such exalting orgasms from her.

"Eat and tell me what made you look so sad all of a sudden." Devin pointed his fork at her plate where she'd been toying with the creamy pasta bake.

"It's a little difficult to concentrate on eating while naked in front of two, fully clothed men," she retorted, uneasy with their probing question. It wouldn't do to let them know she would be sad to leave them. She didn't doubt they would forget her as soon as they returned to their club and took up with someone else.

"Yet you didn't hesitate to obey our instructions," Greg pointed out with a lift of one brow.

Kelsey could concentrate better when they wore their hats and she couldn't look directly into their eyes. "Yeah, well, it's been a long four days since we went to the club."

"Poor baby," Devin mocked. "Finish eating and we'll be happy to pick up where we left off last weekend."

That remark perked her up and she downed the delicious meal in minutes, flushing when both men grinned at her obvious enthusiasm. She was going home soon. What did she care what they thought? After taking the last swallow of tea, she rose and carried her dishes to the dishwasher, her butt clenching as she felt their eyes on her. Her pussy dampened even more, and she squeezed her inner muscles in an effort to hold the betraying juices inside. When she turned and they came toward her, she gave up the battle to hide her arousal. Let them see what their hot looks did to her so they would get on with doing something about it.

But as they steered her to the den instead of the bedroom and settled her between them on the sofa, Kelsey feared they planned another delay. Devin clicked on the television and her favorite movie started rolling. Who didn't love *Indiana Jones*? Right now, she didn't if watching it meant sitting here for two hours without... *oh!*

Greg's deep chuckle rumbled in her ear as he pinched one nipple and Devin scraped his nail over the other one. "You watch while we play."

"But... *ow!*" Kelsey tried shifting away from the stinging burn covering her tender folds, complements of Devin's slap, but his cupped hand prevented her from moving.

"Be quiet unless you need to use a safeword." He pressed against her aching flesh.

A silent huff lodged in her throat as they got busy with their hands and mouths, bringing her to the very edge of orgasm several times only to pull back before she could go over. Frustration pulled curses from her as they thwarted every movement that would get her what she craved. Her nipples throbbed from the sharp tugs and pinches, her abdomen quivered from the brush of calloused fingertips and when they draped her legs over their thighs, spreading her wide, her pussy spasmed, swelled and slickened around their pumping fingers. She glanced down and shivered seeing their dark hands against her pale skin, their fingers pushing side-by-side inside her pussy.

Kelsey closed her eyes and leaned her head back, the boisterous movie theatrics and her pitiful mewls the only sounds in the room as she clutched their thick forearms in a desperate attempt to anchor herself against the rising tide of sensation.

When the small contractions signaling an impending climax began for the third time and were cut off once again, her eyes flew open and she wrestled out of their hold. She sprang up with a demand of her own. "Now." Pivoting on her toes, she stomped down the hall.

"I guess that was mean, wasn't it?" Greg pulled his shirt over his head and followed Kelsey.

"Yeah, but in a fun way. I'm still going to let her know who's calling the shots," Devin replied as he followed him.

Kelsey lay propped up on the bed with her hands on her breasts when they walked in, their wide, sun-bronzed, naked chests drawing her eyes. Without a word, they shucked their jeans and boots and settled on each side of her. They cut off a ripple of relief as Greg rolled her toward him and Devin swatted her butt twice before they maneuvered her the other way for him to deliver two smacks, the slaps hard enough to jolt her with stinging pain and wring a cry from her.

"Last time, baby," Devin growled, pushing her on her back and leaning over. "Don't open your mouth unless it's to use a safeword, welcome our tongue or to suck on dick. Got it?"

"I thought I couldn't... *mmmph*..." He cut off her smiling retort with his mouth and she didn't need to be told twice to open for the intrusion of his sweeping tongue.

And then they went all Dom on her and drove her insane with lust. They each shackled a wrist above her head and pinned her restless legs apart with their heavy thighs. The room spun and lights exploded behind her eyes with the first thrust of fingers inside her pussy and anus accompanied by the dual suction of their hot mouths on her breasts. They rendered her unable to move and left her no choice but to lie between them and quake with the onslaught of pleasure. Bulging muscles pressed against her softer body, their size emphasizing her much smaller stature, turning her on even more. She was still riding the waves undulating through her body when they pulled back, and she gasped the first word that came to mind. "*More.*"

Devin shook his head as he turned her toward him and she came into full frontal contact with all of that hard, warm flesh. "What have I told you about being careful of what you want? Put your leg over my hip." Instead of waiting for her to obey, he lifted her leg himself, draping her calf and foot over his lower back.

The position pressed her slick labia against the hot thickness of his rigid cock. She tried to maneuver up enough to take him in, but he stopped her with a blistering blow on her right cheek and then pulled that globe open for Greg to prod his latex covered cock head against before he slid slick fingers inside her. "We have more, little bit," Greg said as he pulled his greased fingers from her butt. "Deep breath."

Burying her face in Devin's shoulder, she inhaled and held it as he breached her tight resistance with a painful push. She shook, bit her lip and waited until she'd adjusted to the stretch and burn. Her tense muscles slowly relaxed and she breathed easier.

"There you go," Devin murmured, his voice laced with approval that went straight to her heart. Kelsey looked up into his dark eyes and her pulse stuttered at the softening she saw in the midnight blue depths. Bending, he kissed her with as much slow care as Greg worked his cock into her butt.

Their roaming hands soothed her shivers as Greg's whispered, "Easy, Kelsey, slow and easy," settled her reservations and Devin's tender kiss brought a sheen of tears to her eyes. Greg pulled out of her before he'd embedded half of his cock, the emptiness forcing a whimpered protest. She'd just gotten used to the thick, steely penetration.

"How quick you forget we know better than you what you need, and what you can handle." Greg squeezed her sore buttock as Devin released her mouth and made short work of covering his shaft and thrusting between her slick folds.

"Fuck but I love how wet you get for us." He pushed up, filled and stretched her to the point of a pleasant discomfort she'd come to crave.

"And eager for us," Greg added as he re-entered her rectum the same time Devin pulled out of her pussy.

The perfect, synchronized rhythm of one in, one out they set up robbed her of breath and all coherent thought. She trembled from the perfect timing and well-aimed thrusts, her perspiration-damp body sliding against theirs as she basked in their dual possession that kept her sandwiched between them. With each deep plunge of Devin's cock in her pussy, she slid upward, her nipples sliding through his prickly chest hairs before Greg pulled her hips back for his return.

They were careful, too careful. They were slow, too damn slow. And they were good, so fucking good. Her climax broke on a wave of saturating pleasure, sensation after fiery, rippling sensation rolling through her well-used body in a heart-stopping burst of ecstasy that rivaled everything they'd delivered before. She fell asleep in the same position, wrapped around Devin with Greg against her back, their groans of satisfaction bringing a tired smile.

---

KELSEY SPOTTED Jordan and Theresa coming out of the snack shop at the small airport as soon as Greg pulled in and parked the truck. A lump rose to her throat, but she could only deal with one chaotic emotional disturbance at a time. As Devin helped her down from the truck, the lingering soreness from the twenty-four-hour sexual marathon that had ended last night with them double-fucking her again made itself known. Yesterday morning, Greg had cornered her in the stable and with an infectious laugh, yanked down her jeans, bent her over a stack of hay and fucked her from behind. Devin had caught up with her on her walk in the woods just so he could lift her up and down on his cock as he braced her shoulders against a tree. Both men had walked away whistling, leaving her to right her clothes before one of the ranch hands got an eyeful.

It had been hard saying goodbye to Otis and Silas, and the tears that had filled her eyes when she'd fed Cleo her last treat still threatened to fall. But nothing could compare with the sense of loss growing stronger as they walked toward the waiting plane. None of them had said much on the drive this morning, so when Greg yanked her against him and she dared let herself look into his vivid green eyes, she encountered a turbulence he'd never shown before.

"Come back any time you wish, little bit. We're not going anywhere." Greg didn't care what the McAllisters thought. Nothing would stop him from taking one more taste of that sassy mouth. He would miss her, damned if he wouldn't.

Her lips were still tingling and Kelsey was still reeling from the open display of affection when he released her and Devin lifted her by the waist until they were eye-to-eye, mouth-to-mouth.

"You'll always be welcome, baby." Devin caught Jordan's speculative look and Theresa's smile before he kissed Kelsey goodbye, vowing to make Greg pay for how much he would miss the little imp.

Trembling, Kelsey dashed toward the plane, ignoring the desperate pleading looks on Jordan and Theresa's faces. "Later. We'll talk after I get home. Please," she whispered before dashing up the lowered steps with tears running down her face. *More*, she wanted more time with them, but prolonging the inevitable would only ensure the ache now pressing down on her chest would only be worse.

---

*WE HAVE MORE, baby, but you should be more careful of what you ask for.*

Devin's words came back to bite her on the butt Kelsey's first few days back home, and not in the fun way either. She spent the weekend with guilt weighing her down, the hurt both McAllisters expressed on the flight back still gnawing at her. As if that wasn't bad enough, the first two nights spent back in her own apartment, in her own bed, lacked the relief and comfort of home she'd been counting on. The vivid erotic dreams she'd been hoping to dispel by pushing for real-life experiences with her two hosts still invaded her sleep, only now the faceless, nameless man tormenting her in them had been replaced with not one, but two hard-to-resist cowboys.

Kelsey awoke Monday morning out of sorts and irritable, looking forward to returning to work and all the distractions that come with a busy office. She hadn't counted on the crowded subway getting on her nerves, the jostle of rude people being so irritating, or remembered the odor emanating from the crammed together bodies as so distasteful.

Instead of inhaling a breath of fresh air as she left the train and stepped into downtown Philly, her nose twitched with the smell of fumes from heavy traffic, her displeasure increasing with every step she took toward her building. Instead of wading through the hustle and bustle of people either too much in a hurry or too disinterested to say hello or even pass by with a polite nod with her usual indifference, she found herself looking for a stranger's smile and friendly greeting. Horns blared by impatient drivers and cars backfired in tune with muttered curses as people shoved their way to work.

Kelsey reached her accounting firm on the sixth floor of a high-rise with her nerves stretched to the breaking point and her conflicting emotions in a turmoil. Her return home wasn't supposed to be this way. She'd expected to miss the guys, not the people visiting or working on their ranch. The friendly, welcome back greetings from co-workers as she wound her way to her cubicle went a long way in easing her tense irritability. After taking a minute to make lunch plans with two of her closest friends, she reached her desk thinking she was more than ready to settle into the small, confined space and get back into working in the office.

Once again, she thought wrong. In less than an hour she was comparing the constant, monotonous clatter of keyboards and low humming of electronics to the faint trill of fluttering birds, a soft horse's whinny and the distant laughter and clomping hooves of horseback riders. Her eyes kept straying from the computer screen out the large, tinted windows, and she didn't understand why her stomach cramped every time she encountered nothing but a gray haziness and row of rooftops instead of pine tree covered hillsides topped with a cloudless, bright blue sky.

Kelsey spent way too much time over the next few days trying to shake off her discontent and the constant intrusion of her cowboys' rugged faces and their probing, focused eyes whenever they looked at her. By the time she returned to her apartment late Friday night after having spent the evening at a club catching up with friends, a new phrase kept running through her head – *This is not the way it was supposed to be.* Nothing about her return this past week had gone as she'd imagined it would. And it had never entered her head she might miss Montana, the Wild Horse Dude Ranch and the people there almost as much as she'd known she would ache for Masters Devin and Greg.

As she fell into bed praying for a decent night's sleep without dreams guaranteed to awaken her in a needy, aching state, she had to accept being wrong about wanting to come home, and wondered if maybe she had erred just as badly about judging Jordan and Theresa.

Morning brought her no concrete answers to the less than desired outcome of her first week back but a determination to set things right with the McAllisters. After pouring a cup of coffee, she grabbed her purse off the kitchen counter and rummaged inside for her phone. Instead of her cell, she pulled out the phone Greg had programmed their numbers into and handed her the first day at the ranch. She'd never had cause to use it during those too short weeks, but sudden longing to hear their voices poured through her in waves, the ache stirring up those memories she'd wanted so much.

*Come back any time. You'll always be welcome.* Kelsey knew better than to believe they were serious and hadn't given a thought to taking Greg and Devin up on their parting offer. Until now. She tightened her hand around the phone and then tossed it back in her purse. *One thing at a time.* Fishing out her cell, she pressed Theresa's number and said the first thing on the tip of her tongue when she answered.

"Can I come over?"

Theresa's choked voice broke Kelsey's heart. "Yes, of course. If you're agreeable, there's someplace we'd like to take you."

Closing her eyes to stop the tears, Kelsey said the words she knew they wanted to hear. "Sure. I trust you."

She did trust them, she thought as she exited her apartment building and saw them standing by their car, waiting for her with hopeful expressions. But there was one thing she needed to clarify. "Did you mean it?" she asked before getting in. "At the airport, when you said I was more than a case to you."

"Sweetheart." Theresa stepped forward and hugged her, Kelsey's heart stuttering upon hearing her whispered, teary words. "Don't you know you are a daughter to us in every way that matters?"

Kelsey shook her head, choked on a sob and then looked over at Jordan's ravaged face. "I'm sorry. You've been nothing but good to me. I shouldn't have…"

"Enough," Jordon interjected gruffly, pulling her in for a brief hug before ushering her into the car. "We made a mistake in keeping you in the dark and you in not trusting us. We'll do what people should do who love each other, forgive and forget."

Since she had no experience with someone loving her, Kelsey took him at his word and let go of the last of her hurt as they drove out of the city. At first, she thought they were going back to their house, but when they turned in a different direction, she leaned forward from the back seat and asked, "Where are we going?"

"To the cemetery. We thought you'd like to see where your father buried your mother and, if you're agreeable, we can have your father moved next to her."

"Did you tell the authorities in Sweden I don't want anything in that lockbox?" There was no way she could take money she knew came from her father's illegal activities and that had ultimately led to his death.

"Yes," Jordan answered, turning into a beautifully landscaped cemetery. "You can pick a charity and we'll handle the rest. With Lindgren spending the rest of his life in jail, it's now yours to do with as you please." Putting the car in gear, he pointed to the headstone right outside. "That's your mother's grave. The plot next to it is available, if you want to use some of that money to have your father moved next to her."

Kelsey started to get out and then shook her head. There were no memories for her here. All her good childhood memories were with the two people sitting in front of her. And all of her recent memories and the people she needed to be happy now were in Montana. "Sure, go ahead and make the arrangements, but you don't need me here to do that, do you?"

Theresa swiveled in her seat, her eyes sparkling with interest as she asked, "No, so what do you want to do now?"

*Come back whenever you want, little bit. You'll always be welcome, baby.*

She smiled. "I want to return to Montana."

Neither looked surprised, only pleased with her decision. Jordan turned back around and started the car. "Then that's what you should do."

It took her a week of fighting back nerves and making the arrangements to work from home before she was ready to fly into Billings and pick up the rental the McAllisters had arranged for her. She packed two large bags, thinking positive, her new online purchases arriving just in time to go into one suitcase. Six weeks to the day she'd first met Greg and Devin she drove through the gates of the Wild Horse Dude Ranch, her heart pounding so hard, she feared it would burst through her chest.

No one was around as she parked in front of the house and ran her clammy hands down her jeans before carrying her bags inside. She knew right away they weren't in the house, so she hauled her suitcases to the back bedroom, unpacked her new white cowgirl hat, denim skirt and boots, put them on and went in search of her cowboys. Kelsey refused to worry over her reception, to wonder what she would do, how she would handle it if they didn't want her back. Failure was not an option, at least, she prayed it wasn't.

She didn't find them in the stable, but Cleo's welcome was worth waiting a little longer. "There's my girl," she crooned, wrapping her arms around the soft neck. The mare nudged her, looking for a treat. With a laugh, Kelsey found the barrel filled with apples and carrots and picked a large red apple for her.

The stable door creaked open a few minutes later and her heart went pitter-patter at the sound of heavy booted steps approaching down the aisle. She knew before they spoke they were behind her, Greg's curious voice impacting her with the same warm, jolting rush as the first time she heard it.

"What are you doing here, little bit?" The minute Greg spotted her white/blonde hair, his hands itched to touch her. When she turned to face them with the same wary, insecure look in her bright blue eyes and teasing grin, he knew he wouldn't let her leave again without a fight.

God, she loved his nickname for her as much as she loved hearing Devin call her baby. She turned and drank in the sight of their towering heights and Stetson shaded, dark faces. "You said I could return any time I wanted, right?" A welcome grin creased Greg's lean, weathered cheeks as both men took in her outfit, Devin taking an aggressive step forward.

"Yes, but *why* have you come back now?" he demanded, the sight of her impish grin and petite body showcased in that sexy-as-sin cowgirl outfit thawing the cold grip surrounding Devin's chest since she left. Their girl would not be leaving again any time soon.

Kelsey took a deep breath, shoring up her nerve. *It's now or never.* She wouldn't make the same mistake she made with the McAllisters. If they didn't return her feelings, she would deal with it. At least then she would know and could move on.

"Well, here's the thing." She took her hat off and tossed it onto the stack of hay. "After I got back to Philly things started bugging me."

Greg's grin stretched into a smile and Devin's mouth finally lost its tight pinch. "Like what?" Greg sent his hat sailing to land next to hers.

Pulling her top off, she basked in their heated looks as they eyed her pink bra. The girls and slutty bitch did their happy dance, and she felt like doing a two-step right along with them. "Like the noise, the smog and so many friggin' people." She wrinkled her nose in feigned disgust. "I mean, really, who can get any work done with all that going on?"

Devin sent his hat flying and growled, "That's not why you're here."

Her hands went to the side zipper of her skirt as she cocked her head. "I forgot how astute you guys are. Okay, the main reason is... I have a problem I need to work out, and I need to do it here, with your help."

Both men grew tense, their eyes sharpened and they took a protective step forward. "We'll help any way we can, you know that," Greg said.

"It could take a long," she lowered the zipper, "long," she shimmied out of the skirt and stood there wearing nothing but pink underwear and cowboy boots, "long time. So my question to you is, how long can I stay?"

Greg reached out and unhooked the front clasp of her bra. "If I had my way, I'd tie you to my bed and keep you here. Long enough for you?"

Devin shook his head. "That doesn't work for me. I insist we share the burden of keeping her around."

A giddy sense of relief spread through Kelsey's pulsing body and she plowed ahead without reservation. "Maybe we can pick the biggest bed and share it."

"Baby," Devin stripped her panties down and hoisted her

bare butt onto a blanket Greg had tossed on top of the hay bale, "that would be our fondest wish."

Greg spread her legs as Devin settled behind her and reached around to cup her breasts. As he slid his hands under her buttocks and lifted her pelvis for his descending mouth, Greg whispered above her saturated, puffy flesh, "But fair warning, Kelsey. This time around, we don't intend to let you go."

As she closed her eyes and gave herself over to their hard hands and hot mouths, that one word she always associated with her cowboys popped back up. *More, more, more…*

*I can live with that*, Kelsey thought.

## The End

# BJ Wane

I live in the Midwest with my husband and our two dogs, a Poodle/Pyrenees mix and an Irish Water Spaniel. I love dogs, spending time with my daughter, babysitting her two dogs, reading and working puzzles. We have traveled extensively throughout the states, Canada and just once overseas, but I much prefer being a homebody. I worked for a while writing articles for a local magazine but soon found my interest in writing for myself peaking. My first book was strictly spanking erotica, but I slowly evolved to writing erotic romance with an emphasis on spanking. I love hearing from readers and can be reached here: bjwane@cox.net.

Recent accolades include: 5 star, Top Pick review from The Romance Reviews for *Blindsided*, 5 star review from Long & Short Reviews for Hannah & The Dom Next Door, which was also voted Erotic Romance of the Month on LASR, and my most recent title, Her Master At Last, took two spots on top 100 lists in BDSM erotica and Romantic erotica in less than a week!

Visit her Facebook page
https://www.facebook.com/bj.wane
Visit her blog here
bjwane.blogspot.com

Don't miss these exciting titles by BJ Wane and Blushing Books!

*Single Titles*
Claiming Mia

*Cowboy Doms Series*
Submitting to the Rancher, Book 1
Submitting to the Sheriff, Book 2
Submitting to the Cowboy, Book 3
Submitting to the Lawyer, Book 4
Submitting to Two Doms, Book 5

*Virginia Bluebloods Series*
Blindsided, Book 1
Bind Me To You, Book 2
Surrender To Me, Book 3
Blackmailed, Book 4
Bound By Two, Book 5
Determined to Master: Complete Series

*Murder On Magnolia Island:*
*The Complete Trilogy*
Logan - Book 1
Hunter - Book 2
Ryder - Book 3

*Miami Masters*
Bound and Saved - Book One
Master Me, Please - Book Two
Mastering Her Fear - Book Three
Bound to Submit - Book Four
His to Master and Own - Book Five
Theirs to Master - Book Six

Masters of the Castle
Witness Protection Program
(Controlling Carlie)

*Connect with BJ Wane*

bjwane.blogspot.com

CPSIA information can be obtained
at www.ICGtesting.com
Printed in the USA
LVHW011807160820
663340LV00001B/79